LOVE, DANCE & EGG ROLLS

LOVE, DANCE & EGG ROLLS

JASON TANAMOR

Ooligan Press | Portland, OR

Love, Dance & Egg Rolls
© 2022 Jason Tanamor

ISBN13: 978-1-947845-34-3

Ooligan Press
Portland State University
Post Office Box 751, Portland, Oregon 97207
503-725-9748
ooligan@ooliganpress.pdx.edu
http://ooligan.pdx.edu

Library of Congress Cataloging-in-Publication Data

Names: Tanamor, Jason, 1975- author.
Title: Love, dance & egg rolls / Jason Tanamor.
Other titles: Love, dance and egg rolls
Description: Portland, Oregon : Ooligan Press, [2022] | Audience: Ages 13-18. | Audience: Grades 10-12. | Summary: As the only minority in school, sixteen-year-old Jamie grapples with honoring his Filipino heritage while still trying to fit in, but as racial tensions increase, he sometimes wonders if it would be easier to forget his birthright altogether instead of trying to embrace it.
Identifiers: LCCN 2021052637 (print) | LCCN 2021052638 (ebook) | ISBN 9781947845343 (paperback) | ISBN 9781947845350 (ebook)
Subjects: CYAC: Family life--Fiction. | Friendship--Fiction. | Schools–Fiction. | Prejudices–Fiction. | Dance–Fiction. | Festivals–Fiction. | Filipino-Americans–Fiction. | LCGFT: Novels.
Classification: LCC PZ7.1.T374 Lo 2022 (print) | LCC PZ7.1.T374 (ebook) | DDC [Fic]–dc23
LC record available at https://lccn.loc.gov/2021052637
LC ebook record available at https://lccn.loc.gov/2021052638

Cover design by Phoebe Whittington
Interior design by Riley Robert

References to website URLs were accurate at the time of writing. Neither the author nor Ooligan Press is responsible for URLs that have changed or expired since the manuscript was prepared.
Printed in the United States of America

For Bonnie. *The* girl.

1

I'd seen this episode at least a dozen times. Reruns of *The Big Bang Theory*, a show comprised of an ensemble cast of weirdos, had been blaring on the television for an entire week straight. The show was one of my favorites, and I couldn't believe that TV Land was airing episodes back-to-back-to-back.

Sometimes, I'd watch TV Land with my father, who'd usually fiddle with his karaoke microphone like it was a classic car he was trying to repair. He never really paid attention. At least, I didn't think he did. He didn't laugh at the right moments, and he never seemed to realize when the program broke for commercial. I didn't mind. It was one of the few times I spent with my family.

Tonight, though, I was watching alone in my bedroom before hanging out with my two friends, Walter and Dennis.

My mother, per usual, was sitting in the kitchen prepping food for the family. My grandmother usually joined her, humming to herself or laughing at what was playing on the television.

I'd always loved sitcoms. They helped me escape my own life. Mainly because, as I sat watching the seemingly perfect families on the screen—typical American families who fit into society—I couldn't help but think about my own family and wonder why we couldn't be "normal" like the ones portrayed on television.

My father was by no means Dr. Jason Seaver from *Growing Pains* or Mike Brady, and my mother wasn't Lorelai Gilmore or even Samantha from *Bewitched*. We were a multi-generational, bilingual, Filipino family. Something you'd never see on television.

After the current episode concluded, before I could get wrapped up in yet another one where Sheldon makes a fool of himself, a knock came at my bedroom door.

I stood to investigate. On my way to the door, I passed various photographs of me dancing in previous Folk Festivals, the one thing that made me truly happy inside. Scattered between images of recent festivals was a photo of me tilting sideways on the stage last year, as well as pictures from when I was younger, either framed or in plastic inserts so they wouldn't bend or tear. One with my dancing troupe posing for the camera. Another with audience members. Props—coconut shells, a *barong* shirt—from dance routines were splayed throughout my room.

Another knock came, breaking my concentration. Instantly, a note slid under the door, stopping just short of my feet. My father's muffled voice said, "It's from Auntie Marisol." I could hear footsteps disappearing down the staircase.

Auntie Marisol?

The intro to the next episode began, the catchy Barenaked Ladies theme song ringing throughout my bedroom. Before I could get entranced by the gang's next dilemma, I turned off the television.

Anxious, I tore through the contents of the note, staring with raised eyebrows, examining each word as the note shook in my hand. My eyes, red with tears, were frozen open as the news sent a jolt of lightning through my heart. My chin trembled in sadness. It was hard to believe that such a small note had completely rocked my world—it was so little, yet so terrifying.

My phone buzzed. Walter.

The homecoming dance was approaching, and although I knew how important the dance was for most kids at school (trust me, Walter said it was the most important event ever), I now had something much, much bigger on my mind. Something that I'd cherished for half my life, something that had been circled on the calendar for nearly a year now. Something that, unfortunately, was ending.

I sighed, my head downturned and my face puffy. All the life exited my body and my soul. No wonder my father had instantly run off. It was almost as if he knew how I would react, and he wanted me to be alone before he got caught in the aftereffects.

Now, I was stalling, slowly composing myself enough to comprehend the news. The information on the note was plain and simple. No images, no fancy fonts, no slogans, nothing. It was, by far, the most generic piece of bad news I had ever seen.

Please read in its entirety, the memo began. *We would like to thank you for your participation in the annual Folk Festival. It is because of participants like you that this has been a successful event for so long. Sadly, due to the lack of funding, this year's Folk Festival will be the last ever.*

A tradition, one that had run longer than my lifetime, was ending—in two weeks. There would be no more sampling of food from different countries, no more learning about other cultures, no more admiring the different forms of traditional dress, and worst of all, there would be no more dancing.

We take this news very seriously and wish to convey our disappointment in this decision. The Filipino-American Association, along with the many other associations that make up this event, would like to thank you for your contributions to the Folk Festival.

My eyes burned. *How could this happen?* I thought. My hand rose to cover my mouth and then slid down my chest. I felt numb. My thoughts were at a standstill, and I grew unexpectedly cold. *We just practiced all last week at Roger's house. Why didn't she say anything then?*

I scanned the memo over and over, hoping that it would somehow change into something good. But rereading it only sparked anger to rise inside me instead. Pursing my lips, I crumpled the piece of paper in my fist, squeezing the life from it with my bare hand. "How could they cancel this event?" I said to myself. "What in the world were the organizers thinking?"

My muscles began to tense, my lips pressed into a thin line, and sweat formed on my forehead. *What did they know? How could they make this decision for everyone else? I'd like to see them out there dancing.*

A vein throbbed in my neck, pulsing with its own heartbeat, ready to attack.

By now I was fuming, unable to stop my breath from coming heavy with every exhale. "Don't the organizers know that this event is the *only* time I truly embrace my heritage?" But there was nobody to hear my accusations; I was alone in my room, and after this news I felt alone in the world.

Suddenly, the anger turned to sadness. *It's ending?* My heart hurt. The pain pierced through me like a sharp knife, digging deeper into me, betraying me. *How could it be ending?* For years, I had looked forward to this day. It was better than Christmas morning. Even better than my birthday.

I walked to my closet, where my freshly cleaned dancing attire was hanging on a hook over the door—on display for nobody to see. I ran my fingertips over the shirt, the feeling of it reminding me of that day ten years ago when I had first put on the traditional garb for my very first festival.

I pulled the shirt off the hanger, quickly replacing my current shirt with the fancy, see-through barong top. I grabbed the thick, red pants to complete the set, and I felt at home. Comfortable.

There I was, standing in the privacy of my own room, wearing my button-down shirt and tailored pants that stopped just above my ankles. My limbs were equipped with coconut shells, secured tightly by thick rubber bands.

The open floor in front of me was covered in street clothes. But did the organizers of the festival care about what this meant to me? No.

My chest ached and my heart grieved over the news. I'd been dancing in the Folk Festival for most of my life, starting at the age of six with the traditional routines—the coconut dance and planting rice. Eventually I'd graduated to the most glamorous Filipino dance ever—Tinikling. It was the showstopper, the headliner, the closer, the Harry Styles, the—well, you get the idea. Now, with the festival ending, my only option was to make this year memorable. I vowed that those who came to watch the dance would remember me and my partner for the rest of their lives.

I could see it now: Jamie and Rosario, the world champions of Filipino dancing. We could do appearances, tours, and exhibitions well into our old age. The dancing would be much slower, but the appreciation would be so high that audiences would applaud the entire routine. We would be the duo that attendees remembered whenever they spoke about the festival. I would be memorialized alongside Bayani Casimiro Senior and Fely Franquelli, the greatest Filipino dancers of their time. It would be—*buzz, buzz, buzz.* The vibration of my phone interrupted my thoughts. I reached across to pick it up from where it slithered across the duvet, only to realize it was blowing up. Notifications zipped across the screen—texts from my friends.

Where are you?

Wut's takin so long?

I tapped out a quick leaving now, tossed my phone back to the comforter, and turned to the full-length mirror attached to my closet door. Staring into it, I struck a pose that often featured in my routines: my arms crossed over my chest and my knees bent.

My phone, once again, buzzed at me. Another message. Then another.

"I'm coming," I muttered to myself with a heavy sigh.

I took another good look in the mirror before slowly shedding the dance costume and dressing once again in my jeans and T-shirt. As I changed, years of history disappeared before my eyes. Outside of my family and my two best friends, nobody knew about my love of dance. It was my secret.

I tossed the note into the trash, grabbed my house key, and bolted down the hallway to the top of the staircase. A faint sizzling sound came from the kitchen, the sound of hot oil in a pan. *Esssss.* One sizzle after another, a couple seconds apart. *Esssss. Esssss. Esssss.* I knew this sound well, and it could only mean one thing—the Santiago family was cooking. One of the many things Filipino families did a lot of.

I jumped down the last few stairs, flew through the living room, passed my father, and entered the kitchen. The rice cooker was on, and I confirmed that the noise had been the egg rolls my grandmother was frying in a pan of vegetable oil.

My grandmother, who didn't speak a lick of English, was tonging the rolls out onto a paper towel to catch the oil, lining them up like little sardines, one by one. An oil spot expanded underneath the rolls whenever she set one down. As she worked, she hummed an old Filipino hymn.

My phone was still buzzing, a barrage of text messages coming in from my friends. They were asking why I hadn't left my house yet. The football game tonight was a big one against our school's rival. Walter said it was super important.

Dude!

Where are U?

What the hell, man? We gotta bounce!

My mother was at the kitchen table, which she had pushed up against the wall. We never ate together as a family—I mean, I was a busy sixteen-year-old, so my mother used the table as a buffet, prepping the evening's dinner. At that exact moment, she was individually wrapping tiny, cigarette-shaped egg rolls for my grandmother to fry. Spread out in front of her were large, plastic bowls of different ingredients to throw into the wrappers.

"I'm bouncing," I said.

"You're what?" my mother asked.

Ay nako.

She pinched her lips, shaking her head. Her glasses slid over her wide, Filipino nose. "What does that mean? I don't understand 'bouncing.'" She pushed the frames up with her fingertip.

Sighing, I said, "It means to leave."

"Then say you are leaving," she said. "We taught you to speak formally and not in slang." She wrapped an egg roll and placed it gently next to the others. "You sound foolish when you speak like that. Do you use slang in *Tagalog?*"

Susmaryosep.

"No," I muttered. I blew out a quick breath.

"Then don't use slang in English." She stared at me with bulging eyes.

"Fine," I said. "I'm leaving."

"Don't you want to eat before you go?" she asked and then dipped her finger into a bowl of egg whites and sealed an egg roll closed, never taking her eyes off me. Placing the roll on a plate with one hand, she reached for another wrap with her other, filled it with shredded carrots, lettuce, pork, and white onions, then repeated the process of sealing the roll. She never used a measuring cup for the egg roll filling; she pinched the right amount each time. Making egg rolls was an assembly line my mother and grandmother had perfected over time. They were experts in their craft.

On the stove in a large pot, on a burner adjacent to the egg rolls, was chicken adobo. The outer shell of the pot was caked in vegetable oil that had catapulted from the pan of frying egg rolls. The soy sauce base boiled, drowning chicken breasts and legs and bathing white onions and hard-boiled eggs in the bubbly broth. A couple of bay leaves floated around the pot, adding an extra depth of flavor.

I closed my eyes and inhaled the aromas for a moment before telling my mother I was meeting Walter and Dennis before the game. I couldn't count the times we'd spent the weekends together—hanging out, listening to music, watching movies, and sometimes, when we were tired enough, they'd even humored me and learned a few of my dance moves. Ah, those were the days.

"We're going to get pizza," I said.

My mother switched gears, broaching the subject that was fresh in my mind. "Do you want to talk about the festival?" I shook my head. "Are you sure?" she said with a focused gaze. I nodded. "OK."

The fact was that I *did* want to talk about the festival, but not right then. I wanted to dwell in the reality that my dancing career was ending. I had to get going to meet my friends, and besides, I wasn't sure what insight my parents could provide that would really be valuable. My family had been part of the association since arriving in the States (forever ago), and because of that, I was sure my parents' advice would be taken verbatim from the handwritten notice I'd just received. *Were they a part of this decision?* I wondered.

"If you ever wish to talk," she said, nodding slowly with pursed lips. Then, her jaw jutted out, and she wiped the beading sweat off her forehead. "I guess it means you can now start attending school events, like the homecoming dance."

"I guess," I shrugged, my eyebrows raising.

"Things end," she said, "and you should be enjoying high school with your friends." She sealed another egg roll and passed it to my grandmother, who was standing in ratty slippers and a long, flowing flannel pajama skirt that she'd made herself. It fell past her knees and covered her entire body. "Besides, isn't there someone you'd like to go to the dance with?"

I instantly thought of Bethany, the lone goth girl who attended my school. She hadn't attended private school her entire life like me. I only started seeing around her when

I got to high school. We met several times in passing and even had a couple classes together. Conversation flowed so easily with her.

One time, a year ago, during a breakout session in class, we'd ended up in the same group. I couldn't remember how our conversation got to this point, but she told me that she loved breakdancing. I probably conjured the conversation out of thin air because the Folk Festival was coming up, and I'd been thinking about it. Even though I never mentioned how much I loved dancing.

I did remember telling her about a kid who was fire at breakdancing. We talked about dancing for most of the session. The other students in the group joined in as well. One boy even started pop and locking in his seat. We goofed around so much that there wasn't any time left to discuss the assignment. It was a fun conversation. Come to think of it, most of my conversations with her were fun. She always made me feel comfortable, engaging with me in the moment.

When we gathered back in our seats, Bethany answered for our group, freestyling a response like she had a Google bank of answers—some brainiac with hidden knowledge of everything.

I was lost in my thoughts, a wide smile reaching my eyes. When I came back to reality, my mother was staring at me. *How long was I daydreaming?* I thought. Her head was cocked, and her lips were partially opened, waiting for my response.

"Not really," I lied.

"Well, just think about it."

In the living room, my father was singing along to an Elvis song through his karaoke system. His voice was loud and boisterous, way off key, and overall incredibly unpleasant to listen to. Although I couldn't see him, I knew that he was singing to an audience that didn't exist, shaking his hips from side to side, his round pot belly jiggling, and pointing to an invisible fan. His voice was flat, with no range, but he didn't care.

The music played loudly in the background as my father sang his heart out. I imagined his lips quivering as he sang, "Well you can do anything but stay off of my blue suede shoes."

When the song ended, whistles and applause erupted from the speakers. It was completely computer generated, but my father pretended that it was real.

"Mah *me!*" he called out, his accent thick as he ran into the kitchen in excitement. His *tsinelas* slid across the linoleum floor. My father held a microphone with a digital pad built into the side. The gadget was nearly a foot long and had the weight of a five-pound dumbbell. "I got one hundred!"

He was referring to the karaoke game's scoring system. After every song, it would generate a score and punch out the result on a daily leaderboard. To no one's surprise, my father had the top score—and every single one after it. His initials filled the screen, from top to bottom.

My mother acknowledged his achievement with a brief smile before returning her attention to me. "I know you said you were getting pizza, but in case you want to eat, there are egg rolls," she said, craning her neck to where my grandmother had positioned herself.

I stole a quick glance. The egg rolls were now forming a pyramid on the plate.

"Did you eat?" my father asked. His salt and pepper bangs were plastered across his hairline, his side part glistening from the sweat he'd accumulated from all the singing.

If you've ever met a Filipino person, then you'll know that the first thing they ask you is if you want something to eat. The circumstances don't matter—the police could be hauling you away, and they'd run up to you and ask, "Before you're locked up for life, do you want to eat?" Then they would push a plate of scalding egg rolls into your face, while the media snapped pictures of you.

I addressed my father, "I'm going to get pizza."

"With whom?"

"Walter and Dennis."

My father sighed pronouncedly. He ground his teeth and pushed out a half-hearted smile.

Anytime I brought up their names, since forever ago, my father wanted them to come over so he could feed them. When it was convenient, it was fine, but most of the time Walter and Dennis were not in the vicinity.

"Tell them to come over here," he demanded. Like the old Filipino dictator, President Ferdinand Marcos, my father started to direct my mother and grandmother, at once, to triple the order of egg rolls and adobo. He looked like a composer when the musical score picked up, his free hand pointing all around the kitchen. My father barked out orders, "Tell Walter and Dennis to get their butts here this instant!"

Another text message came through.

????

Persistent in his efforts, my father said, "Call them! Tell them there are egg rolls." He pointed to the freshly fried batch with his lips (Filipinos used their lips as an extra appendage, almost like a finger or foot), puckering them out as far as he could, before pointing again at my mother.

Her one eyebrow lowered, an annoyed expression on her face, she said, "They're getting pizza!"

Esssss. Esssss. Esssss.

Don't get me wrong, I loved egg rolls. The problem was that I had them all the time. They were like Oreos in a pantry, a staple in our house. I took them for granted, oblivious to the fact that my parents and grandmother would not be around forever. Also, though, I was extraordinarily late to meet Walter and Dennis.

Another text came in.

For realz?!

"Your grandma is making adobo," my father said, gesturing to the pot with his pointed lips. The broth in the pot was bubbling, the chicken becoming tender. Oil was spitting up out of the pan as my grandmother changed out the egg rolls as fast as she could. My father began to fiddle with the karaoke system, and I groaned internally.

To end this situation—because I knew my parents would continue to ask until I gave in and ate everything they'd cooked and then some—I reached for some of the newly fried egg rolls and popped one in my mouth. The heat burned the inside of my mouth, and I sucked air in sharply through my teeth.

Heetthzz . . . heetthzz . . . heetthzz . . .

When I bit into the tight rolls, the juice squirted out in abundance, scalding the roof of my mouth. The pain was searing, but rather than spit it out and save myself, I just chewed and swallowed faster. I knew that if I dared to spit out my grandmother's cooking, there would be hell to pay.

My mother continued to wrap rolls, my grandmother plopping them in one by one—*esssss, esssss, esssss*—and my father pressed the microphone's keypad to input his next number. There were hundreds of songs programmed into it, from different eras and across different genres. Have you ever seen Asian Elvis sing Shania Twain? It was something.

My father had snuck the karaoke gadget into the States from the Philippines. I had never seen anything like it before. According to him, he'd only paid sixty pesos for it. In the States, it would cost two hundred dollars. I never asked if that was a good deal or not. From his reaction, I gathered it was.

Once I had eaten enough egg rolls to satisfy my parents, I turned toward the door. My grandmother stood, tapping her foot on the floor, waiting for my approval of her egg rolls. "So good," I said to her. Pointing to my mouth, I nodded in approval.

She turned her head, coughed into her fist for several seconds and continued frying. The cough had gotten worse from just a week ago. It sounded like she was a long-time smoker.

"Do you want to bring egg rolls to Walter and Dennis?" my mother called out before I could leave. My head dropped, and I forced a half-smile.

So close! I thought.

"Call them," my father instructed. Tucking the microphone under his armpit, he moved to find some aluminum foil to wrap the egg rolls in to keep them warm.

"We're getting pizza," I said, stopping him before he got too far. My voice stern, I reiterated, "They want pizza."

My father stopped. He swallowed hard. "Oh," he said, his shoulders dropped, and his body caved into itself. He chewed on his lip for a moment and then stopped. He began to fiddle with his microphone again and left the kitchen. In the living room, a Buddy Holly song started.

"I'll be home late," I told my mother, turning to leave. The crackling of egg roll wrappers in vegetable oil stopped me. I inhaled deeply and then pirouetted and swiped a handful of fried rolls from the soaking paper towel like a sleight of hand magician. "OK," I said. "I'll have a couple more." Throwing them into my mouth, I told my family bye and left the house.

The faint sound of "That'll Be the Day" drifted out of the television's speakers from behind the front door.

2

"Large pizza, half pepperoni, half sausage and mushroom," Walter said to the server. His elbows were propped up on the table, his body upright, and his long legs were intertwined underneath the table.

"How would you—"

"Hand tossed," interjected Walter. He then whipped his head so his longish dark bangs moved away from his eyes. "Thank you," he smiled.

The fair-haired teenager jotted down the order and asked what we wanted to drink. I hadn't seen this server before; she must have been new. Usually, we had Lamar.

"Two Cokes and a Dr. Pepper," said Dennis, pointing at me when he said Dr. Pepper.

I raised my hands up in front of me, my mouth partially opening, building into a smile.

"What?" Dennis said. "We get the same thing every time."

The girl smiled. "Alrighty. I'll get the order in," she said. "Lemme know if you need anything." She knuckled the tabletop, her way of saying goodbye, and then tore around the corner into the kitchen, leaving us alone at the table.

Even though the festival was plaguing my mind, it was nice to be with them.

When elementary school had first started, I didn't talk to anyone. I minded my own business, kept my head down, and attempted to learn. My parents instilled the importance of education in me quickly. My mother told me, "We came to the United States so you could go to school."

It took a few months for me to befriend Walter and Dennis, who were neighbors as kids. They had already become friends simply from living near each other. Since we met in elementary school, we've had a tight relationship.

"So, why are you late?" Dennis asked.

I whipped out my phone to check an incoming text message. Rosario. Did you hear about the festival?

Sure did, I replied, Sux! ☹ My mouth twisted subtly.

"Heyo!" Dennis said, waving his hand in front of my face.

"Sorry," I said to Dennis, simultaneously texting Rosario that I'd chat with her later. I slid my phone into my pocket. A second later, it buzzed.

Walter was antsy, his upper body twisting in a knot, turning his attention to the kitchen and the main dining room. He scanned the oversized, circular clock hanging on the wall.

"Who was that?" Dennis asked, nodding.

Shrugging, I said, "Just a friend."

Walter sighed. "Should've called ahead," he said. Then he glared at me under half-lidded eyes. "We're like super late."

"It's not a big deal," I muttered, my breath quickening as I spoke. I was secretly dwelling over the news of the Folk Festival ending. Meanwhile, Walter was making the football game seem like the Golden Globes. As if we *had* to be there on time to walk the red carpet until someone yelled, "Who are you wearing?"

One of the people I actually wanted to talk to about the festival had just texted me. I desperately wanted to check my phone and commiserate with someone who could relate. But I was with my two best friends—who were more interested in football.

"Anyway," Dennis stressed.

"Sorry, was watching nearly a season's worth of *The Big Bang Theory*," I said as a smile grew on my face.

"And that's why you're late?" Dennis's eyebrows shot up.

"Right?" Walter said.

Changing the subject, I said, "Remember when the three of us watched the entire *Seinfeld* series straight through?" My cheeks rounded out into a smile. "It took like two months!"

"I do," Dennis nodded, slightly forgetting about my tardiness. *Seinfeld* was one of his favorite shows. He'd always thought he could play Kramer and loved his physical comedy. "Good times!" he said.

The server dropped our drinks on the edge of the table. Only one of the glasses had a straw. Dr. Pepper. I swiped the drink and took a quick sip.

"Pizza is coming right up," she said, and then she was gone.

Walter sighed again, this time more heavily. "You made us late," he said.

"We're fine," I remarked, turning to him. "The game lasts for, what, three hours?"

Dennis's jaw dropped. His outstretched hand froze in mid-reach of his glass. "Fine?" His head turned down, and his eyes grazed over his long-sleeved shirt, baggy on his slim frame. "Being late because of *Seinfeld* is one thing, but *Big Bang Theory*?" He paused, channeled his inner Jerry, and said, "Really?" Then he collected his Coke.

Walter did the same and downed a swig.

"So, I was a few minutes late," I said, craning my neck to catch a glimpse of how many people were in the pizza joint. I was actually a whole lot of minutes late, because I'd made sure to carefully shed my dance uniform so it wouldn't tear.

The pizza joint was nearly bare bones empty. If I had to guess, the majority of the people heading to the football game. This game was a big deal, at least according to Walter.

"We're going to end up in the nosebleed seats," said Walter. Shaking his head, his gaze darted from me to the kitchen and then back. "So, watching TV is really what took you so long?"

I should tell them about the festival ending. Maybe they would understand. They both knew about my dancing, and how important it was to me, but I bet their lack of interest in my dancing was equal to my lack of interest in football. They just kind of accepted it as something I did, so I didn't say anything. Plus, I hadn't had enough time to grieve the bad news. Instead of confessing, I just shrugged and swallowed a big drink of soda.

I burped, which caused a chuckle from both Walter and Dennis. The spicy licorice taste came up a little, then settled back into my stomach.

"We're probably not even going to be late," I reasoned. "Don't they introduce the players or something first? And sing the national anthem, and . . ." my eyes grazed across the ceiling, "um . . ." then I trailed off, my brain thinking about sliding to the side of the room like a planting rice superstar. A smile reached my eyes.

"What was that?" Dennis said.

"What?"

"That." He pointed at my lips, his head slowly turning toward Walter. Walter was leaning out of the booth, his focus homed in on the kitchen.

Soon after, the server exited with our pizza.

"Did you see his smile?" he said to Walter, but Walter wasn't looking. He had one thing on his mind.

"Finally," he said.

Phew! The arrival of the pizza had saved me from talking about the festival.

The server dropped off the food, told us to enjoy, and then disappeared as the three of us grabbed a few slices each and scarfed them down. While we were eating, I managed to sneak a couple texts back and forth with Rosario. Knowing that she was just as disappointed as I was helped me stave off a total meltdown. We were going to need every bit of support we could get.

Once the three of us finished inhaling the pizza, we rushed out to the stadium.

We could see the packed stadium as we pulled into the large parking lot. There were cars everywhere—some of them even parked illegally. The top of the stadium was outlined in a yellow glow from the lights, and every now and again the noise of the pep band filtered out into the parking area.

The team buses lined the first row of parking. Everyone else found spots behind. After circling the perimeter, we found a spot several rows away from the front gate.

"I told you we were going to be late," Dennis muttered under his breath, and then he sighed loudly.

I wanted to say, "I know, but my Filipino dancing career is over," but I didn't, because they wouldn't understand. Besides, that just sounded awkward and weird. He'd think it was ridiculous. Instead, I brushed him off and looked at the bumper sticker on the car parked in front of us. It read "One nation, one flag, one leader." Another one next to it, read, "My student beat up your libtard."

They must run in pairs, I thought to myself. I looked away and said to my friends, "Sorry guys. After the show, I tried getting out of there, but my parents started pushing egg rolls onto me." And just like that, their moods changed in an instant. Egg rolls, the magical food that made everything disappear. Popular with my white friends since day one.

"Did you bring us some?" Dennis asked, his attitude doing a complete one-eighty. "Jamie, I totally would forgive you for making us late." He smiled impishly.

I shrugged.

"Didn't realize you wanted any," I replied. "I really was just trying to get out of there. Plus, you'd forgive me anyway."

Walter sighed with disappointment. "Still, man," he said, throwing up his hands.

A roar erupted from the stadium, quickly followed by another. Someone was leading a cheer, and the three of us turned toward the sound.

"Dude!" Walter screamed, as the snare drummer rattled off a series of continuous taps. We pushed through the maze of automobiles and entered the stadium.

The football game was in full swing. Students, parents, and alumni filled the stadium to cheer on the Saint Patrick Falcons, their favorite team and our private school's team, in the annual match against our rival, the Westside Panthers. It was a rivalry that went back for generations. Football wasn't really my thing, but to fit in with my friends I had to play the part. I had to act "normal."

The crowd's cheering fell idle; there were some hollers and some whistling, but for the most part, they were quiet. The marching band was playing, and the announcers were bantering through the speakers. From the sounds of the stadium, nothing of interest was occurring on the field.

I walked up the slight incline toward the bleachers, pushing my way through until I was standing in front of the student section. I felt their eyes judging me, scanning me up and down, and I became small, the hairs on the back of my neck rising to attention.

Were they wondering what this Asian kid was doing? Or was it because I was late? They weren't looking at Walter and Dennis that way.

Then I wondered if Nick was here yet. We'd been acquaintances, not the best of friends, but sometime ago he changed. I still can't recall the exact specifics of how our relationship soured, but the turning point was when his father lost his job, and suddenly I became enemy number one. That I remembered. That was when everything had started.

If my life was a sitcom . . .

[JAMIE'S PARENTS find out that NICK is the school racist and save the day by offering him some egg rolls and rice.]

INT. Living Room - Day [music fading into scene]

JAMIE, his MOM, DAD, and NICK are having a confrontation.

DAD: *Nick, let's all calm down. Have some egg rolls!*

MOM: *Have some rice!*

[NICK, *still frowning, angrily takes an egg roll and eats it. Slowly his face transforms, smiling beatifically at the camera*]

NICK: *Wow, these are really good!*

[*Live audience applause*]

DAD: *Nick was on those egg rolls like white on rice!*

[*Live audience groans*]

[*Karaoke machine fires up.*]

[*Roll credits as NICK and DAD sing "You've Got a Friend in Me".*]

[*Fade to black as audience laughs.*]

Cue Emmy nomination.

But this was no sitcom, and since this was real life, my real life, my parents had no clue that their only child was the subject of racial prejudice.

I tried to quell all the disordered thoughts in my brain, pushing them down until my mind was quiet. And just like that, the noise of the stadium tripled.

The game had already started; they were in the middle of the first quarter and neither team had scored. I searched the bleachers and saw the mass of students standing shoulder to shoulder along the first few rows of the bleachers. The school's colors of red and black were spread across much of the home team's side.

"This place is packed."

Pointing toward an empty space about three rows down from the top, Walter suggested, "Let's grab that spot."

"Way up there?" Dennis asked, scanning the area. "There has to be somewhere closer."

"Who cares?" I said. "We're at the game. You can still see everything from up there."

"Fine," Dennis said with a disgruntled sigh.

We shuffled through the rows, the slow trek taking me past fans who'd positioned themselves well before kickoff. Ahead of me, Walter led. "Excuse us," he said. "Sorry."

On the journey up, an elderly white man stared at me from his seat. His gaze was both hateful and accusing. His bright red ballcap, plastered with white block lettering, stuck out like a sore thumb—a modern symbol of bigotry and hatred against minorities.

My heart began to race, my eyes darted around, and I grew paranoid. Since Trump had become president, I had begun to think the worst of people, stereotyping just like many politicians did in order to sow division and strife. When I neared the old man, his eyes focused on the field, and the hairs on my neck rose. Instantly, I soured.

"Pardon us," Walter announced as he marched up to the empty seats. I turned my head away from the old man until I passed him, following my friends until we settled on the edge of the bleachers. Instantly, I could feel my heart rate drop back down to something more normal.

Once settled, Dennis removed his shirt to reveal his chest, painted with the school's logo—a falcon, soaring down to land. Underneath the design, spanning his belly, it read, "Falc U!"

"Nice," Walter laughed when he saw it. They slapped palms, high fiving the accomplishment.

"And that's why you didn't want to sit up here," I snorted. "Dennis, always the Kramer."

He grinned. "Hey, I need to be seen." The two were still high fiving.

I squinted at the lettering, my eyebrows drawing together. I didn't get it. *Falc U!* Then I shrugged. *Like instead of being a high school we were a university?*

Suddenly, the crowd erupted into cheers. Over the loud-speaker, the announcer screamed, "Touchdown!" The band began to play, and as Walter and Dennis started jumping up and down on the aluminum bleachers, I turned toward the elderly man. He was rooting for his team—a fan, just like everyone else.

I scanned the entire stadium, observing the rest of the crowd. For the most part, each person was in a good mood, cheering for their team. While conducting my search of faces, I saw Bethany, sitting alone on a bleacher, away from the rest of the student body. Her personality was so intoxicating. Bethany was everything I wasn't—engaging, confident, and most of all, she didn't seem to care what anyone thought. Plus, the way she looked? Wow!

Tonight, she wore dark lipstick and pale foundation, with heavy, black eyeliner bordering her eyes. Her bangs rested just above her eyebrows, and she'd pulled the rest of her black hair into a tight ponytail. I could only see her shoulders from where I was standing. When I stood tiptoe and leaned to get a better look, I could see she was sporting a pair of charcoal gray skinny jeans and black Chuck Taylors with white soles. She was petite, a tiny punk rocker. She dressed like she was on a mission, something I could *never* pull off.

Even as the noise of the crowd reached deafening heights, Bethany looked bored out of her mind, uninterested in our school's spirit. She kept alternating between checking her phone and glancing around to find something to watch.

During one play, she clapped like she was rooting for someone on the team. A boyfriend? Friend? I looked, but all I could see were white numbers across oddly shaped bodies. She screamed something, cupping her mouth with her hands to create a megaphone, but I couldn't hear with all the surrounding noise.

Honestly, I was surprised she'd even shown up. What was she doing here? A girl like her didn't seem to belong here, but who was I to judge? Out of the entire student body, Bethany and I were the odd ones out—her for being goth and me for being Filipino.

Before I could get too entranced, Walter nudged me and pointed to the scoreboard.

"Did you see that touchdown?" he asked, a wide smile stretching across his face. He was ecstatic, bouncing up and down on the bleachers to show his excitement.

I shook my head. "I missed it, sorry."

"Falc you! Falc you!" Dennis cupped his hands in front of his mouth to amplify his shouts. Of the three of us, he was always the attention getter. One time, he hijacked the school intercom session and read jokes that he'd written the night before. He'd agreed to read the morning announcements, but instead of stopping after the lunch menu, he transformed into Kevin Hart.

"Falc you! Falc you!" Walter followed suit. I watched as the two of them flipped off the opposing players on the field, displaying their enthusiasm for the first score of the football game, before starting the whole process of their high five ritual.

My eyes, once again, drifted over to Bethany. She'd be fun to take to homecoming, but the Folk Festival was the only thing I could think about. *How could they run out of money?*

[On this episode, JAMIE'S dance team has an epic fundraiser teaching random passersby how to plant rice and selling coconut shell novelties for one dollar. By the end of the episode, JAMIE successfully raises some outrageous sitcom amount like twenty thousand dollars.]

The bleacher beneath me started rattling, so much so that I had to catch myself from falling over. At once, the crowd started yelling, "Defense! Defense!"

Walter elbowed me in the side, but I ignored him. "Aren't you paying attention?"

I wasn't. I loved hanging out with my friends, but this was something they were into, not me—my true love was dancing. Now that it was ending, my emotions were all over the place. I just couldn't deal with the game right now. Losing my voice screaming at a game I couldn't care less about wasn't something I was interested in. But I came for them. To participate in typical American pastimes.

"Dude!" Walter said, batting my shoulder with his palm. "Aren't you watching the game?"

"Yeah," I lied, feigning excitement. My eyes fell to the side, away from Walter's line of sight.

"Liar," he said. "Why'd you come if you aren't going to watch the game?" He shook his head. "After all, you made us late."

"Hold on," I said. "I'm only here to hang out with you guys. Whenever I try to bail you get pissed." I shrugged.

The side of Walter's lip curled upward. He slowly shook his head.

"Remember the Macaroni and Cheese Fest at the convention center a couple years ago?" I asked. "You kept saying, 'But we haven't tried all two-hundred flavors.' I stayed. Even threw up the next day! Remember? It was awful!"

"Whaddya talking about?" Walter looked down toward the field and then returned to me. "You're acting weird. What's going on with you?"

What's going on?

Perhaps Walter would understand. Of the two, I was closer to him. I'd spent more time with him, and the two of us had more in common than Dennis and I did. It could be like one of those sitcom moments where the episode ends with a nice chat and the screen fading to black. We would hug it out, and when the screen finally darkened, the audience would applaud.

"Fine," I said. "You know how I dance each year in the Folk Festival?"

Walter nodded. "Yeah."

"Well, they're canceling it after this year." My head lowered as my lips pressed tightly together.

Next to us, Dennis was in an all-out frenzy.

"What kind of play was that?" He directed his distaste toward Saint Patrick's head coach, Coach Priest. His name was Father Walter, but everyone called him Coach Priest. "New coach! New coach! New coach!" he chanted, trying to get other fans involved. He searched the faces around us, attempting to gain support. A couple fans stared at him—one group even went as far as to laugh at him. "New coach! New coach!" he continued.

When no one joined in, Dennis stopped.

Walter's body slumped. "I'm sorry, dude," he said. "I know how important that festival is to you." He reached for my shoulder, patted it, and then stole a look at the field. "And you should know how important this game is to us," he quipped, his head tilting toward the field as if he was only humoring me to begin with.

I heard Bethany's voice in the chaos of screams and cheers. It just stuck out, almost as if I'd committed it to memory. When I found her, she was screaming, "Go get 'em, Sam!"

I couldn't help but smile. My heart warmed.

"Now I know why you're not watching the game. It's all comin' together now," Walter said in a singsong manner. He raised an eyebrow accusingly and pointed to Bethany. She was standing upright with her hands clasped together. He rolled his eyes, his expression turning sly. "I see you gawking at her."

"What? I'm not looking at her," I squealed—but I was.

"If you say so," he muttered and then looked away. Huffing to himself, Walter shook his head. "I guess I thought you were here to hang out with us and watch the game," he said, "not drool over some chick."

"Can't I hang out at the game without being into the game?"

The crowd suddenly went crazy: screaming, clapping, jumping. Fearing he was missing something, Walter quickly turned his attention to the field. "What happened? What'd I miss?" He looked around, scanning the crowd, hoping someone would fill him in with the details. Then he directed his attention to the scoreboard.

"We got an interception," Dennis said, throwing his arms up to fist pump the air. The motion caused the lettering on his belly to elongate down his bony torso.

"Sweet!" said Walter as he watched as the teams changed personnel on the field. Since Saint Patrick's had intercepted the ball, our offensive unit tromped back onto the grass.

With Walter distracted, I stole another glance at Bethany. She was holding her phone up, hiding it behind the backs of the fans in the row ahead of her. A video was playing, and she laughed periodically at the content. Her smile was genuine, and her shoulders gently rose and fell in time with her chuckles. I leaned in closer to see what she was watching, but her screen was too small to get a clear view of from where I was standing.

"Dude!" Walter exclaimed, punching me in the shoulder.

"What?"

Walter pointed to the field. "We just intercepted the ball. If we score, we'll be up two touchdowns," he said. "Watch the damn game!"

Before it could get heated, Dennis interrupted with a heavy groan, dropping his chin to his chest in dismay. "Are you kidding?" he said as Walter looked at him. "Fumble inside the ten," Dennis explained.

"Damnit," Walter said, throwing an accusing look toward me. "See, you're making me miss the game."

I ignored him and stole another look at Bethany. She was typing something into her phone. Then she peered back onto the field, clapped a few times, and after a few glances, returned to her seat. After staring for a few moments, I turned to Walter, who at this point was glaring at me.

"You seriously into that?" he asked. I nodded. "The goth look?"

"It's kinda hot," I said.

He shrugged casually, mumbling snidely, "If you like different."

I couldn't help but chuckle. "I'm different," I said.

Taken aback, Walter said, "What are you talking about? You don't dress like that."

"Not now!" I screamed. "I do on occasion dress in coconut shells and barong shirts." I would fully understand if she felt like an outcast, like she didn't belong. That was one of the reasons why I was attracted to her—why I defended her.

"So, yeah, I *do* dress a little like that," I explained. "How do you not see that?"

"OK," said Walter, his palms in my face. "I'm sorry. You do dress like that on occasion. Just like he," spinning toward Dennis, "does stuff like this on occasion. But that's the key word—occasion." He gestured to Bethany with a quick whip of his head. "She looks like that all the time." Walter returned to me. "So now what you got?"

"You want to talk about looking different all the time?" Walter's lips pursed. He nodded. "I am the only minority in the whole school." Swallowing, I reiterated, "In the entire school!"

Walter's eyebrows shot upward.

"You act like that surprises you," I said, and he shrugged. "You do know that, right?"

"I guess."

He'd hit a nerve, so I raised my voice. Walter still didn't get it, and I was starting to feel sick. "You *do* know that, right?" Then I whipped out my phone, pulled up a text message, and shoved it into his face.

Walter leaned in to read the text: We won't be replaced.

"What is that?" he asked, his head jerking back.

"Nick," I retorted.

"I don't . . . what's it mean?"

What's it mean? I thought.

"It's what those far-right idiots chanted at that white-power rally," I said, before sliding my phone into my pocket. I was breathing heavily now. Walter's face morphed into Nick's and then changed into every racist for a moment.

"I don't look at you like that," he said defensively.

My temper cooled, and once again, he was Walter. "I appreciate that, but some people do. *And*," I said, craning my neck toward Bethany, "some people look at her that way. As being different."

"Yeah," he stretched the word, conceding with a bit of uncertainty. "You're right."

I felt a new, weird distance between us.

Another chorus of cheers exploded from the stands. Dennis screamed, "Go! Go! Go!" He groaned, dropping his head as a deep sigh escaped him.

Distracted, Walter turned to watch the field. "What happened?" He looked around the greenery. "What'd I miss?" The field goal unit was parading out onto the twenty-yard line. Once he figured it out—not that I cared—he returned his attention to me.

"All I'm saying is that you're criticizing her for looking different," I said. "Well, I look different too."

"Again, I don't look at you like that, but whatever," Walter said, playing off my accusation.

Since the country had seen a rise in white nationalism, I'd become very wary of motives. It didn't matter who the person was, if their skin was white, anyone and everyone was suspect.

I had known Walter and Dennis forever. The three of us had history. Yes, they'd never treated me differently, but the fact of the matter was that we were extremely different. My skin was much, much darker than theirs. This was the privilege that both Walter and Dennis had but didn't realize. The Trump presidency had completely changed me. I'd become more conscious, more aware of my surroundings, and more prone to questioning.

"The only difference is we've known each other for years," I said. "You know me. Otherwise, you'd be saying the same thing."

Deep down, I felt that Walter didn't want to address race. It made him feel uncomfortable. I, on the other hand, had learned at an early age that I was not white and that made me different.

One day, on the playground playing kickball, I was rounding third base while another boy, Parker, was heading to second. Another kid in the outfield had a choice to throw one of us out. The pitcher kept shouting, "Get the chink! Get the chink!" The next thing I knew, the ball flew into my legs.

As I walked back to my team's side, I overheard the pitcher saying that he didn't know my name. He and the fielder exchanged laughs, and the game continued. It made me wonder if the only reason he threw the ball at me was because the pitcher also didn't know the other kid's name, and I was easier to describe.

Why couldn't he just scream, "Home plate! Home plate!" Or if he wanted to stay on brand, "Get pasty, get pasty."

Since the country had changed, myself and others were repeatedly reminded that we weren't white. That we were Other. All the far-right talking points revolved around Mexicans and Black people. All Mexicans were illegal. All Black people were criminals. But Asians, we were OK; we were just submissive. The model minority.

One of the first lessons my mother taught me as a child was to not let white people think they were better than me. I understood why she felt that way; more than once white people had made her, and our family, feel inadequate for being immigrants back in the eighties. It still happened now, but my parents, in their old age, had simply quit giving a crap. My father especially—he acted like a war veteran whose sole response to any type of criticism was, "Boy, I spent a lifetime fighting for your rights. Nothing you say is going to rile me up." My parents were quite possibly where I had gotten my anxiety from. After all, feeling inadequate was something I was experiencing first-hand. Hence, the numerous messages from Nick.

"We obviously have different perspectives," Walter said.

Nodding, I replied, "Yes, we do, but this impacts my perspective more because I'm the one who is different. And," I paused, lazily pointing to Bethany, "she's different as well."

Our little charade must have been enough to garner attention from random bystanders, including Bethany. Walter nodded in her direction. "Well, now she's staring at you," he said.

Walter turned to watch the game. He was cold for the next few minutes, his posture stiff and tense. He didn't say a word to me. I still wasn't sure if he had that much disdain for Bethany, or if it was because I was ruining the football game.

I turned slowly toward Bethany, my interest sparked by Walter saying she was looking at me. As soon as I caught her eye she looked away. I kept my gaze on her regardless, and I was happy to realize that every so often she would sneak a look at me, smiling out the side of her mouth. It felt like we were vibing.

"You should ask her to the dance," Walter suggested, though he still refused to look at me. He was talking about the homecoming dance, the most important dance of the year. "You two would make a good couple." His voice turned sarcastic, and I sighed internally.

"Ha, ha," I said. "I'm sure she has a date already."

Honestly, I wasn't sure if she had a date, or if she even wanted to go. Maybe she was with the football player. Sam, was it?

The fact was I had no intention of asking anyone to the dance. I was flat out not going. Sure, deep down I thought I should go because it was part of being in high school and assimilating into American culture, but the homecoming dance was the same night as the annual Folk Festival. I wasn't going to miss that, especially not now that it was the *last* Folk Festival. It was the one place I felt comfortable in my own skin—sometimes overly so, confident, to say the least.

The first half of the game was nearly finished, and Saint Patrick's led Westside by ten points. During a timeout, one of Westside's cheerleaders started dancing to the music playing over the loudspeaker. She performed a montage of TikTok moves, the crowd cheering her on as she struck a pose toward Saint Patrick's bleachers. Fans from our side started screaming, but nobody made a move—until Bethany ran out onto the field.

She found a spot on the small patch of grass adjacent to the short retaining wall and started moving her torso from left to right. Her arms extended out, away from her body like she was measuring her wingspan. Then she curled her left wrist, her forearm and elbow following suit, until both of her arms were flowing like soft waves across a river. Her right foot lifted, pushed into her inner left knee, and her body collapsed like an accordion until she was on the floor, breakdancing in a circle. She helicoptered for a few turns and then stood up and posed.

The student section went nuts, roaring and blasting cheers to the other team's stands. The cheerleader across the way did a quick robot, stopping suddenly with a sharp gaze toward Bethany.

Bethany, standing with perfect posture, flopped to the ground into a centipede. When she got near the sidelines, she spun her leg around, gliding onto her back until she was windmilling for several rotations.

I was floored. My jaw dropped so low that it nearly gathered dust from the ground.

Then the referee's whistle blew, and the players entered the field.

Bethany jumped to her feet, climbed over the retaining wall, and returned to her seat, all to a round of applause from nearby spectators. Taking a bow, she smiled with profound energy.

All I could say was, "Wow! She slayed it!"

Next to me Walter muttered, "Showoff."

Suddenly, I didn't feel so angry.

3

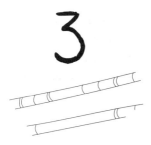

Whenever Nick entered a room, I swore "Uptown Funk" played overhead. He walked like a heavyweight boxer about to knock out his opponent in the first round—a swagger that made heads turn. And he had the attitude to match. He brimmed with confidence, and the entire student body could see it. Nick knew exactly how to act and which words to say, and he did so at every opportunity. This was how he'd ended up as student body president, also known as, the most popular boy in school.

The crowd in the student body section split in two as soon as Nick showed up. They were like peasants seeing royalty, throwing rose petals at his feet as he graced them with his presence. I watched from afar as one part of the section moved one way and the other half went the opposite. Wherever Nick decided to pass, the crowd accommodated him. It was difficult not to. He commanded attention—a quick smile and flashing blue eyes—with each step. Sometimes he weaved left to right, and other times he circled just to bask in his legions of fans. I'd experienced a similar feeling at the Folk Festival, basking in all the positive energy.

Everyone loved Nick. Well, except for one person. I had the text messages to remind me: 14/88.

Walter elbowed me. "Look who showed up," he said, gesturing in Nick's direction.

My eyes locked on to where Walter was looking, and suddenly my heart raced.

I know, I thought. *I could feel it.*

I swallowed the buildup of saliva in my mouth and bent my knees to slink down into the crowd of heads around me. Nick had every right to be here; he was a student after all. I'd argue that the majority of students would rather have Nick at the game than me. That poll even included me, who solely came to the game to hang out with my friends.

I ducked behind the person in front of me, squeezing myself in between Walter and Dennis. Dennis looked down at me, slid over a tad, and continued to watch the game.

"Just try'n relax," Walter said.

"I am," I answered, even though I wasn't. My eyes followed Nick as he greeted students with high fives, handshakes, and waves, engaging with teens as if he were running for office. He posed for selfies, his broad shoulders swaggering from side to side to accommodate each person's phone. Smugness radiated off him in waves. He enjoyed the attention, and although he was nowhere near me, his presence caused my gut to turn. He was one hundred percent a dickhead, or as I liked to call him, Nickhead.

"Maybe he'll stay down there," Walter said. By now, my head was pressed up against Dennis's body, my cheek every so often grazing against his skin. "Oh, wait, never mind."

"Huh?"

Walter shushed me and said, "Just keep still."

That could only mean one thing: Nick was getting closer. "Uptown Funk's" catchy beat was getting louder, the *doh, doh, doh doh doh, doh doh, doh doh doh,* pumping through my chest, making it hurt. Deep down I knew there wasn't music playing at all; rather, it was my heart, thumping in terror. I gritted my teeth until they hurt.

I peered out into the stands, catching a glimpse of him, following his every move. A few rows in front of me, one boy screamed, "Nick!" and the two bro hugged. They whispered a few words to each other, and in less than ten seconds Nick was engaging with another student, who then welcomed another student, then another—eventually, half of the row was fawning over Nick.

Walter's mouth dropped open, careening into a slight smile. "How nice would it be to be *that* popular?" I craned my head toward him, crouching even more in fear now that Nick was getting closer. "Sorry," Walter said. "You have to admit, everybody loves him."

Well . . . I thought.

Over the speaker system, the broadcaster said, "And now it's the start of the fourth quarter." Fans in other sections of the bleachers, away from Nick, rose to cheer their respective team.

"Go get 'em!" a group of mothers cheered.

The Falcons rushed the field to get into formation. The players from Westside greeted their counterparts on the grassy area, lining up in a row across the field. I slid in closer between Walter and Dennis to hide from Nick's view, shaking my head at Walter's comment. It made me wonder if he secretly had a crush on Nick.

When I snuck a peek at Walter's face, he was almost salivating as his eyes followed Nick. My fingertips started to sweat while my heartbeat played "Uptown Funk" in double speed. I swore Nick had a radar for these situations, always homing in on me like a heat-seeking missile. Sandwiched between my two friends, I said, "Let me know when Nick leaves."

A girl screamed off to the side. "Nick! Got a date for homecoming yet?" Her voice was loud, meaning he was getting closer. "If not, I'm available."

I crouched lower, my knees almost buckling. The *doh, doh, doh doh doh, doh doh, doh doh doh*, becoming louder and louder.

Nick shouted back to the girl. "I'm keeping my options open." Then he laughed and the music picked up.

I looked up to my friends. "Is he gone yet?" Neither Walter nor Dennis responded. I was uncertain if they could hear me over the football game, so I asked again. "Is he gone yet?"

Aren't they listening?

Again, there was no response. Instead, Dennis was screaming at the referee. He was sweating at this point, his body slick from the crowd's energy and body heat. My face rubbed up hard against his belly, the sweat soaking my cheek.

I tugged at Walter's shirt. "Did Nick leave?" I asked again, this time with greater concern. The crowd was silent. Then, fans of the home team began cheering.

"Yes!" Walter said. His arms flew up to the sky. My two friends began jumping on the bleachers, the force of which caused me to grab ahold of their waists.

"Nick's gone?" I said.

"Yes! Yes! Yes!"

I didn't realize that Walter was screaming at the outcome of the referee's ruling until I stood up to see Nickhead right in front of us. Surprised at his discovery, his eyes flashed, and his eyebrows lifted. "Well, what do we have here?" asked Nick. He looked like a kid on Christmas.

Walter spun around and looked at me. "I didn't tell you it was clear!"

"How's it going, Walter?" Nick said.

Walter's legs nearly buckled. He seemed smitten by Nick's popularity. He slid across the bleacher as far as he could without falling off, leaving nothing between Nick and I. "Want to join us?" Walter asked like a fanboy.

Nick's eyes burrowed into mine, and although he didn't say anything, I was reminded of a conversation we had when we were alone in the school bathroom back in junior high. He'd bowed and tucked his bottom lip under his front teeth, squinting his eyes and laughing—his classic Asian face. The bathroom was quiet, and I was secretly willing for someone to enter. Another student. A teacher. Anyone!

"Aw you roshing your hands?" His phony Asian accent was annoying and more than that, supremely racist. It was also inaccurate, but I'd learned to expect nothing less from Nick.

I ran out of the bathroom, the *doh, doh, doh doh doh, doh doh, doh doh doh* fading out of my head.

"No," Nick said to Walter. "Just came to enjoy the game." Then he slapped me hard on my shoulder.

Ow!

The pain brought me to my feet, and Nick smirked at me, pointing to my cheek. He clenched his teeth, his lips holding in a smile. "Well, you guys enjoy," he said and then walked away.

"What was that look for?" I asked.

Walter took out his phone, snapped a pic, and then showed it to me. Part of Falc U was smeared across my cheek. Only it was in reverse, the words reading, "U laF." The *c* in Falc U had not transferred, so conveniently the message spelled out, "You laugh." Because, of course it did. It was Nick. Everything he touched turned to gold.

"Never mind that," I said. "What were you thinking inviting him to join us?"

"I was thinking he's high-key the most popular dude in school," Walter said, "and it wouldn't hurt to be seen with him."

"Even though you know he's super racist?"

Walter shrugged. "I don't think he's that bad." Then he returned to watching the game.

What!

Thinking about Walter's statement made my heart hurt. An emptiness settled in the pit of my stomach. My mouth dried up, and I closed my eyes. I wanted to say something, but instead I remained silent. I just took the comment and buried it down in my soul. We'd just discussed this about Bethany, about being different, about racism—so why would his mind change now?

My jaw clenched and the cords in my neck went rigid. I just stood there in a huff, breathing heavily as the game carried on. The rest of the stadium was lost in its allure, but none of it seemed to matter right now. The only thing I could do to feel better was steal a glance at Bethany, who was watching the game with ambivalence. Just looking at her made me feel better.

Then, Walter screamed at the field. "Worst call ever!" It made me shake my head. *Kind of like when you said that Nickhead wasn't that bad,* I thought. I wanted to speak up, say something about Walter acting like Nick but to a lesser degree. White privilege. This was my opportunity.

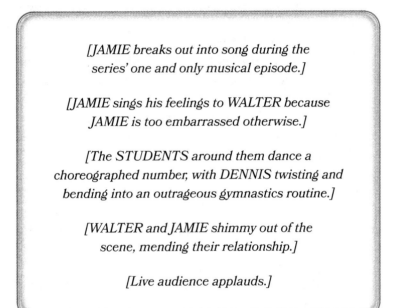

[JAMIE breaks out into song during the series' one and only musical episode.]

[JAMIE sings his feelings to WALTER because JAMIE is too embarrassed otherwise.]

[The STUDENTS around them dance a choreographed number, with DENNIS twisting and bending into an outrageous gymnastics routine.]

[WALTER and JAMIE shimmy out of the scene, mending their relationship.]

[Live audience applauds.]

But instead of standing up for myself, even to one of my best friends, I chickened out. "I can see why hanging out with Nick would be cool," I said.

What was I saying?

Deep down, I thought covering for Nick would lighten up Walter's opinion about Bethany. It was a weird theory, but it was something. I couldn't believe what I was saying. I gulped, "We're all good."

Then, some seats opened up near the student section, in the first row. Dennis pointed to the opportunity and asked if we wanted to move.

"Let's do it," Walter said, as if everything was back to normal. I just stayed silent and followed the two of them down the bleacher stairs, passing the elderly man with the bright red hat. When I snuck a look in his direction, I noticed the hat read the name of a local grocery store chain. The slogan was underneath it, giving the perception of another infamous motto.

Since the election, anytime I saw a red hat with white lettering I expected the worst. Images on the internet of angry white men with red hats screaming into the camera, flipping people off with spit flying from their mouths, flashed through my brain every time I saw a red hat with white block lettering. It was a knee-jerk reaction to all the stories that went along with the images.

The old man and I made eye contact. He nodded and then returned his focus to the field. I breathed a sigh of relief, realizing I'd gotten myself into a tizzy about presumed racism, when I was really struggling with my own culture.

I sat and watched the game from my new seat, not saying a word to either of my friends, only sulking quietly to myself. Walter and Dennis watched in silence.

I looked up at the scoreboard: Saint Patrick's was now up by three touchdowns. I watched as the final minutes of the game ticked down until it finally ended. The team launched onto the field, shouting and cheering. The cheerleaders followed closely after, and the crowd erupted with hollers. Fans around us hugged and high-fived. We won, but I didn't care. No matter how much happiness and joy filled the atmosphere, I felt depressed. How could I not?

Soon after, the stadium emptied, each person, couple, and family retiring to their respective lives. I did the same. With hardly a word spoken about the incident with Nick, the ride home was quiet. When my friends dropped me off at my house, I bid them adieu and walked the lonely path up my front steps to my happy place.

The encounter with Nick had dampened my mood, like always. When I felt dejected and insecure like this, I drowned myself in food. The fridge held the key—egg rolls, white rice, and chicken adobo. I made a beeline for the fridge as soon as I entered the house and quickly made myself a plate.

I leaned against the kitchen counter as I ate. From where I stood, I could see my father asleep on the couch, my mother and grandmother having already disappeared to their rooms. The dim glow of the television created a faint spotlight on his slumped figure. His head drooped down onto one shoulder, his beloved karaoke microphone resting on his belly as he dreamed the night away.

When the gadget was idle for extended periods of time, it went on auto mode and began cycling through various songs in its catalog. It was a feature designed to entice participants. The song playing now was by Miley Cyrus. The words crawled across the screen and a dot bounced on each word that, in this case, should have been sung by my father. With him passed out, the scene was like riding in an elevator—no words, just electronic music.

Digging into my food, I thought about the Folk Festival. A wave of emotions hit me at once—agitation, anguish, despair—exploding from the pit that I'd buried them into. It was the gateway to my Filipino culture that I didn't share with my family, that I only experienced with other Filipino kids. Now I felt hopeless, like my one and only safe space was turning on me. First Nick, then Walter for some reason, and now the Folk Festival. What was going on?

When I first began dancing, the coconut dance, also known as Maglalatik, had been my introduction to the spotlight. I was so nervous! Twelve dancers participated, wearing coconut shells cut into halves that were attached to our hands, elbows, knees, waists, and shoulders by thick, elastic bands. Our objective was to hit each shell in time with the beat of the music, as part of a choreographed routine.

When the dance began, the music was slow. As the routine progressed, to dazzle the audience with dance moves and hand-eye coordination, the music got faster and faster. The entire event only lasted a few minutes, but afterward the audience was left mesmerized.

Onlookers always talked to us after the event.

"That was so amazing!" people would say.

"Wonderful!"

"A perfect performance!"

Their comments felt like reviews of a Broadway show. They treated us like celebrities, acting like adoring fans that wanted nothing more than to speak to us and praise us for our efforts. I was able to glimpse into Nick's life. It gave me confidence for the first time, a sense of normalcy that had nothing to do with the color of my skin. We all looked like each other, and people only saw us for our talent.

The stares gave me a feeling of being seen in a positive light, instead of being looked at as a second-rate citizen. I was from another world, not a third world. I was . . . I was a human being.

People would beg to take pictures with us and inquire about autographs. Often, people would ask if they could wear the coconuts to see how difficult it was to have them on while dancing. They were surprised to find out the edges of the shells would dig into their skin, piercing them when they moved. At times, I had the marks to prove it. This only added to the mystique of the Filipino Dancing Troupe.

The memories brought a smile to my face. Hanging with the other dancers and basking in the attention of impressed fans brought me the greatest feeling in the world. I was filled with helium, my body floating off the ground in an intoxicating high, and nothing could bring me out of it.

Before I could fall deeper into a trance, the instrumental Miley Cyrus song ended, and fake applause emanated from the living room. The video game music tallied up a score, and my smile widened, amused. I finished off the rest of my late-night snack and retired to my bedroom.

My fancy, embroidered short-sleeved shirt hung on a doorknob in my room. The thick pants draped over the hanger. Recalling my years of dancing made me happy, and in that moment, I wanted nothing more than to drag that feeling out for as long as I could. So, I decided to once again, change and rehearse.

I still could *not* believe the Folk Festival was ending. It was weird—the more I thought about it the more it brought back wonderful memories. But it also brought a heavy dose of sadness. It was bittersweet at best.

Staring into the mirror, fully dressed, coconuts attached like I was a rejected Teenage Mutant Ninja Turtle, I jumped out a couple feet. Mentally playing the music in my head, I smacked the coconut shell on my right palm against the shell attached to my left knee. My palm then slid up toward my upper body, the shell striking the one secured on my left shoulder. Then I kicked my leg up, my body twisting one way, and mimicked the action with the shell attached to my left palm. I struck each shell in rhythm, adding in a couple dance moves in between, and danced the routine from beginning to end. The shells struck one another with solid hits, a unique experience not unlike a tap dancer tapping on stage. I wondered if I was too loud for my parents and grandmother.

As I stood in the mirror, striking the pose I normally did on stage, faint artificial clapping from the television rose through the floor. Closing my eyes, I slowly began to cry. I'd been holding in my emotions since I'd heard the news, putting on my brave face for my friends and the public. Thinking about it was too much. My knees buckled, causing me to fall to the floor. The edges of the coconut shells dug into my thighs. I cried even more, so much that I wasn't even making noise anymore—just a babbling baby with red cheeks and a flood of tears streaming down my face. My body convulsed with twitches that I couldn't control.

My dream was ending and for what? A crappy real life dictated by racists like Nickhead? A life predetermined by a rise of white nationalism? By people that only cared about those who looked like them?

I leaned into the mirror and smirked, copping a disgusted look at my face. It still had smeared lettering on it. I realized that if I didn't do anything, didn't stand up for myself, that this was what my life was going to be from now on—an eternal message that told racists to laugh at me.

Even when Nick didn't get to me, he got to me.

4

I woke up earlier than usual and sat on my bed evaluating my life. I was extra mopey, thinking about all that had transpired the day before. Three issues clouded my mind. The first was of course, the Folk Festival. The second, Nick's continual harassment.

When Nick first started picking on me, my plan was to just allow him to get his fix until he grew tired of ridiculing me and eventually stopped. It had started in the sixth grade. I thought it would have changed by now.

Last night was no different. He had sauntered in and made his presence known, playing the all-American boy to his legions of fans. The oblivious students wanted a piece of Mister Popularity, disregarding the fact that Nick was a friggin' racist. But why would they care? Just like Walter, all the other students were white like Nick.

The third issue was the homecoming dance. Both Walter and Dennis wanted to go, mainly because it was the first year we, as sophomores, could go. It was all they talked about. I'd never really thought about it, since the festival landed on the same date, but Walter didn't know that. I'd just said that it was ending. He knew about my dancing but didn't care enough to get invested. Neither of them did. Not seriously, at least. But if I did go, perhaps it could be with Bethany!

I scanned my bedroom to see my dance uniform hanging bravely on a hanger on the closet doorknob. Then all the photographs from past festivals. The visuals made me smile. Not a whole lot, but still.

My parents were in their bedroom conversing in Tagalog; I could hear their voices trickling through the walls that separated my room from theirs. My ears perked up and I stiffened, my focus turning toward the muffled sound of their conversation. Then I heard footsteps.

My father poked his head into my room. "Do you want to eat?"

Outside, from the hallway, my mother screamed, "Ask Jamie if he wants to go!"

Addressing her, my father said, "What?" My mother repeated the request. "I am!" he screamed, before groaning. "We're going to eat Chinese," he informed me. "Want to go?"

"I thought they cooked yesterday."

His lips pursed as he looked back over his shoulder. "Your mom has a coupon; we're all going to go," he said. "Me, your mom, and your grandma."

"Sure." I shrugged, holding back my own thoughts. "That sounds good. I'll be right out."

I didn't really want to go to the buffet. I still felt like grieving the festival, but I didn't have another reason for getting out of bed today. Sulking in my misery had sounded like a plan worth pursuing, even though I knew it would just make me more miserable. Chinese food was a good enough incentive to get me moving, to get me motivated, and to get me dressed.

"Also," my father began, "I want to talk to you about your grandma."

"Is something wrong?"

"We'll talk about it later."

"OK . . . I just need to change," I told him, and my father nodded. Then, his eyebrows lowered, and he inched closer to me. Pointing to my cheek, he said, "What happened to your face?"

My eyes narrowed. "My face?"

He pointed his lips and extended them. "Your cheek."

U laF.

My mouth opened and an awkward chuckle escaped. Blushing, I began rubbing at the ink until my cheek hurt. "Nothing," I said. "It was for the football game." I kept rubbing until my skin burned, though I couldn't tell if the heat emanating from between my fingertips was from that or a result of my embarrassment. "It's from Dennis."

"Oh," my father said. "Do you want to call him? See if he wants to come and eat?"

"No." I sighed, looking for a response he would accept. "He has homework," I lied.

"Oh," he said again. "What—"

"Walter does too." After last night's comment, I really wasn't in the mood. I knew I'd get over it, just not yet.

My father stopped and stared down at the carpet for a moment. Then he decided to respect my privacy for a change and left, closing the door behind him. "Ma *ma*," he called out to my grandmother. "Get dressed. We're going to eat."

I slid out of my bed, made it quickly, and got dressed. As I threw on clothes, my eyes were drawn to all the photographs documenting all the years I'd given to the association. Then they moved back to my performance attire. Seeing everything at once made me think again of the first time I danced, a bittersweet memory in the wake of the news about the festival.

Before I could start to reminisce on my entire dancing career, my mother opened the door. The doorknob turning startled me. My right knee kicked up, my foot suspended in the air, and I pirouetted with elegance to address my mother. It was a classic Tinikling move.

"Are you ready?" she asked.

I stole a look at my barong and smiled. "Yeah, I'm good."

We left the house and piled into the car.

On the way to the buffet, my father was belting out the lyrics to a song on the radio, singing in his loud, spirited karaoke voice. My mother talked about what she wanted to eat, to no one in particular. My grandmother and I were in the back seat, both looking out our respective windows.

Suddenly, something caught my attention: blue and red flashing lights.

My father, messing up the lyrics with different words, had gotten caught up in the song and had somehow forgotten he was driving. We were getting pulled over.

After the car slowed to a stop, my father hit the flashers. Behind us the police car's lights intruded through the back window, the brightness of the bulbs forcing its way into the back seat. My mother began to settle into her seat as my grandmother stared aimlessly out the car's window. She turned toward the sirens, the bright lights drawing her in. I, meanwhile, started to hyperventilate.

My father, on the other hand, raised his hand up, as if to say, "I got this." A little thing about my father. He was born during the President Marcos era. He had been a teenager at the height of martial law, so he was no stranger to the current happenings in the United States— the protests, the opposition, the crooked politicians. He had lived through it successfully and had come out the other side. He honestly believed that the current political climate would be exactly the same as his teenage experience—that it too, would pass. Therefore, his confidence was through the roof.

I was not as easily convinced. I was living it for the first time.

"Don't say anything," my father instructed us, shushing us in case we didn't hear. Eyeing the rearview, he called out to my grandmother in Tagalog, "Ma ma, please don't talk."

My grandmother nodded, laughing. "Claudio," she began in her native tongue. "Always causing trouble." Then she shook her head. After a second, she turned to me. "He's always challenging authority."

What does that mean? I thought.

My father and grandmother exchanged a couple words, until my father repeated his command.

Craning my head, I could see the officer—a white officer—marching toward the car, his right palm resting on the butt of his gun.

I began to freak out.

White officer? A car full of minorities? Tap, tap, tap, and then outcries for justice! This never ends well on the internet!

I imagined Shaun King pushing our story on his social media sites, asking for the name of the police officer. "We need to know who this officer is. He just shot up a car full of Asians." There would be thousands of shares, and the video would garner millions of views. "This family was only going to the buffet," King would tweet. "What is this world coming to? We. Are. Better. Than. This."

Cars zoomed by the cop, and a couple of the passersby stared at the situation. The officer looked friendly enough with his half-smile—very non-confrontational. When he reached the car, he tapped on the window with his knuckles. My father nodded and slid the window down. As he did so, the police officer stepped back, adjusting his position to prepare for the worst.

When the coast was clear, the cop peeked into the car. His eyes scanned the back seat and the passenger seat, before saying to my father, "Can I see your license and registration, please?"

My mother sat like a statue. She didn't move, she didn't speak; it was as if she had fallen asleep with her eyes open.

My father dug into his back pocket, his upper body leaning far into the passenger seat. My mother, centimeters from my father, remained still. He pulled out his wallet and slid out his credit card. Handing the officer his Visa, he stated in Tagalog, "You are very ugly."

My grandmother burst out laughing.

My father was the type, growing up during the martial law of late '70s and early '80s in the Philippines, who believed that any police official was the enemy. He had his share of run-ins with Marcos's administration, many of which were with corrupt officers, so the badge really affected my father, like some sort of PTSD. It brought back a slew of memories for him, and it was times like this he'd go into opposition mode.

The police officer glanced into the back seat, squinting against the glare of his headlights. I forced out a smile and then waved with a fragile wrist.

Please, don't shoot! I thought, terrified.

"This is a credit card," the officer said, returning his attention to my father. He was well composed, a professional. My father pointed to the piece of plastic, nodding his head in ignorance. "This is not your driver's license," the policeman said sternly. "Please hand me your license." He returned the credit card, pushing it toward my father's face.

My father, feigning ignorance, retrieved the plastic and then slid out his insurance card. He held it up to the officer's face.

The cop clenched his jaw, baring his teeth in a grimace.

"Your driver's license," he reiterated, slowly and clearly, enunciating each word loudly in his annoyance. It always confused me, why people thought repeating the same thing over and over but louder each time would make them easier to understand—it didn't.

My father scratched his head. "Lie sense," he said slowly.

"Yes, your license. I need to see your driver's license."

My father then shook his head.

After a moment, the officer closed his fists and mirrored steering a wheel.

"Oh," my father answered. "So sorry." He exchanged his insurance card for his license. The officer told us he would be back in a minute, the relief clear on his face, and then disappeared into his car behind us. "Pig, oink, oink," my father said, imitating a pig's sound.

My grandmother laughed even harder.

"Dah *dee!*" my mother said. Rattling out Tagalog, she muttered, "We're going to get arrested."

My father stopped joking. At least until he caught a glimpse of my grandmother in the rearview mirror, and together, they burst out laughing.

"Dah *dee!*" my mother screamed. She elbowed him. "You're setting a bad example for Jamie."

I shook my head. *Bad example? More like a badass example.* If only I had a sliver of the courage my father had.

"He knew I was joking."

"You don't know how it will affect him," my mother said.

The two argued for a moment in rapid Tagalog until my father twisted his upper body to face me, resting his elbow on the back of the car seat. "You knew I was joking, right?" he said to me.

I nodded.

The officer returned to the driver's side window. Slipping the license back to my father, he said, "You were driving under the speed limit." The officer looked down toward the road, pointed into the distance. "It's forty-five here. You were doing thirty." His hand showed four fingers, then five. "Four, five," he said. "Forty-five."

My father nodded. He quickly took out cash. Four five-dollar bills. Handing the money to the policeman, he offered, "Four fives." Nodding his head, my father pushed the money toward the officer.

The officer, visibly shaken, looked back to his car. I followed his gaze and saw the patrol car's camera. All I thought was, *Please don't put this on social media. Please don't put this on social media.* I could imagine that tweet from King. "Officer bribes Asian family to *not* issue a ticket. Spread this video around. We. Are. Better. Than. This!"

My father's arm extended farther out the window. He was leaning out of the car, pushing the money toward the policeman.

"No," the officer said. Holding his hands up so we could see his palms, he said, "You're free to go." He started waving to my father, gesturing for him to continue. Then he pointed down the road.

My father continued his assault. "Four fives."

Backing away from the car, shaking his head, the officer said, "Bye-bye." He glanced at his patrol car again. Flicking his wrist down the way we were heading, he instructed, "Go!" Then he grabbed his imaginary steering wheel and moved his fists from left to right.

In today's world, there were two different types of minorities—my generation and my father's. He and my mother came to America back when being politically correct was non-existent; when commercials boasted Asian families saying into the camera, "Ancient Chinese secret." There were no cell phone cameras, no social media sites, and people were accountable for their actions. All of this contributed to his mentality. To put it bluntly, my father did not give a shit.

I didn't think the officer was a bad person; he handled the situation that was in front of him. But between the media, society, and Nickhead, my first thought was how badly it could end. My father, though, had a different perception. He just saw police as pigs.

My father nodded lazily, rolled up the window, and started the car. Shifting into drive, he muttered, "*Tarantado*," which was the closest translation to "asshole" in Tagalog.

My grandmother laughed. "Claudio," she whispered.

As we drove off, I spun around to see the officer walking back to his car. His head was down, and his gait didn't have that confidence it once did.

We drove for a few miles until we arrived at the restaurant. The buffet's glitzy sign greeted us, blinking above the filled parking lot. The only spot my father could find was at the far end of the property, on the other side of the entrance. The four of us walked the distance to the front doors together, toward the wave of soy sauce mixed with fried breading drifting out of the vents.

My grandmother grabbed my arm and used my body as a crutch. We walked slower than my parents, who were gaining distance as we marched toward the doors.

"Are you doing OK?" I asked.

My grandmother smiled, nodding as she continued to walk toward the entrance.

She came to live with us when I was eight. She was the typical grandmother: she brought us useless gifts, made us clothes that we would never wear, and she was always elated to see us, oftentimes overly hugging and kissing us as a greeting.

It was weird at first, those initial days she'd lived with us. I didn't really know what to say to her; I'd never had a grandparent this close to me. My other ones were still in the Philippines, so meeting someone who knew my father as a kid was exciting.

One day, my mother came into my room and asked if I had any pants or shirts that needed mending. My grandmother was a seamstress, so she offered to sew patches or mend any clothes that were ripped or on the verge of ripping. My wardrobe doubled instantly, and it was then I began a relationship with her. She introduced me to *champorado*, a chocolate oatmeal-type dish, which soon became my favorite Filipino meal.

Soon, we reached the buffet's entrance. A hostess seated us at a table and told us where to find the buffet, plates, and cutlery, pointing to the islands of glass windows in the center of the room. I followed her finger, the bright lights and aromas of different countries competing for my attention. It was impossible to choose what to eat here. Was I in the mood for Italian? Sushi? Fried chicken? There was so much to choose from, your standard Chinese-American buffet.

The establishment was jam-packed with hungry patrons, stuffing their plates and their faces, often at the same time.

"Go ahead," my mother said, and then she helped my grandmother into her chair.

I zigzagged through the maze of aisles and filled my dish until it looked like a volcano of food piled on top of each other. Fried rice, egg rolls, Mongolian beef, crab rangoon, sweet and sour pork, black pepper chicken, and two fried chicken legs, all crammed together in the center.

Balancing the plate in my hands, I returned to the booth.

My father was on the phone, talking to a friend. He was talking so loud, I could hear him before I could see him clearly. He laughed and said in Tagalog, "We're eating Chinese."

My mother and grandmother had already vanished from the booth and into the buffet, so when I sat down, I succumbed to the embarrassment of my father alone as he barked out Tagalog into the phone's receiver. Instantly, my mood swung to the negative, and I scanned the tables that surrounded us, waiting for a snarky remark or a funny look.

For some reason, his Tagalog voice was always much louder than his English voice. "It's fine to use our house," he said, smiling widely. "No, no, no." My father laughed. "Not a problem at all."

Sensitive to what patrons nearby were thinking, I threw down an egg roll, quietly listening to the one-sided conversation. *When will this be over?* I thought.

[SHAUN KING turns to the camera. He is sitting in the booth next to JAMIE and his family, eating a plate of different types of food.]

[PATRONS look condescendingly at JAMIE'S FAMILY.]

[SHAUN pulls out his phone, his thumb on the Twitter app.]

SHAUN: Are we better than this?

My father's voice brought me back to the restaurant. "Jamie and the dance troupe need to practice," he said.

The conversation was about me, but nobody around us knew what he was saying. I leaned in to hear more, picking at my food so the chewing wouldn't distract me from eavesdropping.

Soon after, my mother returned with a plate of crab legs. My father passed her the phone, gesturing with his lips to talk.

The abrupt action took her by surprise. "Who's that?"

Pursing his lips, my father said, "Just answer." He then grabbed a leg from the plate.

Collecting the phone, my mother said, "Hello?" A slow smile formed on her face. "Oh, hi, how are you?" My mother listened for a moment. "We're all here, even Jamie."

I cut her a look, my eyes fluttering. Surely the people around us knew I had to be Jamie, right? My name didn't translate in Tagalog, and they had mentioned me twice. People had to be wondering what the hubbub was.

I ate my food slowly, half-listening to her conversation, but also attentive to my surroundings. The bearded man nearly choking on pizza. The wrinkle-skinned woman who looked like she smoked a carton of cigarettes between each bite of noodles. Her reverse-bob hairdo was a dead give-away—a patriot mom only wanting what was best for her country. *OK, I'll just say it*, I thought. *Karen*. And I couldn't ignore the older white man with a large crucifix across his shirt shouting out his religious beliefs.

It was nice to know that Chinese food could bring people of varying opinions together. Again, Asians were submissive. So, I guessed it was OK to eat their food.

My mother began to talk louder, almost screaming, and my attention returned to her. Whoever was on the other end had to be going deaf. "We can stop by later," she said. "Maybe after we bring Jamie home. He probably won't want to come."

Here they were, flaunting their ethnicity while I was trying to hide from it, dodging glances from people who probably thought I would steal their job or benefits from under their hard-working noses. I felt the looks on me, waiting for me to speak to see if I spoke with an accent, or if I spoke in a different language. They were waiting to judge me, to justify their behavior should a call to immigration be necessary.

I sunk down into my seat, my head down. Were people staring because my mother was being loud? In my mind, they, like Nick, all wanted us to go back to our own countries. They wanted to poke fun at us. They wanted to—

My mother hung up the phone. She addressed me. "Do you remember Chit?" I shook my head. "Chit!" she yelled, astonished that I didn't know who this person was. "You remember Chit. He was your confirmation sponsor."

My father, meanwhile, took the plate of crab legs. My grandmother waddled back to the booth with her own plate.

"Yeah," I said. "I remember." I really didn't, but it was the only way to end this episode.

"He's coming to the Folk Festival."

The news alone should have brightened my day, but the embarrassment was so overwhelming, I simply shrugged and dug into my meal. I couldn't admit it was cool around these ever so important non-Filipinos.

After the short exchange, my mother stood to find food. My father followed and my grandmother dove into her food.

"How are you enjoying everything?" I asked quietly so no one could hear me speaking in Tagalog.

She swallowed a cold piece of shrimp, nodding. "It's good," she said. "It's nice to get out once in a while." Then she went into a coughing fit, one that ran long enough that I got nervous.

I slowly turned to the table of six next to us, watching to see if her ailment had distracted them enough to investigate. But instead, I saw that they were eating in silence. Not once did anyone in their party turn toward me. They were all shoveling down Chinese food, breadsticks, or fried chicken.

In one corner of the restaurant, a Pakistani family ate in silence. In the other, a Mexican family enjoyed each other's company. White families were scattered about enjoying their meals. There were several other Asian families—Thai,

Korean, and I believed Japanese—all eating in peace. And Karen was marinating on her plate of noodles. Either America wasn't as scary as I'd pegged it to be, or egg rolls really did bring people together.

Regardless, my insecurity still got the best of me. However, my self-doubt did not last too long, as once my mother and father returned, they told me what they had wanted to discuss.

In English, my father said, "We're going to send your grandma back to the Philippines."

What?

The news about my grandmother shocked me. It wasn't something I expected from my parents. The rest of the time we sat in silence until we headed home, full to the brim. I couldn't stop thinking about why they would send my grandmother back when she'd been here for so long.

Over the next couple days, they slowly broke the news to my grandmother. I only got bits and pieces, as school and the Folk Festival dilemma clouded my mind. But the times I was around, it was like a pop star's farewell tour, one long montage down memory lane. The three of them reliving various recollections, like the days when my mother and father were dating, laughing at how different they were as young adults. It was weird to hear about my parents as single people before I was born.

"I wasn't sure why your mother liked your father," my grandmother told me. My father chuckled as I stole a look at him. Then my mother reached for his hand and pulled it into her. "Not because of your father's doing," she said, "but because your mother's family was so well off." My grandmother looked at my parents with flashing eyes. "The two were just so different," she added. "She could have been with someone of the same status."

I wouldn't be here if she had, I thought.

The television barked some dialog, and the audience clapped. The network was airing reruns of *Cheers.*

My mother's hand grazed my father's forearm. "Your father was," pausing to look at him, "*is* the bravest and most generous person I know. That's why I fell in love with him."

The two shared a look. My grandmother started to cough, and my father released his gaze to escort my grandmother upstairs to her room.

"I'll be right back," he said.

My mother and I looked toward the television and sat in silence. I was half-listening, my thoughts now on performing my final dances.

There were footfalls above us, maneuvering through the hallway until they stopped in my grandmother's room.

"How are you doing?" my mother asked.

I knew she was inquiring about the festival from her solemn tone, but I still wasn't ready to talk. That part of my heart was still recuperating from the news. I'd gotten over it a little but had managed to avoid the topic for the most part, only sharing some texts back and forth to Rosario. To someone who could honestly relate.

"I'm fine."

"Do you want to talk about the festival?"

Shaking my head, I said, "Not really." I turned to her. "It's ending . . . there's nothing really to talk about."

My mother slowly nodded, her lips pointing ever so softly. "Your confirmation sponsor is coming," she said. "That's nice of him."

"Yeah." *Chit was it?* I thought, and then I turned to the TV.

The slight tension in the room wafted around us. To avoid talking about the Folk Festival, I watched the show for a couple scenes, until my father returned.

"Everything all right?" he asked, feeling the thickness in the room.

The side of my lip curled, and applause broke out on the television set. With my grandmother retired for the night, it was one of the few times I had my mother and father alone. Just the three of us.

"Everything is fine," my mother replied. "Just watching television."

On the TV, Sam Malone joked about his days as a baseball player. It was a typical sitcom formula, a set-up from a supporting cast member, and the punchline delivered by the star. The scenes always flowed so seamlessly. The laugh track kicked on, and my eyes were drawn to the show but then shortly fell over to my mother.

"Just like old times," she said.

A rumble above us disrupted the moment. A long stretched out coughing fit ensued, and my father soon disappeared to check on my grandmother.

My mother and I looked at each other. Then, before the silence could linger, she said, "Are Walter and Dennis coming to the festival?"

"No."

"Are the three of you, OK?" she asked. "Usually, you're over at one of their houses, or they're over here, or . . ." Then she stopped talking.

Was it that obvious on my face?

I was still a little bitter about Walter's attitude at the game. Plus, with the festival next weekend, I wanted to focus all my energy on that, knowing that my relationship with Walter and Dennis would work itself out. It typically did.

"We're fine," I muttered. "They're planning on going to the homecoming dance, and they're super excited about it." My mother's eyes narrowed. "The festival and the homecoming dance are on the same night." Her mouth circled, as if she hadn't put two and two together.

Her chin jutted out, almost like she knew the dilemma and why there was friction between us, but that was only part of the story. "Well," she said, "you should at least tell them the dance and the festival are on the same day."

"I plan to," I said.

"I'm sure they'll understand."

5

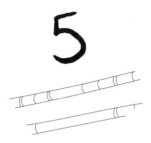

At school, students were laughing more than usual, happy just to be there. With everything going on in my life, the atmosphere just seemed petty. Irrelevant. A couple of students were playing catch in the hall, and at one point I had to duck out of the way of an errant football.

I walked quicker, rounding the corner when I passed two kids, who were chatting nonstop about how excited they were for the upcoming football game, the homecoming game, the big one before the dance. Naturally, this conversation sparked an interest in the previous game against Westside, and the students stood around recalling specific plays that had occurred.

"That breakdancing battle was the best part," one boy said to his friend. "How rad was that?" He half-attempted a robot with his right arm, bending it into a ninety-degree angle and letting it swing like the pendulum on a grandfather clock.

When I saw this, I cracked a smile. *Bethany*, I thought. The game was days ago, yet her impact was living on so vividly.

All around the school were signs promoting homecoming. As I walked down the hall toward the cafeteria, I saw that the old, defaced signs had been replaced with new ones that featured James Bond posed in his suit with a gun pointed toward the words "007 Homecoming Dance." It practically screamed the theme to everyone who walked past.

I entered the cafeteria and took a seat in between Walter and Dennis, who were watching a video of a far-right rally that had occurred in downtown Portland and was rumored to involve a couple of football players at our small private, suburban high school. It was one of a continuous parade of rallies that seemed to never end.

Instantly, my gaze went to where the players were sitting, eyeing them as they entertained themselves at their table. I tried to decipher which players, if not all of them, were bigots.

A high-profile right-wing group was from nearby Vancouver, Washington, but the members spent a lot of time protesting in downtown Portland. Walter and Dennis were scanning the footage to see if they could find out which football players were there.

"How did they even find out about this?" Walter asked, leaning closer to the small phone's screen, squinting to see.

I took a quick glance at the footage. It was filled with a thousand or so tiny, unpixelated faces. The volume was muted, so it was difficult to get the full impact of the rally.

"I think you're wasting your time," I said.

Walter ignored me.

Dennis jumped in, "How crazy is it knowing that some of our beloved football players could have been at this rally? Or any one of 'em? A bunch of racists spouting their views."

Thinking about Nick, I muttered, "Is it?"

My mind shifted, and I scanned the long tables for one person—Bethany. We'd shared a moment at the football game, but it was different than our previous run-ins, where we just exchanged subtle smiles and curious looks. It was the in I was looking for with her. She had always made me feel good when we interacted, but add in the breakdancing? Seriously, I was smitten. Just like the boys in the hall, she had an impact on me. The more I thought about her, the more interested I became.

[BETHANY, the neighbor who always lingers around, completely invisible to JAMIE, walks in and out of JAMIE'S house, striking up conversation with his parents, while secretly fawning over him.]

In this episode, BETHANY is the only character with an obscure but necessary item that JAMIE needs to conclude the show.

[Cue the heart-eye graphics.]

BETHANY is now on JAMIE'S radar.

[After the last commercial break, JAMIE fantasizes a montage of rom-com moments between them, like picking up her dropped books or having to hold hands for some contrived reason.]

[JAMIE fawns hardcore.]

My friends were scarfing down food next to me, shoveling blindly as the video ended—especially Dennis. He acted as if this was his last meal, like a prisoner on his way to death row.

The video ended and Walter and Dennis returned to reality. The motion distracted me, and I saw that Walter's attention was now on the table of football players.

"You're never going to know which ones were there," I said.

"Maybe you're right," Walter said, and returned to his lunch. "But it's still crazy to think about."

Again, I muttered, "Is it?"

"Creamed chicken on a biscuit is the best school lunch ever," Dennis said, in between bites, interrupting our conversation. He wasn't even chewing, only swallowing as soon as the food entered his mouth. "Seriously, best hot lunch ever," he proclaimed through a mouthful of food.

"Remember when you read the announcements, and you replaced what was really on the menu with creamed chicken on a biscuit hoping that it would magically come true?" I asked.

We laughed.

"It didn't," said Dennis.

Walter scooped up a serving for himself. He, on the other hand, savored the taste and relished in its flavor. He closed his eyes with each bite, almost like it would heighten the experience.

We'd quasi made up, without so many words, and it was fine with me. It was a recipe we deployed whenever there was tension: a long, drawn-out text chain over the course of two days. Then, add in a speckle of time. Finally, a stilted conversation where we pretended nothing had happened. We had a lot of history together, and one disagreement wasn't going to tear us apart.

As for me, I sat with a full tray, the hot lunch untouched and instead, stared around the room examining face after face after face—until I spotted Bethany sitting in the corner of the cafeteria.

She wore a long, plain black skirt and orange short sleeved shirt with a white cat decal on the front. Her striped socks stretched the length of her lower legs. She looked like something out of a Tim Burton movie as she perched on the edge of her seat, a small distance away from the next student.

Her knees were facing the girl next to her, who was gabbing with Bethany as the two alternated bites for chitchat. Bethany randomly picked at her food, spearing the biscuit before letting it drop back to the plate, nodding to the girl or smiling whenever the girl became animated. The girl dressed like every other person at school in a loose blouse that fell over blue jeans—very regular and forgettable. Was she at the football game too? I wasn't certain.

Whatever the case, I just stared, wondering how I could talk to Bethany about her epic windmill without sounding like too much of a tool.

Bethany poked at a piece of shredded chicken, smothered it in the creamy base, and threw it into her mouth. She chewed slowly, almost oblivious to the taste as she concentrated on her plain-Jane friend's story. She didn't pay attention to anyone else but the girl. It was something I'd noticed the handful of times I had talked to her. She was always fully engaged with the person she was speaking to.

I was enamored with her, totally lost in her presence. The looks at the game were the closest I'd come to making a true connection with her. Sure, I playfully flirted with her the random times I'd talked to her, and our conversations were a lot of fun, as if we'd known each other forever. But I had never made a move.

One time, I left class and literally bumped into her while she was standing by her locker. I apologized, and we talked for what seemed like only a few seconds. She mentioned something about my haircut, saying how much she liked it. It caught me off guard. My hair was the last thing I cared about. The fact that she'd noticed gave me butterflies.

The next thing I knew I was late for class.

All our conversations were so fluid, uninterrupted, like our lines were scripted. I felt like I was flirting with her, but maybe I wasn't. She never made me feel uncomfortable, which made it so easy to talk to her. At the game the looks felt different, and that scared the crap out of me—in a good way.

"Why aren't you eating?" Dennis elbowed me hard. He was nearly finished with his lunch. Scoping out the line at the front of the cafeteria, he said, "I may go up and get seconds."

I looked down, apathetic in my purchase, and then shrugged. "I guess I'm not that hungry," I replied.

"You didn't even touch your food."

"Just not feeling it," I said.

Dennis slid his tray out in front of him. Drooling over my lunch, he asked, "Mind if I feel it?"

"Why not?" I pushed the food over toward him and returned my gaze to Bethany. She was speaking while subconsciously grazing her fingertips across her phone. The girl slid a forkful lazily into her mouth, her eyebrows rising whenever Bethany said something interesting. She chewed in a steady rhythm, almost mechanically, as if eating was a means to function rather than a means of enjoyment.

I continued to stare at her until Walter pounded me on the shoulder.

"Unbelievable."

"Ow!" I said, whipping him a look. The other students sitting at our table began staring as I rubbed my shoulder with my palm, wincing at the pain. "What was that for?"

"I'm afraid our friend, Jamie here," he said, turning to Dennis, "has other ideas for lunch." He started laughing so hard his body started to quiver, almost causing him to fall off the bench. "He apparently wants what *she* has," pointing toward Bethany's table. "I'll pass."

"Hey!" I yelled, louder than I expected, and it startled me enough to look around at my surroundings. "Why are you being so mean?"

Walter rolled his eyes and turned his head to avoid a confrontation.

"Seriously," I said. My eyes darted around the cafeteria—a few tables of students were looking in our direction. To my right, I scouted out a table full of cheerleaders. Several of them wore jerseys of their favorite Saint Patrick's players or of their dates for the big dance. One was glaring at me, waiting for the argument to escalate.

I panned across the table full of band members. A tuba player was sitting sideways on the edge of the bench, practicing his instrument. The low-pitched horn bellowed across the cafeteria—it sounded like he was summoning whales. A drummer twirled a stick in-between his fingers, watching me with a keen interest.

"What?" Walter said. "Just giving ya' shit."

My attention rolled back to him, passing the table full of football players who were causing their own ruckus at their table: daring one of the team members to drink as many cartons of milk as he could in one minute. In front of him were rows of cartons, waiting to be drunk.

Then I said to Walter, "Sure you were."

He shrugged, and as usual, I did nothing. Instead, I noticed Bethany glancing at me. Her friend had left the table, and Bethany was sitting alone.

Our eyes met, and when they locked, I couldn't help but smile. Just like that, my annoyance with Walter disappeared.

At first, she just stared at me, but when I kept smiling my goofy grin, Bethany eventually closed her eyes and ducked away with a slight smile. I wasn't sure if she was flattered or terrified, which made me nervous. So much so, I softened my smile and dropped my eyes to the table in fear. After staring at the space in front of me for what seemed like hours, telling myself repeatedly that everything was cool, I stole a look toward Bethany's direction. *Be. Brave,* I told myself.

Even though I was born in America and spoke without an accent, I was a brown skinned Filipino kid trying to avoid the Nickheads of the world. I could walk into a room and immediately know which kids had issues with me, just from the way they looked at me or the way they spoke to me. It became a lot more common in 2017 when the new administration took office.

One day, I was with my grandmother at the grocery store, who was looking for the ingredients to make *hopia* for a dance practice at our house. I didn't notice the three white kids who were following us down each aisle, acting like they were shopping. When we got closer to one of the kids, he stepped away from his siblings and said, "We're going to send you back to Mexico." He laughed as he and his brothers ran away down the aisle. I remember standing there thinking, *I'm Filipino.*

Since then, I developed this new sense of awareness when it came to racism, direct or indirect. Whenever I was in public, I consciously avoided looking people in the eyes, fearing that a comment or a look, like what Nick had mastered, would crush any confidence I had. If I did catch someone in a grocery aisle or department store, I quickly nodded and smiled, feeding into the Asian stereotype that we were all submissive.

Even now, I had feelings of insecurity, like ghost hunters who felt cold spots in an abandoned house. I'd become conditioned to the far-right propaganda. That I don't deserve to be here. That I'm inferior. I had the text messages to prove it, subtle as they were.

You know Harry Potter isn't real?

Then, something happened.

Turning to Walter, I said, "Are they blasting 'Uptown Funk'?"

Walter, sitting aloof, looked up to the ceiling, his mouth turning downward.

I pointed up. "Do you hear that?" I quickly checked the table full of band members, wondering if it was them. The tuba player was eating his lunch in silence, his instrument leaning on the floor against him. My eyes traveled down the entire table, but there wasn't anyone playing music.

Dismissing my question, Walter said, "Uh, no."

"You don't hear that?" I asked again, turning toward Dennis. "Please tell me you hear that."

"Hear what?" Dennis said.

Walter shrugged and shook his head. "Sorry. We don't hear anything."

For good measure, I checked each table to see if anyone was blasting music. Sadly, nobody was. The other students were all digging into their meals and chatting amongst themselves, lost in their own lives.

LOVE, DANCE & EGG ROLLS is taped in
front of a live, studio audience.

[Guest star and part-Filipino singer, BRUNO MARS,
slinks into the cafeteria, singing and getting everyone
involved in an "Uptown Funk" flash mob.]

[JAMIE thinks BRUNO could earn him enough cool
points to make all these uncomfortable feelings dissipate.]

[Too bad it isn't sweeps week yet-and the
series doesn't have the budget!]

In reality, this could only mean one thing-Nick was in the vicinity.

I searched all three entrances. No sign of him yet. The imaginary tune grew louder inside me, and when I swung my head around toward the main entrance of the cafeteria, I saw him.

Nick entered the cafeteria in grand fashion. He strutted like a model on a catwalk, his tall, toned body moving gracefully through the room. As soon as he reached a table, a boy was quick to greet him. If the boy was any quicker, a secret service agent would have jumped in front of Nick.

"Hey!" the student shouted.

Nick flashed a smile, his teeth twinkling under the bright bulbs of the overhead lights. The loud greeting triggered a couple of the football players to look in Nick's direction. Nick's chin jutted out as he nodded to the jocks. "Sup?" he said, then smirked.

He walked by another table, winked at a group of girls, then continued on his path like a random twister touching ground on a Midwestern farm. Nick was unpredictable and greeted anyone who would let him, which seemed to be the whole cafeteria.

A boy eating popcorn from a bag waved to Nick, who in return stopped in the middle of the cafeteria, opened his mouth, and urged the kid to toss him some popcorn. The boy did, launching a kernel like a medieval catapult launching rocks into enemy territory. A collective group of heads slowly turned, watching as the tiny kernel entered Nick's mouth.

His popularity made me sick.

I wanted to leave right then, but suddenly Nick approached our table and smiled out the side of his mouth. "Gentlemen," he said, burning his gaze into me. I tried to look away, but his stare kept drawing me back to him. A magnetic force that couldn't be stopped.

"Hey Nick," said Walter.

Dennis lowered his chin and dished out a gentle nod.

Me? I just sat low into my chair, my eyes moving from Nick to the tabletop and back in a rapid motion. A hole opened in my stomach, and whenever he looked at me, I looked away.

"What's going on?" asked Walter.

"Not much," said Nick. "Just trying to find something to eat."

I could tell he was staring at me even though he was talking to Walter. His vision was burning a hole into my face like a heat gun.

"That's all," he said.

I twisted my body subtly away from him, toward Bethany's direction, and we made eye contact.

"There's creamed chicken on a biscuit," Dennis said behind me.

"Yeah?" Nick said. "Is it good?"

"It's the best lunch ever." They all laughed.

What is he doing? I thought

I was quiet, still looking at Bethany, whose eyebrows had furrowed. Her stare then brushed across Nick and back to me.

Nick moved closer to me, his body inches from mine. Everything about his posture threatened violence. My muscles tensed up in a matter of seconds. All my fears came out at once. My heart rate quadrupled.

"I'll have to try it," said Nick. "Thanks for the recommendation." He left shortly after to visit another table and never looked back.

My mouth was dry as I clenched my fists, nerves coursing through my body. I'd never been in a real fight before, and honestly, I had no idea how to protect myself. What was I even thinking? He was gone, off schmoozing another group of students, but here I was stuck in a state of high anxiety. If only I fit into the Asian stereotype that we all knew martial arts.

[JAMIE springs to his feet and then squats in a martial arts stance. Begging NICK to come forward with his best shot, JAMIE mocks him with his fingers, curling them into his palm, motioning for NICK to make a move.]

JAMIE: If you want to fight, then let's fight.

[NICK charges.]

[JAMIE systematically beats NICK up like Bruce Lee.]

[Cue a fight sequence that is choreographed skillfully and artistically.]

[NICK turns to flee the scene.]

NICK: You haven't seen the last of me.

My reverie ended as quickly as it began.

I turned my head. My eyes caught Bethany's and a calmness brushed over me. Her sad smile spoke volumes—I was a pathetic tool.

As tough as I tried to be, I knew deep down that I would have gotten my butt kicked in front of my friends, my crush, most of the student body, and some kid drinking several cartons of milk.

My thoughts were interrupted by the football players booing as their teammate lost the milk challenge. A couple students laughed out loud, while others clapped obnoxiously. A teacher entered, did a looky-loo around the cafeteria, and stopped when she spotted the milk cartons. "I better see those in the trash," she said, meandering over to the table full of jocks to stop their game.

She mouthed a few words, and after a short exchange between her and one of the players, the teacher started laughing. "I know you guys are just joking around," she said and left. If that was me, she would have waited until I cleaned up.

Bethany dropped her phone to the floor. She leaned back to reach for it but missed it by a couple hairs. She leaned farther back, her legs swinging off the ground and nearly lost her balance.

I hustled over, sliding into action, leading with my right leg, my left leg dragging behind me, strong and flexed. Auntie Marisol's voice in my head screamed, "Perfect posture!" I tipped sideways like a teapot, my hips square as I picked up the phone in one swooping motion. It was the signature move of the planting rice dance.

Bending upright, I returned the phone to Bethany, hoping that she hadn't noticed that unintentional bit of dancing. With the Folk Festival on my mind, and how much I'd been practicing it was hardly surprising it happened automatically.

Bethany thanked me for returning her phone, her eyes wide. "That was a neat little move," she said. "Do you dance?"

My mind suddenly screeched to a halt, and my eyes bulged in embarrassment. Even though I knew she breakdanced, and we'd talked about dancing before, I had never dreamed of disclosing my secret to anyone outside my circle. *But she seemed so sweet and nice*, I thought. *Maybe I could . . .*

My heart suddenly started to race, and the pace of my breathing shortened. Frozen in place, I opened my mouth and lied, "I . . . I wasn't dancing." My tone was defensive. *She could not know about the Folk Festival,* I thought.

"Oh," she said. Her eyes creased as her lips pressed tightly together. Shrugging, Bethany added, "It looked like a dance move to me. It was pretty cool." She slid over to make room. "Would you like to join me?"

Would. I. Like. To. Join. You? Uh . . . Was Fely Franquelli one of the greatest Filipino dance choreographers of all time?

I stood frozen, my eyes fully open, goggling at Bethany as she sat waiting for an answer.

Well? Was she?

I bit my bottom lip, and my cheeks rose into a silly smirk.

Uh . . . yes. The answer is yes.

Nodding like a bobblehead, I said, "Sure." But instead of sounding confident and cool, my voice came out squeaky and insecure, sounding more like, "Sheer!" I couldn't believe this was happening. This was my first conversation with my crush in a public setting—the cafeteria during lunch-where everyone could see us, and it was already going horribly. To make matters worse, I pointed to the decal on her shirt. "I like your cat shirt," I said. To her, I was certain it sounded like, "I leak your Kate sheert!" And then I meowed, curled in my fingers, and flicked my wrist. But I couldn't stop. I kept on meowing for a while. I was nervous to the core. I was talking to a girl! *The* girl!

"You're funny," Bethany giggled.

I chuckled nervously, my lips knotting together as I tried my very best to be cool. My cheeks grew warm, and I started to blush.

"Sorry," I said. "I was . . . never mind."

Eventually, I relaxed. Once my brain settled back into normalcy, I stuck out my hand.

"I know we've been in class before and chatted a couple times, but we've never formally met. I'm Jamie and you're Bethany."

She smiled, swaying left to right like a smitten sapling. "Indeed."

"You're just so different," I said.

"How so?"

How so? Uh . . . "Just that you seem different from everyone here, and when you're different, you tend to stick out." I looked around the cafeteria, gesturing to each table. "You have the jocks," I said, pointing to the players, as my mind drifted to thoughts of the far-right rally.

I guess when you all look the same, you don't easily stick out, I thought. I kept staring for longer than I'd wanted to before moving on.

"Then the brainiacs, and over there," twisting my body toward the drama club, "you have the acting club."

Bethany extended her arm, stoically drawing out an imaginary audience. She was playing along. "You mean the *thespian* club?" she announced, like a stage actor reciting his lines. She laughed to herself.

I laughed with her. "Right, thespian."

At first I thought Nick's appearance was something awful, but now I didn't see it that way. It created an opportunity to talk to Bethany. She scooted over to make more room for me. Behind us, Walter was calling my name, but eventually, his voice faded as I lost myself in Bethany's presence.

Next to me a girl bumped me as she stood. "Sorry," she said, but I didn't pay any attention to her because the top of my wrist was grazing against Bethany's side. Simultaneously, we looked down at where we were touching. Just then, the bell to end lunch period sounded.

I floated on cloud nine for the rest of the day.

6

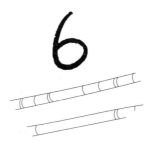

The fact that it was a weekday didn't stop my family from hosting a mahjong marathon; nothing stopped Filipinos from hosting a mahjong marathon. Tonight, the tile-based card games were happening at the Santiago house, and the place was bustling. This choice of venue was mainly so the Filipino Dancing Troupe could practice in our large basement area. The festival was rapidly approaching, and we had to practice.

Inside the kitchen metal spoons were hitting metal pans creating a continuous banging, and noodles sizzled as they hit scalding water. A vinegary smell tickled my nose, and I could tell they were making *pancit*, a Filipino noodle not dissimilar from spaghetti. In between, egg rolls fried in a large pan of vegetable oil. Chicken basked in a curry-flavored broth. Fish broiled in the oven.

My father took mahjong seriously. He was a purist, having collected many sets of original tiles. He would always say that you could tell if a tile was real by biting into it. "If it's solid against your teeth, it's probably real." Authentic tiles were made from bone and backed with bamboo, so my father would scoff at newer mahjong sets that were constructed out of plastic. He went to great lengths to find these sets—Oriental stores, import/export stores, and even various gift shops in Asian massage parlors. Sometimes, Chinese restaurants offered gift shops for customers—a few rectangular glass cases filled with Buddha statues, paper accordion fans, vases, and, if you were lucky, the occasional mahjong set. I wondered if that was why we hit up the Chinese buffet so often.

Mahjong was the Filipino version of gambling. "Back then," he said, "we didn't play for money. We played for dry goods or crops." During one backyard marathon, my father and three of his friends had roasted an entire piglet. That night the game went on for something like eight hours. "We rotated seats and took turns turning the *lechón* over the open fire," he'd said. "Every hour we'd switch." After two rotations each, the piglet was cooked, charred exactly how Filipinos liked it—with the meat moist and the skin thick and crispy like a leather belt. And the winner walked away with enough meat and dry goods to last a month.

This generation, however, gambled with money. Money would exchange hands with every game, and whomever had the most loot at the end of the marathon—usually around midnight—would win a little trophy.

Slowly, some of the visitors braved the karaoke machine. Auntie Racquel picked up the karaoke microphone and picked a song by Taylor Swift. As the music started and she got into position, I turned to my father. "Auntie Racquel is pretty good," I said, a slight tease in my voice. "Your high score might be in jeopardy."

"That's OK. It's just wonderful to see the house so full, it's like being home again. I haven't seen Auntie Racquel since she got back from the Philippines." He glanced over at the machine and smiled. "I'll just have to knock her off the top spot!" he responded with a wink.

With the festival drawing near, many "relatives" found ways to participate. Their children were in the troupe, or they showed up for support. I use the term relatives loosely. The fact was that everyone in the Philippines was an uncle or aunt or cousin, according to my parents. This was how my father introduced each of them. "This is your Uncle

Max," or "Have you met your Auntie Gemma?" or "You know Uncle Jimmy!"

This was not true at all. All these Filipinos were just really, really, good friends of the family. And the auntie or uncle title was given to any Filipino older than you.

Being around Filipinos was vastly different than being around white people. Although my personality stayed the same, my perspective changed. I felt very Filipino around my white classmates and very white around Filipinos. There was never an in-between—I was equally as uncomfortable. I was, in fact, Other. But at least here, I was safe.

So when people came over, dishes in hand—because God forbid they didn't—I stayed silent and greeted each guest with a smile. I pointed the way to the kitchen, through the maze of chairs and tables. "You'll see Lola when you enter." My grandmother greeted each person with a kiss to the cheek and then everyone in the room began speaking Taglish, a combination of English and Tagalog.

"*Magandang gabi*," Uncle Max said to my father. "How are you?"

"I'm good," my father said. "*At ikaw?*"

Uncle Tony sidled up next to me. "Jamie, *kumusta*," he said. "Are you ready for the Folk Festival?"

I shrugged, the reminder bringing me down even though I knew they were here for the dancing troupe.

"I guess," I said. "It just sucks that it's the last one."

Uncle Tony ruffled my hair with his palm. "It'll be fine," he said. Then he moved off to find where the food's aroma was coming from. "*Kumusta*." His voice trailed off as he disappeared into the kitchen.

I surveyed the area, doing my part to greet everyone as they entered. My father pinched his lips together and gestured to the card tables that were set up throughout the house. He took one seat and called for Uncle Diosdado to join him. Uncle Diosdado plopped down in the seat, his beer gut drooping past his waist, almost striking the bottom of the table, and the two began shuffling the tiles into one large pile. Auntie Gemma and Uncle Pedro squeezed into the remaining seats and started positioning all the tiles face down into the tabletop.

Auntie Gemma slid her chair as far as she could under the table to make room for others walking throughout the house. "*Ay nako*," she said. "Tight squeeze." My father laughed, and soon after all the mahjong tiles were facedown and ready to be dealt out. I stood in my position in the entryway of our house until the traffic died down. Auntie Marisol maneuvered through the maze of tables and chairs and then bolted to the one long table dedicated to food that was pushed up to the wall. She piled some food onto a plate and then rushed over to me.

"Ready for practice?" she asked, throwing an egg roll into her mouth with ease. Auntie Marisol was our coach and the sister of a friend of my parents. She had been the coach for years and had seen many kids pass through her tutelage.

I nodded with slight disappointment.

"It's your last dance." She chewed the roll and then swallowed. "Let's go out in style." Then she smiled and found a place to sit in the living room.

It was weird to think about the last Folk Festival. Even though everyone here was to show support for the Filipino Dancing Troupe, I couldn't help but wonder if these mahjong sessions would continue after it was over. I felt sad, not only for our dance team, but for people like Auntie Marisol, who'd dedicated her life to teaching us these dances. And to the Filipinos who came for the company. And for my father, who loved seeing his friends.

Auntie Racquel was now singing Nine Inch Nails, but she couldn't keep up with the lyrics, even though they were scrolling across the screen. She was always one word behind, so it sounded like an echo as she sang, "Head (Head) like (like) a (a) hole (hole)."

After a few stanzas, she examined the microphone as she turned it around to stop the song. "*Ay nako*," she said. "*Susmaryosep*."

My father ran over to assist, taking the gadget and stopping the sound. The fake audience booed, and a score generated of sixty. Auntie Racquel laughed. My father laughed with her. I turned my attention to Auntie Marisol, who was finishing off her plate.

"I'll be down in a minute," she said.

I nodded. Just then, my grandmother brought out a bin full of barbecue pork kabobs. I took a deep whiff of barbecue sauce smothered over scalding pork before heading downstairs for rehearsal.

This would be the final go around, the final performance that people would hopefully remember for years and years. I was both stoked and sad just thinking about it. As I got down to the bottom step, I saw Rosario and Arthur talking next to a giant wooden carving of *The Last Supper*. Next to them was a barrel man—a wooden sculpture of a man inside a barrel—which I grabbed as I casually walked up to the pair.

"Sup, guys?" I asked as I pulled the barrel off the little Filipino prop, revealing his ginormous wooden penis. I snorted as Rosario growled and swatted the toy away from me.

"Oh my God," she said with an eye roll. "Grow up, Jamie!" While she was saying this, Arthur grabbed the matching barrel woman and gave me a wink.

When Rosario turned back to continue their conversation, he brought the figure up to her face and yelled, "Look out, torpedoes!" Two torpedo-shaped boobs sprung up and shook like a diving board after a jump. Rosario groaned and stomped away, muttering about how she should hide the toys the next time.

When Auntie Marisol arrived, we began the rehearsal with the planting rice dance. All members of the troupe, even the youngest kids, got into rows, and we began to dance in unison when the song played. We danced to the tune of "London Bridge is Falling Down," stepping forward and backward as if we were grabbing rice from a basket and planting it in the ground.

"Perfect!" Auntie Marisol said, as we finished the dance. I moved off to the side, waiting for instruction. She scanned the room. "Where's David?"

David appeared, wide smile and all. As the two of them had a brief conversation, I looked at the other dancers and wondered if they were sad about the festival ending. Some of them had only been dancing for a few months, but others had been dancing for years. I was curious to know how the end of the festival was affecting them.

"OK," said Auntie Marisol. "Let's practice coconuts."

I slipped on my coconut shells, secured them around each limb, and fell into place. Roger, Arthur, and the rest of the older kids got into position. A more difficult routine, we rehearsed the dance when the music kicked in: clapping our shells together in rhythm and dancing a synchronized number. At one point, we sounded like tap dancers. The music played overhead alongside sounds of clicking ivory as the smell of soy sauce filtered down into the basement. My stomach growled, and I thought about running upstairs to throw down some egg rolls but stopped when I noticed two of the girls setting up two-by-fours. My eyebrows furrowed—Tinikling already?

A couple of the middle-school-aged boys walked two long bamboo sticks to the center of the room and placed them on top of the two-by-fours.

"Are we doing Tinikling now?" I asked.

Auntie Marisol nodded without ever making eye contact, her gaze wandering around the room. She narrowed her eyes, tilted her head, and then said, "Rosario, where's the tor . . . "

Rosario slid up next to me. She leaned into the coach and said, "The what?"

"The tor—" Auntie Marisol said, dragging the word out. "—pedos!"

Rosario sprung in front of me, whipped out the barrel woman, and lifted the wooden barrel off of her. Two pointed boobs came at me at a hundred miles per hour.

[The show parodies THE MATRIX, and when the two missile shaped boobs come near JAMIE, JAMIE slowly bends backward, his feet still placed flat on the ground, while his torso defies gravity and runs parallel to the floor.

[Enter neato special effect.]

[JAMIE'S arms flail like he is wading backward in a pool. Instantly, his voice transforms into a low sounding growl.]

JAMIE: Boooooobs!

Auntie Marisol fell to her knees in laughter. Rosario dropped the toy and ran away, giggling at the prank. The rest of the troupe joined in. I stood with reddened cheeks, realizing that it wasn't just the festival that was ending, it was the family atmosphere.

Before we could get too caught up in the hysteria, Auntie Marisol said, "OK, enough fun. Let's practice." She looked down at the bamboo stick setup. "Rosario, Jamie, get into position."

I went to one end, and Rosario went to the other. As the girls took their positions at the end of each pole, I slowly exhaled and closed my eyes. *This is it,* I thought. I still couldn't believe it was ending. Before I could dwell in the misery, the girls started banging the bamboo against the wood. They struck the poles together and then slid them across the two-by-fours at a moderate pace. It was an Asian double Dutch.

Clank, clank, swoosh.

Clank, clank, swoosh.

When the music started—a slow tempo song—and the right moment came, we leaped into the middle and danced a few simple steps. As we loosened up, the song changed to a faster one, and I could feel the energy passing through me. My knees kicked up as the poles slid under me, and at times the bamboo was moving so quickly that it looked like there were more than two sticks. We caught a rhythm and the beat picked up until Rosario and I were moving like Michael Flatley in *Lord of the Dance*.

Clank, clank, swoosh.

Clank, clank, swoosh.

The music started to fade out, the girls slowed down the speed of the poles, and once the song disappeared into silence, I jumped off to the side. Upstairs, the fake applause from the karaoke machine roared into the air. I closed my eyes, and even though I knew the clapping was for whoever was singing, I imagined being on stage in front of an audience.

Our coach shouted, "Do it again!"

As the rest of the dance troupe sat around the room and watched, Rosario and I rehearsed for a second time. My knees were tired from kicking them up, trying to prevent the bamboo poles from hitting my ankles. As we danced together, our bodies facing one another, we grabbed each other's hands and began to step in between the poles faster and faster.

I was just getting warmed up.

The sounds of the poles hitting against each other became louder, and when they finally reduced in speed, Rosario and I spun around so our backs were facing each other. Some of the members clapped.

"Perfect!" Auntie Marisol yelled.

One younger dancer mimicked my movements off to the side. He was next in line for the torch, but sadly, there wouldn't be a next time.

Clank, clank, swoosh.

Clank, clank, swoosh.

I was like a football player running through an obstacle course made of rubber tires: my knees hiking higher with each step, the poles nearly striking my feet.

The consistent *clank, clank, swoosh* motion of the poles made me dizzy as I watched my feet lift off the ground in between the bamboo. I started to sweat as adrenaline coursed through my body. My heart raced, the beat pumping through my chest. Shaking my head, the scene surrounding me returned to focus, I screamed, "Faster!"

Clank, clank, swoosh.

Clank, clank, swoosh.

I spun around, Rosario followed suit, and I repeated, "Faster!"

The girls working the bamboo poles increased their motion, striking the poles and sliding them into each other. When the poles struck each other, they sounded like thunder. I looked up at Rosario. Her forehead was glistening, and a smile escaped her lips.

We continued the faster pace until the routine was over. When the song stopped, Rosario jumped away from the poles and bowed. I, however, folded over and attempted to catch my breath. Breathing heavily, I uncurled my upper body and threw my arms up to the ceiling, lost in my own personal victory. The rest of the dance troupe erupted into applause.

Upstairs, the karaoke was going strong, and the aroma of Filipino food lingered, filtering down the stairs. Someone was singing Maroon 5, and judging from the random thumps against the ceiling, I guessed that they were dancing along too.

Auntie Marisol checked her watch. She was on a tight schedule. "Time to eat," she said. "You have one hour." The dancers hustled up the stairs, starting with the youngest. "Then we go again," she called after us. "But for the Tinikling, we'll practice with the alternates, Eleanor and Jamie, and Rosario and Ruben."

Dishes of food were spread across the table in an orderly fashion. Plates and bowls of different noodles, like *pancit luglug*, were on one side of the table. Main dishes, such as chicken curry and *dinuguan*—a spicy pork dish—filled the middle of the buffet. Large bowls of white rice covered the rest of the table.

In between were platters of egg rolls, a Tupperware full of barbecue kabobs, pots of vegetable stew, various chicken courses, a fish complete with head, eyes, and skin, and an eight-piece bucket of Kentucky Fried Chicken.

My grandmother was humming softly to herself as she stood in front of the stove tonging egg rolls in and out of the frying pan. When she saw the parade of dancers marching in, she smiled. I kissed her on the cheek and told her that everything smelled delicious. She nodded and continued with her task.

One of the younger dancers, Esmerelda, stood on tiptoe in front of the table of food. Her head tilted from side to side to see what dishes were available. I pointed out the *dinuguan* and Esmerelda's head swiveled left to right. She bit down on her lip and said, "No, thank you."

"You don't like pig guts?" I teased, with a wide smile.

"No!"

Then Esmerelda found a plate and meandered to the front of the line. Shortly after, the line began to fill with hungry dancers.

Tongs, oversized spoons, and large forks rested on top of each of the dishes. The dancing troupe ate first. Standing in line behind a pair of younger dancers, I glanced at the fish. While the children were filling their plates, I reached over and scooped out the eye with my finger. Before anyone could notice, I slid the eye into my mouth and chewed. The texture was spongy, but essentially, it just tasted like fish. Then, I piled on a white rice base, flattened it to accommodate the main courses, and piled each dish on top of each other. After swiping three barbecue kabobs and a handful of egg rolls, I moved to the dessert table.

Esmerelda walked by, her own plate towering with food. Eyeing my dish, she said, "Where is your *dinuguan?*" Then she laughed and continued moving.

In the living room the roar of the television mixed with Taglish from the mahjong tables. It was difficult to decipher between the two, as often, when a game became too intense, bystanders loitered around to cheer on their favorite relative.

At the dessert table, I immediately saw some *biko*, a sweet rice cake that's sticky to the touch. I'd have to come back for some later when I had room on my plate. I did, however, grab some of the *ube halaya*, which I would drop off to my father. He loved that purple stuff, but I wasn't a fan of yams.

I entered the living room, scanned the different tables, and saw my father. He was sitting in a game, his tiles in a row in front of him. Some were standing upright, others on their side; his formation stood like a miniature Stonehenge. There were dollar bills stacked together next to him.

A friend of my father's stood up from his seat. "Jamie," he said. "You can have my seat." He gestured to the open seat and disappeared into the kitchen.

When my father saw me, he slid over a bit to make room. He observed my mountain of food and said, "There's *biko*."

"I saw, but I didn't have room on my plate," I replied with a smile.

My father nodded. "Oh."

"But I did get you some *ube*," I said, moving the dessert to a napkin and then placing it next to him.

He thanked me and then continued to play in the marathon.

Behind me, a new song was beginning: Madonna. Craning my head, I saw two Filipinas standing in front of the television while one held the microphone. The women were swaying side to side in unison. They had smiles on their faces, each having the time of her life.

One Filipina started to sing. "Get into the—"

The other, pulling the microphone away, said, "Not yet." The song's introduction continued to play, and while the two were laughing at the one's error, the words began rolling across the screen. ". . . the groove. Boy, you have to . . ." The Filipinas quickly started singing until they were back in sync.

I smiled and returned to my food.

Patricia exited the kitchen with a handful of egg rolls. She threw one into her mouth, chewing quickly.

"Is that all you're going to eat?" my father asked.

Patricia smiled and nodded her head. "I can't eat that much while dancing." She rubbed her belly, then threw down another egg roll. Her eyebrows shot up. "I'm not like this one," she said, referring to me, "who can eat whatever he wants." I blushed and looked down at my mountain of food.

"I have a high metabolism," I defended myself. My father just laughed and then returned to the game. Patricia walked into the living room to watch the singers perform.

There was clapping from some of the mahjong players. Seeing my family interact with their friends made me happy. We were one huge family, really. It was why I loved the Folk Festival so much. It was one of the only venues where all of us could get together. There was so much comradery.

Watching them made me wonder about the other Filipino kids in the dance troupe who also grew up in the US, if any of them were the only minorities at their schools like me. If they had the same feeling I did. That although I felt very white around my family and embarrassed and uncomfortable at times, I felt very much at home. I felt very comfortable in my own skin. I felt . . . like a Filipino, even though I was still Other.

Two players sitting across from each other began sparring back and forth in Tagalog.

"This hand is mine," one man said.

The other just laughed and shook his head. "Not if I can help it." He then pointed to his stack of tiles with his lips.

Their conversation made me smile. My father laughed at their trash talking, and I laughed with him. Tiles steadily built up in the middle of the card table, and the pot of cash slowly grew. I looked in amazement at the amount of money that was in front of me.

The only thing my father needed was *lechón*. I ate my plate of food slowly. It was a school night, and it was getting late, but at that moment, I felt alive and energized. I felt accepted. I knew it was just the high from practicing our dances, but I didn't want it to go away.

Rosario walked by with a plate of *biko*. When she passed by, the entire table of players, led by my father, stopped and clapped.

"What was that for?" Rosario asked.

"For dancing in the Folk Festival," my father said.

Rosario rolled her eyes and chuckled. "Well, thank you," she said, her eyes moved toward me and widened.

The way everyone treated the dancing troupe was the opposite of how Nick treated me at school. They just clapped for two of the dancers—for no reason at all! Hoping to drag out these feelings for a little longer, I stood from my seat. The players stopped what they were doing and clapped. I shook my head and then bowed. I revisited the food station and selected some dessert. I still had forty minutes until the next practice session.

The two women in the living room waited for the karaoke machine to generate a score. When the machine pushed the results onto the screen, one of them screamed. A perfect score. Her name moved up the board.

"Uncle Claudio!" My father twisted his upper body. "Look," she pointed to the screen.

My father leaned out of his chair to see the television and saw the scores. There was a new name sitting in third place. He smiled. Nodding his head, he said, "Ah, very good!"

"We're going to get every high score." The two women searched for another song and entered the code into the microphone. The B-52's. Instantly, "Love Shack" began playing, the drum beat kicking into gear. Rosario jumped to her feet. She grabbed my elbow, and I nearly dropped my dessert. "Jamie, we need a male to sing."

"But my *biko*!"

The lyrics rolled onto the screen.

"C'mon!" she said, pulling me into the group. "Put your plate down!"

I dropped my rice cake on an end table and joined in at the next opportunity, singing, "—by the side of the road that says fifteen miles to the—"

Rosario and the Filipinas screamed, "Love shack, love shack yeah."

Together the three of them sang the next verse, dancing side to side. Rosario bumped her hips into mine. Eventually, my body loosened up, and I gave in and threw myself into it. Even though I sang my parts off-key, the next few minutes were a blast.

A sensation of happiness settled within me. Seeing how excited and happy everyone was made me realize something—I really did love my family. And part of it was being Filipino.

7

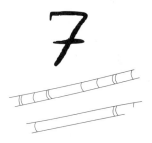

I stared blankly at the test, wracking my brain for answers.

The festival was ending, and homecoming was around the corner, which meant I had to somehow tell Walter and Dennis that I wasn't going. And then there was Bethany, but all I could think about was this damn test.

The test question was torturing me more than Nick ever had. I needed to put down an answer and move on to the next one before time expired. I had already spent way too much time lingering on this question and still had a handful to go.

How many valence electrons does carbon have?

Scanning the physical science question over and over, I closed my eyes and inhaled deeply. How many valence electrons does carbon have? This was a very good question. My mind was like a slot machine: three separate reels spinning round and round, hoping to stop on the right combination. But when they stopped, the big loser sign just flashed at me, over and over again.

Unable to drum up a response from my subconscious, I looked around the room and exhaled heavily. Every student had his head buried in the surprise test. Just a few rows ahead, one test taker had his eyes tightly closed and was muttering to himself.

I feel you, I thought.

Sarah, the brain of the school, was flying through her exam, marking answers down faster than I could read each question. I tried to catch a glimpse of her responses but stopped, fearing that I would get caught cheating. Getting in trouble before the Folk Festival was not worth the risk.

Instead, I sat in my seat in disbelief. I could not believe that the teacher had sprung a surprise test on us.

How many valence electrons does carbon have?

I fiddled with my pencil as my eyes shifted from left to right, watching each student fill out answers with much more ease than I. My eyes continued to pan right when something stopped them—Nickhead. He was eyeing me and mouthing the words to something.

I tried to make out what he was saying but couldn't. "What?" I mouthed back at him.

"What did you get for number six?" he whispered, holding up the number on his fingers. He was ducking behind the student in front of him, using her body as a shield against the teacher, while periodically checking to see if she saw him. It was funny to watch. Nick was so much taller than the girl that he looked like a Whac-A-Mole, his shoulders falling lower and lower as his head shot up.

Craning my head to look behind me, I returned to Nick and said, "Me?" pointing to myself with my thumb.

He nodded emphatically. His teeth were clenched, and his eyes had narrowed. "What did you get for number six?"

Is he serious right now?

Dropping my chin to find number six on the test, I looked back to him and shrugged.

How many valence electrons does carbon have?

He pointed down to his test booklet, tap-tap-tapping the sheet firmly, and then checked the front of the class with a quick glance. "Hey!" he whisper-shouted, ducking back behind the girl in front of him. "Number six."

My shoulders shot up even harder. I mouthed, "I don't know."

My eyes widened as Nick's face turned red and his forehead wrinkled. He was going to kill me because I wouldn't give him the answer that I didn't even know to begin with. If I could only explain. If I could only inform him that I too, did not know the answer. If only I could Whac-A-Mole him.

Then, something changed within me. "OK," I whisper-shouted. A student nearby looked at me. I feigned an apologetic smile, then stole a quick look at the teacher. She was writing in a notebook, completely ignoring our class.

I turned to Nick and then held up three fingers. Nick dropped the tip of his pencil to the paper. As I watched him write in the response, reality hit me hard, and caterpillars began to squirm in my stomach. The short burst of confidence quickly faded. Swallowing the lump that formed in my throat, I thought, *What did I just do?*

I willed the answer to be correct, even answering three to the question on my own test. If it was wrong, at least I could show Nick that I had answered the question the same. *He's logical, right?* I thought. *Right?*

From the front of the classroom, the teacher gave a five-minute warning.

"Start to wrap things up," she said aloud. Her heels clicked on the tiles below her as she paced the front of the room. The clicking only made things worse—it sounded like a clock counting down the remaining time.

My fingertips started sweating. I had just answered three to number six, and there were still fourteen questions left. I rushed through the rest of the questions, answering with my gut reaction. I circled the first answer that came to mind: meter, six hundred and fifty grams, atom, homogenous mixture. And so on and so on until the teacher announced that we had to put down our pencils.

A collective sigh blew out into the atmosphere. One boy was still frantically writing down responses. If he pressed the lead into the paper any harder, smoke would have appeared on the sheet. "I said all pencils down," Miss Jennings called out.

The kid's body deflated. "C, C, C," he said quickly, then he surrendered his pencil, groaned, and slid down in his chair.

I snuck a look at Nick, who was smiling to the student next to him. "Aced it," he said.

"No way."

"Sure did," said Nick. Then, as if he knew I was eavesdropping, he turned to look at me. "Thanks to Jamie and his Asian smarts."

Asian smarts? I thought. *This boy was full of stereotypes. What's next? Commenting on my driving?*

I couldn't take much more of this. I turned in my seat until I saw Bethany with her chin propped up on her closed fist. Instantly, the caterpillars emerged as butterflies, a complete metamorphosis from what I'd been feeling while dealing with Nick. My heart jumped for joy. I was paralyzed in a state of extreme happiness. Her eyes locked onto me, and she smiled before glancing at the clock.

"Class is over," our teacher announced. "Please read the next three chapters for tomorrow." The bell marking the end of class sounded. Luckily for me, this was the final class of the day. I stood and stretched.

Nick brushed past me, causing me to lose my balance, and said, "Thanks for the help. I knew I could count on you." A student nearby overheard Nick, and her indifferent expression transformed into a smile. She pressed her hand against her chest, her lips partially open as her eyes gleamed at Nick's sincerity.

"That was so nice of you," she said to me, her palm grazing down my shoulder.

What the . . .

Then she left the class, leaving only Nick, me, and Bethany in the room. Nick twisted his lips into a smirk, his eyes boring into mine. His stare scared me down to my heels, and I stumbled back a couple steps. He looked toward the entrance—nothing. The gesture was subtle, but Bethany noticed right away. She stood and rushed to my side, getting into Nick's face. "Why don't you leave him alone?" she said.

My eyes widened, my brows raising and then pulling together. I was mortified. This diminutive girl was standing up to this larger-than-life racist. I stood there calmly, taking the situation in stride. "It's OK," I said, pulling Bethany toward me. Her arm was slender, her skin as soft as gardenias.

"It's not OK," said Bethany.

The air grew heavy; the silence became unbearable.

"C'mon," I said, breaking the tension. "Let's get out of here." *Who am I?* I gestured toward the door, but as I guided her to the exit, Bethany dug in her heels and stood firm, solid as a rock. I couldn't believe how strong she was. It must have been from all the breakdancing.

Turning to me, Bethany said, "Why do you let this douchebag pick on you?" Nick and I both tensed—me out of fear and him spoiling for a fight now that he had me in private. Bethany stared at me; her eyes filled with anger.

Seeing how angry she was caused me to wonder: *Are you upset with me or him?*

"You should stand up for yourself," she told me.

I could practically see the smoke billowing from Nick's nostrils. He was like a bull ready to charge. Nick then swung out around Bethany, stepping in front of her to focus his attention on me. He looked to the classroom door, checking again to see if anyone was entering. When no one did, he said, "You won't stand up for yourself. You're not man enough." Then he smiled.

After another look to the doorway, he moved in closer until his face was just inches from mine. His breath was warm on my face. "Are you?"

I flinched, closed my eyes and scrunched my face to prepare for the worst. My heart was in overdrive. I held in my breath until I became woozy.

"Or you going to Kung-Fu me?" he said. "Huh, Wong?"

Wong? That's new.

"You think that just because you're popular that you can treat people like that?" said Bethany, who had stepped in between us. I could feel the back of her shirt brushing up against me. "Yeah," she said. "I know your kind: cool guy out in the open, asshole in private." She nodded. "I have friends on the football team."

Nick was stunned into silence.

I opened my eyes, and the top of her head was covering Nick's chest. His eyes were narrowed. He was fuming. Then he smirked, and a softer persona came out. "I was just messing with him," he said. Then, as if I'd entered another dimension, Nick said, "I've known him for years. We're actually best buds."

Best buds?

"Isn't that right?" he asked with a devilish smile.

His eyes locked into mine, their forceful stare burned into me. The hairs on my neck tickled me as they stood on end. Slowly, I started to nod. "Yeah," I muttered, turning away from him.

"You need to get lost!" Bethany said, then grabbed my hand and tugged. I followed, and we walked out of the classroom, not looking back.

Bethany twisted to stare Nick down. "Loser," she said.

My heartbeat subsided as we walked farther down the hall. She had done the impossible: She had stood up against Nick. She was like Supergirl, swooping in to save the day, and the coward in me had just buckled. It only solidified how I saw her. She was my hero.

The halls were deserted. When we got to the front yard of the school, Bethany said, "Why don't you stand up to him?"

"I don't want to talk about it." I released her hand.

She raised an eyebrow as she looked at me and opened her mouth to speak, only to close it again. Clearly, she had an opinion but wasn't willing to share it.

"Are you waiting for a ride home?" I asked. I looked toward the parking lot. My car keys jingled in my pocket with each step. "My car's—"

Bethany pointed down the road. "I walk to school," she said. "I only live a few blocks that way." She bit down on her bottom lip and her eyelashes fluttered as she smiled. "Would you care to walk me home?" She moved in closer to me; one eyebrow raised for a brief second. "I'd hate for you to get your butt kicked when I'm not around. I don't want to see anything happen to that pretty face of yours."

Burn, I thought, but then my spirits lifted. She was flirting, and I adored it wholeheartedly. I let the intoxication consume me. *I'd hate for you to get your butt kicked when I'm not around.* The statement made me smile. I repeated it a few more times. My face warmed, and my heart danced.

"Sure," my voice crackled a tad, "that would be nice." I shook my head and laughed. "I mean, walking you home, not getting my butt kicked." I hid my face from view so she wouldn't know I was blushing.

Flashing her teeth in a grin, she said, "I knew what you meant."

"I'll just leave my car here," I said, glancing toward the parking lot.

We started down the sidewalk. Various students loitered around the school grounds, some playing catch with a football, others just standing around and chatting. Two first-year students waiting for their ride looked down the street at the empty road. Not a car in sight.

"What're you doing for homecoming?" a round-shaped boy asked.

His friend, a skinny boy with train-track braces, replied, "Just staying home."

"Same," the round boy said. "It sucks that freshmen can't go to the dance."

Their conversation faded as we passed.

I wish I had that problem, I thought.

Then I peered over to Bethany, who was staring ahead with a slight grin frozen on her face. A small part of me grew excited about the dance, but then I dismissed it with a quick shake of my head. I could only have one thing on my mind—the Folk Festival.

Kicking leaves along the pavement, I muttered, "Thanks for coming to my rescue." I pinched out an embarrassed smile. I felt pathetic, and hearing those words come out of my mouth literally made me pathetic.

Bethany nodded and cracked a smile. "Well, if you would've done karate on him, then maybe he would've stopped."

"You mean Kung-Fu," I said. "There *is* a difference." There was a bitterness in my voice, and suddenly I became miffed at the remark, always thinking the worst. Bethany grabbed ahold of my wrist and playfully squeezed. My eyes instantly drew to my arm.

"I know," Bethany remarked. She bumped into me, her shoulder touching mine. "I was joking."

"It's not funny," I said, slowly sliding away.

Bethany picked up on my aloofness. "Are you mad?" she asked, moving toward me to narrow the distance between us. She let go of my wrist.

I shrugged and said, "You may be joking, but what you did was exactly what Nick did back there: making an off-color comment and then apologizing."

She pressed her fingertips to her chest. "Oh . . . I—I'm sorry," she said. "I didn't mean for—"

"It's fine," I replied, shaking my head.

Bethany grabbed my arm, stopping me mid-step. "No, it's not fine." She shook her head. "I didn't mean to make you feel bad," she said. "It was a dumb joke, and I'm sorry." There was sorrow in her eyes. "I don't want you to think I'm like Nick at all. Sometimes I forget I'm—"

"White?"

She pressed her lips together. "I was going to say privileged, but that works too." Then she loosened her grip on my bicep and brushed her palm down my upper arm. Nodding, she said, "OK?"

Comment aside, her soft touch comforted me, and I felt accepted. Wanted. It was hard not to. Every inch of my body tingled, and I felt like I could float away and be happy solely with this feeling.

"OK," I said.

I closed my eyes, and I thought about a life with Bethany. The two of us together. Our own family. I took a deep breath.

"Can I ask you something?" she said, disrupting my daydream of marriage, three dogs, and a vacation home on the coast.

We continued forward at a steady pace.

"Anything."

"How did it get to this point?" she asked, glancing back over her shoulder at the school, even though we'd traveled a good distance. "With Nick, I mean."

Oh.

"It started with the test. He was staring at me, trying to get answers from me." I shrugged exaggeratedly, rolling my eyes for added effect. "He literally asked me what the answer was to a question that I was stuck on. How many valence electrons does carbon have? When I told him I didn't know, he got angry." I sighed heavily and continued, "Seriously, this is my life." I stared down the road aimlessly.

Flashing a wide smile, Bethany said, "No, I mean, how did the whole picking on you start? From the beginning."

"Oh." *Where to start?*

Before I could go on, Bethany said, "The answer, by the way, is four." I looked at her, my eyebrows furrowing in confusion. "There are four electrons in carbon's outermost valence shell." I then realized that not only was she cute, she was also smart. My mind brought me back to our break-out session. I sulked silently and my chin dropped, realizing I had gotten the answer wrong. Which meant that I had told Nick the wrong answer. I just sighed.

"I'm assuming you got it wrong," she said.

Twisting my lips into a pretzel, I nodded. *And so did Nick,*
I thought.

"So," she prodded gently, "tell me how this all began."

I sighed as I tried to pinpoint when exactly it had
started. The good thing about going to a private school was
we had all the same classmates, from elementary through
high school. So, I got to know all the students. Even the
bad ones. That was how I'd become close with Walter and
Dennis. Which led to the bad thing about attending private
school—we had the same classmates. Namely, Nick.

"The teasing started early, back in the sixth grade," I
said slowly. We picked up the pace a bit, our steps falling
in time with each other. "When I first entered the room,
I realized that I was the only minority. It was like looking
at a color palette of only white paint," I said. "Seriously,
I could sit by Frostline, Paper White, Mother of Pearl, or
Apparition."

Bethany snorted out a giggle. "Apparition," she said
softly. Her laugh made me happy inside, and I stopped
talking to bask in it.

"That hasn't changed the entire time I've been here. Being
the only kid that's different has never really bothered me—or
at least, it shouldn't have. I just tried to fit in where I could."
Saying that made my gut hurt—of course it bothered me.

Bethany nodded with great interest.

"Walter and Dennis lived a couple blocks away from
me," I continued. "They were neighbors, and all three of us
rode the same school bus together. We got along instantly."

"I don't really know them, but they seem nice," she said.

"They are, once you get to know them," I nodded in
agreement, though I was thinking about Walter's initial
reaction to Bethany—he hadn't been so nice then. But he
was still my friend. One of my only friends, in fact, and I
felt like I had to cover for him, even though Bethany didn't
know what he'd said. "Walter's kind of obnoxious, but he
means well," I tacked on.

We passed a park, where some kids were playing basketball while others sat on the swings, rocking slowly back and forth. The air was slightly chilly, but overall, it was a nice fall day. I paused and licked my lips for a moment to wet them. I wasn't sure why my mouth was suddenly so dry.

"My whole world was the two of them," I said, a soft smile on my face as I reminisced. "We did everything together: rode bikes on the bike path, waded in the creek, spent the night at each other's houses . . ."

"It sounds like you had a great childhood."

And that's not even the half of it, I thought. *The dancing was the best part.*

I nodded slowly and closed my eyes for a moment, remembering. Back then, I could be myself. I had my friends and my dancing troupe, even though none of my Filipino "relatives" went to my school.

"I did," I said. "Everything was so different back then." I glanced at her and shrugged.

Bethany pursed her lips and smiled out the side of her mouth. "What do you mean, different?"

"Just the way the world is now," I said, shaking my head. "I'm starting to question everybody. Look at things differently. Even people I've known for years and years, I feel like I can't trust. It's weird to admit that, especially about Walter and Dennis." I thought about Walter, and it bothered me. Was he looking at the world differently, too? "Maybe they secretly have issues that are now becoming more obvious."

Her eyes narrowed as she looked at me. "That's interesting."

"I mean, don't get me wrong, we're still close."

"I'm sorry you feel that way," she said. "Have you talked to them about this?"

I haven't.

I shook my head.

When I didn't speak, Bethany said, "So what about Nick?"

"Nickhead?"

My favorite laugh returned. "That's funny," she muttered. "Nickhead."

"Right." I realized I was stalling—just like always, hoping that things would just pass. "He transferred in from a different city. I think we were in fourth grade. The factory his father worked at closed down, and their headquarters offered him a job somewhere else." I sighed heavily and pointed downward in a sharp stabbing motion. "Milwaukie, Oregon. Apparently, racists are not only drawn to Portland but to the suburbs as well. Why it couldn't be Milwaukee, Wisconsin? I have no idea."

"Of course," Bethany said, rolling her eyes.

"Although Nick was in the same class as us, he had the body of a tenth grader. Or maybe I was fourth grader with the body of a fetus. I wasn't sure."

Bethany giggled. She knuckled the back of my hand. "You're so funny," she said.

You make it easy for me to be myself.

"What got me was his first couple years at school, he sat quietly on his own. Nice as could be. I actually approached him. We were sort of friends—I even went to his house a bunch of times. But then he changed." I grimaced, recalling how my father had forced egg rolls onto him when he'd first moved to town. I'd told him there was a new kid at school, and suddenly, I was a drug dealer peddling Filipino food. "Just like that." *Maybe I shouldn't have stopped bringing him egg rolls?* With a quick sigh, I pursed my lips. "Then, word got around that his father's company was sold to a Japanese firm, and the firm moved production back to Japan. The plant closed, his dad was laid off, and they started having money problems."

"I can see how that would be stressful for him," she pointed out gently. I eyed her for a moment before nodding in agreement.

"But it was weird how he just changed." My shoulders shot up high, my shrug reaching the sky. "He'd make comments like how his father would only buy American made televisions and cars or something. Like out of nowhere."

"Do you think Nick associated the Japanese firm with you and began hating all things Asian?"

Oh my God! My head whipped over to Bethany. I'd never even thought about that. I just figured he preferred GE over Sony.

"Come to think of it," I said, a realization dawning on me for the first time, "he started coming to school wearing shirts with American flags on them." My gaze darted to the sky, trailing outward until they returned to Bethany. "I remember thinking that it was odd, because before he always dressed very preppy."

"You mean like he does now?" she said. And I snorted.

We approached an intersection and stopped as a car drove through. I looked both ways, took Bethany's arm, and led us across the street. "Nick used to be the quiet kid in school. That was until he started dressing like a," I air quoted, "patriot."

I was floored at this discovery, my lips partially opening in disgust. "That's when he started with me."

"Crazy," she said, "he's so well liked by everyone in school." I looked at her with knotted lips. "Well, almost everyone."

"True statement," I said, slowly nodding until my mind drifted off. "Nick blames me for what his father's company did to his family," I turned to Bethany, who looked at me with tightened lips, "and he's been taking it out on me ever since."

"He's been doing it for so long, and he knows he can get away with it," she commiserated.

I nodded and continued, my voice tainted with bitterness. "And with the world the way it is now, it's never going to stop. Especially since he's so well liked." I shook my head. I realized I was in a no-win situation. "No one knows about the shit he puts me through."

I pulled out my phone, showed her the continual text messages.

We will be back!

The OK emoji.

"I don't get it," she said. "What's that mean?"

Shrugging, I said, "They're white power phrases or something." I scrolled through the random texts from the most popular student in school. "I had to look them all up."

"Why don't you turn him in?"

"And say what?" My eyebrows curved downward. "The coolest guy in high school is racist?" She nodded, like it was that simple. "Show them all these messages that don't straight out say anything?" Shaking my head, I said dejectedly, "Thanks, I'll pass."

"It might work."

"I think your privilege is getting the best of you," I said, as the bitterness returned.

Bethany pinched her lips tight. Nodding gently, she muttered, "I'm sorry."

It was silent for a few seconds. *What am I going to do?*

As if Bethany was reading my mind, she said, "Listen. He's an idiot who thinks he can get what he wants by intimidating you." She rolled her eyes. "Which is why you, and *only* you, need to stand up for yourself."

If only.

"One day," I said and turned to her with a faint smile. I fell silent for a few moments as we walked.

Bethany rubbed my shoulder with her hand, caressing my arm softly. "Something obviously radicalized him."

"I guess," I said. "My fear is that with the rise of white nationalism, Nick will only get worse." We stepped onto a small bridge built over a creek. "And who knows what he's capable of."

"Right," Bethany expressed softly. "There have been a lot of incidents in the news involving white supremacy."

I looked down at the water, tiny ripples gently flowed toward the bank. "The water looks pretty," I said, changing the subject.

Bethany leaned over the rail to look, going up onto her tiptoes. "It's beautiful."

I began to relax, suddenly feeling much better. Any retribution Nick had planned would have to wait until later. I stared at our reflections in the water. Bethany's pale skin and dark clothes contrasted against each other, and I saw what the Nicks of the world did—a kid who looked different. It was more apparent than ever.

"Just because you'll get out of high school and away from Nick, doesn't mean that the prejudice will stop." Turning to me, Bethany said, "For it to stop, you have to actually do something about it."

What she said was true, and I forced a smile. "I know."

I know, I know, I know!

We fell silent for a few moments, admiring the creek. Then, without saying a word to each other, we continued across the bridge.

"Where are you from?" she asked. I was quickly learning that she was full of questions, which wasn't something I was used to.

"Here," I said. "I was born right here in the good old Pacific Northwest."

The corners of her mouth turned downward. "I meant, what nationality are you?"

Realization dawned on me, and I nodded. "I'm American, but my parents are from the Philippines." I'd never really exposed my race to anyone. I wasn't sure where she was going with this.

"How cool," she said, before narrowing her eyes. She was curious. "Why does Nick call you Wong? The Philippines were ruled by Spain before the United States took over."

My eyebrows shot up. Her knowledge impressed me. She was like a *Jeopardy!* contestant on a five-day winning streak. *What is, "Wow, this girl is smart?"*

"How did you know that?" I asked. "Oh, and Wong is new. Today's the first time I'd heard it."

She blushed. "I did a research paper on the Spanish-American War."

"Ah," I said.

"So, if anything, to be accurate," she said, "Nick should call you something like paella instead."

"What!"

"*That* was a joke," she stressed. Her jaw clenched and her smile faded away to be replaced with a frown. "A knock on how ignorant Nick is."

I wanted to be mad, but I couldn't stop myself from breaking into laughter. "That was funny," I said. "And cute."

She sighed heavily, almost as if she was relieved by my reaction. "So, do you speak the language?" she asked.

Nodding slowly, I said, "Pretty much. It's hard not to when you grow up in a bilingual household." I copped a look at Bethany out of the corner of my eye. She wasn't trying to use my race against me. Instead, she was genuinely interested in getting to know me. This gave me warm fuzzies.

Licking my lips, I continued, "I don't have a reason to speak Tagalog outside my home, so I don't. I was born here. I consider myself an American. That's my ethnicity, but I think Nick only sees race." We walked through an empty parking lot and then came across a main street, a couple cars passing us by. "My mother wanted me to only speak in Tagalog, but it didn't stick. I wanted to assimilate."

Suddenly, our hands touched as we walked. It felt like an electric shock, and I glanced at her just in time to see a faint blush. Being near her made me feel like Jell-O; I wanted nothing more than to hold her hand.

Turning to her, I explained, "None of the kids at school spoke another language, so I didn't want to either. It was hard enough to fit in, being the only kid with brown skin." I'd never thought about it until now, but maybe there were some white kids who spoke French or German. Maybe I wasn't so different.

"Do you think it would have been different if Nick wasn't around?"

"You mean, would I be more Filipino if ignorant people didn't exist?" Bethany pursed her lips and nodded. "I doubt it," I shook my head. "I've never been to the Philippines. I was born here. I'm American. It's just that my skin is brown." I sighed in disgust, thinking about how much I hated people like Nick.

We continued our stroll down the sidewalk. "You mean, everything you *perceive* to be American?" I wasn't sure what she meant. "America is all about diversity, right? It's about the freedom to be different," she said. "That is what's wonderful about being an American. We can be different."

"It's easy for you to say that," I said. "No offense, but you're white. Sure, you dress like this," I gestured to her outfit, "but you could easily not and fit in just fine." I stewed for a second, my gaze darting anywhere but on Bethany.

"You're right," she said softly. "I didn't think about it that way."

Thinking about this made me angry. My nostrils started to flare, but when I looked at her, I saw the interested and sweet person that she was. Instantly my body relaxed.

"That's why I try to assimilate," I said. "It's much easier that way." She looked at me with a keen interest, her eyes wide and inviting. "It doesn't matter anyway," I shrugged. "People like Nick do exist."

Bethany was intrigued. I continued to walk straight but could feel her attention locked on me.

We entered the cute downtown area of Milwaukie. The suburb was next to Portland, but its downtown was quaint and more bearable. The street was quiet, only a few cars were parked in front of the multiple businesses on the block. My mind was at a standstill.

"I can't believe you didn't want to speak Tagalog all the time," she said, her mouth dropping open in disgust. "I would love to speak another language. I'm so jelly." I dismissed the comment, brushing her off. "So, tell me this: what is something Filipino that you can't get enough of?"

[JAMIE looks into the camera.]

JAMIE: Dance, baby, dance!

Inside, my soul lifted. I wanted to say that I loved dancing in the annual Folk Festival. The one time of year I could truly be myself: embrace my Filipino roots; accept being Other with all the different kinds of Others at the Folk Festival; taste other cultures' food, enjoy other countries' heritage, and watch other kids dance their native routines. But I didn't. I couldn't drum up the courage to be me, to confess. Instead, I lied. We were getting along so well, and I couldn't bear the humiliation if she didn't think it was cool. I imagined watching her hold in laughter as I told her about the mahjong marathons and karaoke competitions that took place while we practiced our moves.

"I like my grandmother's egg rolls," I offered.

"Well, duh," she said. "Who doesn't like egg rolls?"

I smirked internally at the thought of my father finding out and demanding that I bring her a dish of Filipino food. He was always so giving, unlike me.

I changed the subject.

"What about you? Why do you dress like that?" I gestured to her almost all-black outfit: a thick, black velvet skirt that stopped at her knees, contrasting against her pale white skin. With it, she wore fishnet stockings, leather platform boots that were tightly laced up her ankles and shins, and a black cardigan sweater over a white button-down shirt, whose cuffs were rolled up to her elbows. Fingerless gloves adorned her gentle hands.

Bethany stopped and delicately held her skirt, bobbing into a light curtsey before smiling at me. "You like?"

Nodding, I said, "Yeah, it's different. You look like a badass!"

"I like the style," she said casually.

"Badass!"

She lowered her chin, her cheeks turning red. "Thanks," she said with a smile, "but I like to think I'm an individual, a non-conformist who lives by her own rules." She turned her head toward me slightly. "But mostly, I love the style."

If only I could be as comfortable with myself as she was with herself. Not only was Bethany pretty and intelligent, but she was also confident. I caught her eyes. A sparkle developed inside them. We were sharing a moment, but I wasn't sure what she was thinking.

Did she find me pathetic? Was she really into me? Could she tell that I was really into her? She may be interested in my background, but how would she act in front of my family? Or a bunch of Filipinos? Or coconuts shells? My mind raced.

"What about you?" she asked.

I shook my head, my train of thought slowly returning to the present. "Me?"

"Yeah." Bethany swayed her hip into mine. "Ever thought about painting your fingernails? Or maybe wearing some eyeliner?" Her cheeks rounded into a smile. Then she stepped ahead of me, spun around, and walked backward. She jutted out her chin and moved her head side to side to assess my face. "I think you'd look great with some dark eyeliner."

Blushing, I said, "I don't know about that." I chuckled, "I like to stay under the radar, not be out in the open." Bethany pirouetted and walked alongside me. "It's hard enough dodging Nick now. I don't want to give him anymore ammo."

Bethany shrugged, a slight smirk escaping her mouth. "I don't know," she sang playfully. "I think it would be hot." Then she grabbed my hand, "but I guess I understand." We walked the remaining distance to her house in silence.

8

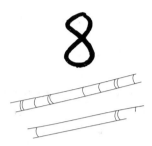

After Bethany and I arrived at her house, we had the most awkward but glorious hug.

I said goodbye and then walked the few blocks back to school to retrieve my car. Being alone brought a mixed range of emotions. I only thought about the festival a little bit; I couldn't stop thinking about Bethany. I was almost excited to go to school so we could talk again. How crazy was that?

I replayed our conversation as I passed some of the same landmarks on my way back. When I crossed the bridge over the creek, the butterflies resurfaced instantly as I remembered that part of our conversation.

I hopped in my car and drove home. As I neared my house, all the feelings about my secret life entered my body—the Folk Festival was ending. For good.

Frowning, I opened the front door and called out hello to my father, who was at his post by the karaoke machine. My grandmother was sitting on the couch, staring aimlessly forward while she talked to him about something or another. They were laughing, and every now and again, my father's attention would move from the television to her.

Were they talking about old times? Reliving old memories?

My mother poked her head around the corner in the kitchen, a damp towel in her hands.

"There you are," my mother said. "I need you to take your grandmother to the store to get some fabric."

"O . . . K," I said, stretching the word out and wondered why.

"I think it's important for you to spend time with her before she goes back home," my mother said.

Often, when my parents were away at work, I sat in the living room with my grandmother, watching television. It was a way to try to get to know her. We talked about her life in the Philippines and what my father was like as a child. She told me she had learned to sew from her mother, who'd hemmed the clothes of all the neighbors. It was how she'd made her living in the Philippines, and why my mother had her mend all my clothes. Hence, the visit to the fabric store.

"I don't know," I whined. I'd just spent the last hour or so with Bethany, and I hadn't had a chance to unwind. Plus, the festival was coming up. "Can't you take her? I just want to relax."

"Relax?" my mother said. "You've been out of school for . . ." looking at the clock, "over an hour. Where have you been?"

I didn't want her to know about Bethany just yet. My father was within earshot, and if he overheard our conversation, I could imagine him jumping at the chance to serve someone new Filipino food. The door with Bethany was just opening. I didn't need them to barge in with their abrupt Filipino-ness.

"I had to stay late for an assignment," I lied.

"Jamie," she said. "It's important to your father and I that you spend time with her before she goes back to the Philippines."

Right, I thought. *The Philippines.*

I sighed. "Fine," I conceded.

"Ma *ma!*" my mother called out. "Jamie is going to drive you to the store."

A second later, my grandmother shambled into the kitchen with a static smile that had probably been stretched across her face for a while.

"Hi," I said, leaning in to kiss her cheek. "I'm going to take you to the fabric store."

On the car ride there, my grandmother just stared out the window. The radio was low, playing softly. I didn't really know what to talk about, so I asked her if she was excited to go back to the Philippines.

"I'm happy to see my children," she said. My father was the eldest of ten, and the rest of his siblings were in the Philippines. None of them had the funds or desire to come to the States. "I haven't seen them in a while."

"I bet they will be happy to see you," I said.

She turned to me, placed her fragile palm on my arm, and said, "I bet your father will be happy to get rid of me." Then she laughed like it was the funniest thing she'd ever heard.

"Can you tell me about my father?" I asked, my eyes staring at the road ahead of me.

The traffic was horrendous: cars often stopped for minutes at a time on busy streets. The Portland area's evening commute lasted forever and traveling a few miles took close to an hour. I pumped the breaks and then slowed to a stop behind a row of cars at a red light.

"Is there anything interesting that I don't already know?" I asked, which really could have been any number of things. Like with my grandmother, my father and I had a superficial father and son relationship. We never really had any deep conversations.

"Did you know that your father was once part of an activist group?" my grandmother said.

I instantly thought about the protests in downtown, how violent they'd become, and how the police would disperse crowds with tear gas. The scenes looked like something out of war-torn Afghanistan. *Was he one of those activists risking his life night in and night out?*

I turned to look at her. "I knew he was involved somehow," I said, "but not to what extent." The reality was, it was one of the only things that I knew about him.

A sly smile appeared on my grandmother's face. "He was following in his father's footsteps."

My grandfather?

"Your grandfather was a big opposer of President Marcos," she said. "And your father wanted to be just like him." She coughed so deeply that I could hear the phlegm bouncing in her throat. After the coughing fit subsided, she continued. "When your grandfather died, your father continued his work. Even though there was a new president, a lot of the old regime's policies and officials remained." She cleared her throat, causing the crackle in her voice to disappear. "By then, most everyone knew his name, and who he was fighting for."

This part of my father's story was one of the reasons that I held him to such a high standard. And possibly why he had that "screw you" attitude. I only wished I could be more like him. Especially now that I knew it was a passed-down tradition, I felt like I was failing our family name.

Santiago, I thought. *More like Suck-tiago.*

I struck the gas pedal and continued to the fabric store.

"That's actually why he and your mother came to the United States," she said. She quickly coughed and then pressed her fingertips to her chest.

What? I'd always thought they came here so I could go to school. To get an American education. That was what they'd always told me.

"I didn't know that."

"Yeah, back then, in the Philippines, anyone who spoke up against the government got put on a blacklist. Your grandfather did and soon after, your father." Her eyes closed softly. "He kept telling me that the new president was different. That things would change." She shook her head and then laughed. "But they didn't," she continued. "He was still associated with his father's legacy, well after your grandfather had died. I respected him for that, even though I thought he would get killed."

Killed?

"Imagine having to look over your shoulder every day," she said. Then a proud smile drew on her face.

I felt a similar feeling with Nick.

"One day, he and your mother were out, and a police officer stopped them," she said. "They were checking people's IDs against the list, and your father's name was on it."

Oh. My. God!

My grandmother, talking slowly as if another coughing spasm was approaching, swallowed. "Somehow they got away, and the next thing I knew he and your mother were fleeing to the States." She exhaled deeply, pushing down her cough for another time. "I didn't see him again until I came here."

Wow, I thought. Not seeing your son for years. What if all that was taken away from me? By wanting to be American, and shying away from my culture, was I taking my family for granted?

The store was within sight, but a long line of cars turning in the intersection kept us waiting. I was leaning forward to see where we were in line, when my grandmother poked me on the hand. I turned to her, my grandmother's eyes flashing with urgency. She wanted to tell me something. "Don't tell your father," she said, "but Claudio is not his real name."

I felt like the Tasmanian Devil suddenly bum-rushed me and threw my life into disorder. What was she talking about? My father wasn't really my father?

To Be Continued...

NARRATOR: That's all for this season. Stay tuned until next season to find out what is going on.

Viewers search for spoiler alerts online, only to discover one of the main characters had a sketchy, private life that would ruin the series forever.

"His real name is Rigoberto," she said. "He changed his name when he left the Philippines."

Who was this man? I tried to process the information as I crept slowly toward the stoplight. My father was this kick-ass activist who had to flee the Philippines and changed his name in the process? I felt like the world was shifting—my loud, embarrassing dad, a badass? Why didn't I know all this? How—

HONK!

A car blasted its horn behind me. Shaking my head, I noticed the huge space between us and the car ahead, so I stepped on the gas and turned just before the light changed to red.

We entered the lot and pulled into a spot. "Thank you for telling me," I said. "It really gives me a different perspective on my family." Inspired by this more positive outlook on my heritage, I decided that I was going to tell Bethany about the Folk Festival.

When we entered the store my grandmother stood at the front, by the registers, staring into the large warehouse filled with fabric. There was a faint smile on her face. It could have been because of any number of things: the times she and her mother sewed together, the reality of going back home, or something completely ridiculous like the elevator music that was playing—maybe it reminded her of my father's beloved karaoke machine, and how she would miss him.

[RUN DMC song begins to play loudly.]

[GRANDMA can suddenly speak English. As credits roll up the screen, GRANDMA turns to camera.]

GRANDMA: That's a wrap.

[Fade to black as audience laughs.]

An employee greeted us, asking if we needed any assistance. Addressing my grandmother, I said in Tagalog, "What're you looking for?"

My grandmother smiled. "I need fabric," she said. "I promised your mother I would fix some of her clothes."

I turned to the woman, who was leaning in with curiosity. She was nodding gingerly, her eyes wide open and her lips forming a circle, ready to ask questions if she needed to.

I suddenly felt like my grandmother for a moment: a non-English speaker, exposed like a goldfish in a tank, and I froze. There was that feeling of insecurity again. The feeling that people were judging me, thinking I was uneducated, and looking down at me because of my brown skin. I started to panic. She must think that neither of us could speak English.

Closing my eyes, I blabbered awkwardly under my breath. "Uh . . . um . . ." It was like I was at the Chinese restaurant again. People waiting to see if I could speak the language. I swallowed hard.

[Translation appears at bottom of screen.]

[Actors crane heads to read lettering, to see what the audience sees.]

[Live audience laughs.]

Gritting my teeth, I addressed the clerk and stammered, "Fabric?"

"Of course," the woman replied. She pointed to the back corner of the store. "Just holler if you have any questions."

I nodded and quickly escorted my grandmother through the store.

The worker disappeared down the main aisle and turned a corner. I watched her, wondering if she was telling her co-workers about her experience with us. I could see it now: "This Korean kid and his grandmother have no idea how to speak English." My insecurity turned rampant once again, and I lost that warm glow I had from hearing about my father.

This reminded me of the time someone cut in front of my father and I at the hardware store. My father had been scanning the signs above the aisles, searching for some drill bits. Standing in front of the register line, he'd spun around to scope out each sign, and when he couldn't find the winning aisle, he started for the register. It just so happened that another customer—a white guy—was shuffling around the corner and had walked up to the cashier, oblivious to my father. In all fairness, my father was uncertain and didn't commit to a line.

My father started cursing the man out in Tagalog, using his karaoke voice to make sure he was heard. That voice was so commanding that pretty much the whole store heard him. I could hear the conveyor belts by the cash registers screeching to a halt. When the guy turned to address my father, an argument ensued.

At first the dispute was fair, each man hurling insults at one another like a "yo mama" roast battle. Then, the white guy said, "Why don't you go back to where you came from? We speak American here!" By now, a crowd of shoppers had begun to gather. My father, who'd been speaking in Tagalog the entire time, stared the man down. In heavily-accented English he said, "Why don't you make me?"

I had never been so terrified in my life. In today's political climate, the man could have whipped out a Glock and begun firing. A debate on the cable news would ensue, with the far-right-wing extremists siding with the white guy and preaching about immigrants, and the far-left-wing zealots preaching about most homegrown terrorists being right-wing extremists. There would be massive protests, and the issue would be drawn out for months.

Back then, though, it was nothing like that.

"Why don't you make me?" my father said again.

I saw the guy begin to tense, ready to pounce on my father. He started to talk down to my father, like an adult patronizing a child. Attempting to intimidate my father, the white guy kept uttering, "What did you say?" He moved in closer to my father, puffing out his chest to appear more threatening. If it was me, I would have buckled under the threat and said, "Nothing," and then let him proceed. But when my father didn't respond the guy became angry. He repeated, "What did you say?" Again, my father stood as still as a statue in order to address the situation.

Store workers had started to approach the scene. They moved in from all directions, all aisles, swarming the area like a SWAT team. Before the store personnel could break up the fight, my father squatted into a martial arts stance. He stared the white guy down. Then, my father began to shift his body from side to side, rocking in a motion that was ready to attack. Bouncing on his toes and dancing on the balls of his feet, my father exhaled slowly. His lips pointing to the ground, directing the guy to where he'd end up.

"I said, why don't you make me?" Then he slowly raised one hand, flipped his palm up so it faced the ceiling, and crooked his fingers, gesturing for the man to make a move. "This won't hurt a bit," my father said.

I was stunned. I had no idea if my father even knew martial arts. Instantly, the guy's demeanor softened. He backed off and raised his hands up to my father. A peace offering. He turned his head from side to side, let out a hard sigh, and nodded at the employees and shoppers.

Returning to my father, the man said, "I was just joking." He slid to the side of the aisle and gestured for us to go ahead of him. The scene quietly dispersed, whispers floating around as the other customers left to continue their own missions.

I should have asked him then if he knew martial arts, but I didn't. I was so impressed by what happened. He was larger than life.

At the fabric store, my grandmother stood aimlessly, scanning the entire place. When my heart slowed to a calm, I looked around the store to find that people were minding their own business, looking for their own fabric and craft supplies.

Suddenly, my grandmother ventured down an aisle and began picking out fabric as if she had been in the store before. She measured out what she needed and walked it over to a nearby employee. I watched from afar as the worker cut off the amount my grandmother indicated and packaged it in plastic. The whole exchange was fluid, as if the two spoke the same language. While the worker was wrapping the fabric, my grandmother grabbed the yarn she needed and placed each style on the counter.

I walked toward my grandmother. The woman assisting her smiled. "It looks like you're going to make something nice," she said. My grandmother nodded, lost in her own world but just attentive enough to get through her day.

I retrieved the merchandise, and together we walked toward the register. I turned my head and saw that the worker was continuing with her task of stocking shelves.

Everything was in my head. Just like at the Chinese restaurant. Just like at the football game with the red hat. The entire episode. Nobody was poking fun at us, at me. Even though my grandmother couldn't speak the language, she was still a person who could communicate with other humans.

With the legend of my father the activist and my non-English speaking grandmother maneuvering through a retail store like an episode of *Survivor*, I knew that I could learn to stand up for myself. Not everybody was like Nick, and I was destined to prove it to myself.

I paid for the goods, and we exited the store.

9

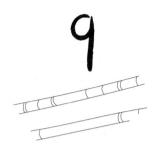

It was a week before homecoming, which meant that the last festival was coming up as well. I did everyone—Walter and Dennis, that is—a favor by skipping the final game that led to the big dance. As predicted, Walter had given me an earful. My phone blew up.

It's the last game B4 the dance!

I thought you said the homecoming football game was always against the worst team? That doesn't sound exciting. I texted. Plus I don't want to ruin it with my not wanting to be there.

He replied with another attempt to change my mind, but when I explained about my grandmother's condition, and that she was going back to the Philippines soon, he dropped it.

Tell her I hope she is all right. Then, I miss her egg rolls!

I replied with a thumbs up and then added, Maybe we can hook up this weekend some time? I miss hanging.

Rad!

For the first time since I heard about the Folk Festival, I didn't feel so anxious, so rushed. I promised my mother that we would have a family day together. One of the last before they sent my grandmother back. And by family day, I meant we basically lounged around the house, each minding our own business. My father had the television buzzing with headline news, but when I threatened to stand up from the couch, he flipped the channels until an episode of *How I Met Your Mother* appeared. On the screen, the gang was discussing Barney's playbook.

My grandmother sat in between my parents hemming various pieces of clothing as she and my mother spoke about my grandmother's trip to the Philippines.

"I wish we could go back home," my mother said.

My father was fiddling with his karaoke microphone, inspecting every inch, flipping it round and round as if he was tuning the engine of a Pontiac GTO, getting it primed for the next dance rehearsal.

As she folded and stacked a shirt that she'd finished hemming, my grandmother said, "I'm excited to see," coughing into her fist, "how much the country has changed." She picked up a pair of pants. "But I'm mostly excited to see relatives that I have not met, like grandchildren."

My mother placed her palm on top of her hand.

This gesture warmed me inside, and I started to feel differently about my family in relation to sitcom families. We were our own brand of normal. Instead of a network sitcom, our family was on cable.

The television blinked, and then suddenly, the karaoke menu appeared.

"Dah *dee!*"

"I'm just making sure it's ready," he said.

My grandmother laughed. Then she coughed out the melody until it hit the bridge section. While they were arguing about the machine, I texted Rosario.

One week!

Let's go! she replied. I wonder who's closing out the fest?

I gave a look to no one in particular. It me!

LOL. Got that right!

Then I changed subjects. How you holding up?

The television began to change colors, the episode transforming into a computerized menu of titles.

Meh . . . you? texted Rosario.

Same. Nothing new but I kinda met a girl.

What? You're in love? LOL

I shook my head, a smile forming slightly and I typed, LMAO. No . . . maybe . . . Then the winky face emoji.

Wut she like?

I did my best to describe Bethany.

A song fired up. Michael Bublé.

"Dah *dee*!"

"I have to test it!"

My parents started bantering loudly over the music as if they were screaming. All the while my grandmother continued to hem, laughing periodically at the scene around us. I couldn't help but chuckle, typing away about Bethany and how she made me feel. The day was just flying by. Then, my grandmother announced that she had run out of thread, so we had to make another trip to the yarn store.

Gotta go, I texted. See you soon?

And then we were out.

The errand was short, as my grandmother knew exactly what she needed and exactly where it was. We were only a few steps out the store when Bethany texted me, asking if I wanted to hang out. I couldn't help but smile at my phone.

Replying, I texted, At the store with my grandmother. Later?

She answered back, saying that she wanted to meet her.

I don't think that's a good idea, I replied. She's very tired and wants to go home to go to bed. The excuse just came out of nowhere. I cut my grandmother a look. She was staring into la-la land, but given her failing health, she was perfectly upright and had all the energy in the world.

Please? Bethany texted. It's beautiful out. Wouldn't she rather be outside?

Though she couldn't see me, I shrugged as I replied, I don't think so.

Can you ask her? A few seconds later, she said, I would love to meet her.

OK, I replied. I asked my grandmother, who agreed without hesitation, saying that she would love to meet my friend. I texted back, How about the park off Monroe?

I'll see you in a bit.

There were still a couple hours until sunset, so it would be fine.

I pulled into the park.

The park was a small patch of greenspace with a single hiking trail that led into a flowery range of landscaping. A couple garbage cans with pet bag stations were at each entrance.

As we exited the car, a woman walking her dog disappeared down the trail.

Bethany was already there, sitting on one of the two benches. She was sporting a more comfortable outfit than she'd normally wear to school: dark trousers with holes in the knees and a button-down sweater over a tank top. Her Chuck Taylors kicked back and forth while she waited. Even dressed down, she was beautiful. Seeing her made my heart flit.

She waved to me from afar, her legs stopping and crossing underneath her. Was she nervous too?

The evening was calm: there was no wind and the air was cool.

"This is my friend, Bethany," I said, helping my grandmother to the bench beside her.

Bethany reached her hand out for a shake. "It's so nice to meet you," she said.

My grandmother's eyes fell to Bethany's small hand. Delicately cupping her palm into Bethany's grasp, she shook it softly.

A text message came through: Walter. Dude!!!! Did you hear 3 of the football players got kicked out?

What? I replied.

Yeah. 4 being at a white power rally downtown!

Then I texted, Crazy! Even though I didn't think it was.

Would they get canceled? I thought.

No cap. LOLOLOL. They said they attended as a joke. Maybe, I guess.

A joke? I thought.

But whatevs. Dennis is coming over, Walter texted. We're gonna hang n nail down our homecoming plans. U should join 2. Thinking we could coordinate our outfits like a team of spies.

The plan actually made homecoming sound like fun. I missed hanging out with them. If nothing else, we could get a cool photo of the three of us. I could go with Bethany, the two of us dressed sharply like Bond and a Bond girl. She'd look amazing. Plus . . . wait. The Folk Festival. They didn't know that it was on the same day. I had to tell them soon.

My eyes darted around me until they found Bethany.

I didn't want to tell Walter about Bethany, so I removed her from the scenario. Sorry, out with my grandmother. Had to run errands with her. By then it will be too late. I sent the text, then I slid the phone into my pocket.

"Sorry," I said, patting my phone. "Walter wanted to hang out."

"That sounds fun," Bethany said. "I'd love to hang out with them someday."

Someday.

I nodded. My gaze drifted toward my grandmother. She sat on the edge of the bench and looked around the greenspace, unaware of what was going on. I felt much more awkward than when I'd last seen Bethany. I wonder if this was proof of what I'd been fearing. When she and I were alone it was magical. With my grandmother here, it was strange. How would it be if she came over to meet my parents? A circus with trapeze artists and a juggling clown on a unicycle?

Leaning into me, Bethany whispered, "Can I talk to her?"

"Sure," I said, laughing nervously. "I'd have to translate though."

Bethany's eyebrows shot up. "Will you?"

"Of course."

Bethany pointed at the costume necklace that my grandmother was wearing. To be honest, I hadn't even noticed it, and I'd spent the entire day with her. "That's very nice," she said. My grandmother turned to her with a smile frozen on her face. "Your necklace," she pointed. "It's very nice." Then, Bethany traced her neckline to where a necklace would fall onto her.

I waited for her to finish and relayed the information in Tagalog.

My grandmother nodded and said thank you. I couldn't help but smile. "I like her sweater," she said. "I used to make them back home."

"What'd she say?" Bethany asked in a hurry.

"She said thank you, and that she likes your sweater." I turned to my grandmother, to see if there was anything else she wanted to say. Then I remembered, "Oh, she said she used to make sweaters back in the Philippines."

Bethany kicked her shoes out in front of us, her legs straightening. Then she clapped softly. "That's so cool!"

I never really had to act as a translator before. This was a first.

Bethany tapped her lips with her finger. "I want to ask her something, but I can't really think of anything," she said. Then she shrugged. Although she was speechless, she seemed to enjoy the moment.

My grandmother leaned in to me and said, "Is she coming to the Folk Festival?"

The festival?

Bethany tapped my shoulder. "What'd she just say?" She lifted her face, a smile forming on her lips.

My lips opened, my jaw falling farther and farther. "Before I tell you what she said," I began, "I have to tell you something."

My grandmother was staring at me. *Ay nako!* I need to answer her question. Raising my finger to Bethany, I turned to my grandmother. "I don't think so," I said and shrugged.

"OK."

"I have to talk to her real quick, though," I said. "After that, we can go home. OK?"

My grandmother smiled and then turned away and started humming.

When I looked back to Bethany, she was smiling. "Everything all right?"

Everything was ... OK? Suddenly, a pit opened in my stomach, my nerves were starting to get to me. Should I break it to her slowly? Or just come right out and say it?

I love to dance! I thought. That didn't sound cool.

"What is it?" she asked, her hand accidentally touching mine. My eyes went straight to where she touched me. "You can tell me anything."

Just tell her!

Evening was setting in. The air was cooling to the point that my grandmother shivered. I didn't have much time before the park would close. I was stalling.

"Since you're not going to talk to me, can I ask *you* something?" She blinked at me once, her playful mood shifting.

Yes! I bought some time!

"Are you going to the homecoming dance?"

Ay nako!

Her eyes met mine. "I mean, do you have a date yet?"

My eyes flashed in false excitement, and it took all my strength to push out a smile. I wanted to go. *To hang out with Walter and Dennis, and to go with you!* I thought. I hated that I had to turn her down, but she had set up the opportunity like a perfectly set volleyball ready for a spike.

"No. I don't plan on going to the dance," I said.

She sat back and whispered *oh* under her breath. She tried not to frown, but I could see her bottom lip starting to quiver. Her grip loosened, and her hand laid limply on top of mine.

Tell her about the Folk Festival! my inner voice screamed. *Tell her that, of course, I want to go to the dance. I love dancing! I have the coconuts at home to prove it!*

"It's not because I don't want to go," I said, shifting in my seat. "It's because I have another dance I have to go to."

My grandmother laughed for a reason I would never know. Her voice broke the tension between Bethany and me. My focus returned to Bethany, who was now staring at me with sad eyes. "Another dance?"

"Remember in the cafeteria when I picked your phone up off the floor?" She nodded. "You thought I did a dance move, and I said I didn't."

"Yeah," she said. "It was pretty smooth." She imitated the move with her upper body, tipping over sideways. Then she smiled.

"Well, I lied. It *was* a dance move."

Her eyebrows lowered into a frown. She looked disappointed in me. Bethany's lips opened and closed like a fish, her gaze darting around the park. When she gathered her thoughts, she returned to me. "Then, why did you tell me—"

Raising my hand, I said, "Let me explain. See, there is this Folk Festival that I have been dancing in for years. It's a Filipino thing." My heart began to race. "Actually, it's an Asian thing," I said. "I've been dancing in it since I was this tall." I raised my palm flat against my stomach to show how small I was when I'd started dancing. "That's why I can't take you to homecoming."

Bethany displayed a confused look. "Why were you afraid to tell me?"

The night was approaching fast, the air temperature dropping at a quick pace. My grandmother crossed her arms together, placing her hands on top of her biceps.

"I'm almost finished," I said to her, rubbing her back with my hand. Turning to Bethany, I said, "Well, the festival is the same day as the dance, and it's the last one ever. It will be the last time I dance these three routines." I started to become emotional, my eyes tearing up. "That move I did in the cafeteria is one of the moves I do in the planting rice dance."

"Planting rice?" she asked, a smile brushing across her face.

"Planting rice, or Pagtatanim," I said to impress her, "is the act of planting rice in the field. Dancers bend sideways, stooping down to the floor," I outstretched my arm to simulate planting rice, "and our back legs stay locked, never leaving the floor."

I shrugged and waited for a response. She said nothing, but she was curious, leaning into me.

"It's a fluid dance with many dancers," I said, swallowing. "There are other choreographed parts to go along with planting rice, but for the most part, the song mimics a typical day of rice farming."

"Why didn't you tell me this?"

My shoulders raised. "I was embarrassed," I said. "I didn't think it was cool enough. I didn't think you would like me if I told you." Bethany rose to her feet. With both hands, she pulled me toward her. We stood close, looking each other in the eyes. My grandmother gazed at us and coughed. The fit was short, but it took a while for her to catch her breath. Bethany reached for her, gently rubbing her shoulder with her hand.

"I'm almost done," I said to my grandmother. "I'm telling her about the festival, and how I'm dancing in it."

My grandmother smiled. "Oh, I bet she would love to watch."

"Maybe," I answered.

Bethany turned to me. "What were you two talking about?"

"I was just recapping our conversation. Anyway . . . where was I?"

"You were saying how you were embarrassed about your dancing."

"Right," I said.

"Listen, not only do I find you wildly attractive," she said, "but I am fascinated with your life."

Wildly attractive? Looking down at the grass, I kicked my foot out in front of me.

"I'm sorry. I should've told you sooner."

Bethany pursed her lips tightly and nodded. "Yes, you should have." Then her face lit up. "What if I came to watch you perform?"

My shoulders sank. "I don't know," I said. "It's something I've always done just with my Filipino community." The thought of having her there scared the crap out of me. It took a lot for me to even talk about dancing. Performing in front of her was another story.

"Why hide it?" she said. "Because you're ashamed?" I slowly nodded, my eyes moving away from her.

My grandmother was now humming an upbeat pop song. I couldn't tell what it was, or where she'd heard it from. The radio? Karaoke? I dismissed it and turned to Bethany.

She sighed, shaking her head. "Do I make you feel that way?" Her eyes began to wander, and I imagined her replaying every conversation that we'd had in her head.

I didn't answer. I just sat there, staring. The truth was Bethany didn't make me feel that way. I just was nervous— make that terrified—about opening up my entire life to her. If I felt very Filipino around a bunch of white people, how would she fare around a bunch of Filipinos? Just thinking about it shook me. I wasn't ready to go there. At least not yet.

"So, whaddya say?" she said, her eyelashes fluttering.

"I-I can't."

My grandmother began coughing, non-stop. She keeled over on the bench, her fist closed in front of her mouth. "I'm sorry," I said, standing to leave. "I have to get my grandmother home." Then I helped her up and walked toward the car. "I'll call you."

10

The weekend was nearly over, and I felt horrible about Bethany. I avoided her the rest of the weekend, not on purpose, but because I had felt I had to make it up to Walter and Dennis. The juggling act was going awry. The three of us hung out at Walter's for a few hours. They gave me the lowdown on the homecoming dance (I'd still hadn't told them), and afterwards, we binge-watched a *Scrubs* season. Dennis's choice. However, I kept checking my phone to see if Bethany had texted.

I felt like this until I eventually slept, but when I woke up, I was in a deep sweat. My gut was twisted in knots. My face was pale, and my cheeks were hollowed. Playing the scene at the park in my mind, over and over, I thought about the best way to apologize to Bethany.

Sitting on my bed, cross legged in the center of the duvet, I typed out an apology, adding teary-eyed emojis to convey my sadness. I checked the time. There was still an hour before school started, but I couldn't wait until then.

Sorry I've been distracted this weekend.

I wasn't sure if she would reply or not. Perhaps she was getting ready—doing her makeup or sorting through her closet for an outfit. The wait was killing me, adding an extra dose of stress I wasn't counting on.

A few moments later, she replied. You hurt my feelings ☹ Why have you been avoiding me?

My stomach collapsed in on itself, and all the air disappeared from my lungs. I felt even worse now.

That wasn't my intention, I tapped out. Can I make it up to you?

She didn't reply for several long minutes, and a pain started in my gut.

Remember when I ran out to the field and started breakdancing?

Yeah! My face brightened as I remembered how she had stolen the show, commanded the crowd's attention. You were awesome!

I wish you would show me how awesome YOU are.

Ouch.

What was I doing? I'd told her about the festival already. I'd introduced her to my grandmother. What was wrong with me?

Breathing out a heavy sigh, my head dropped to my chest.

Think, think, think, think, think . . . I know!

My fingers went into overdrive. Would you want to come to a rehearsal? It wasn't the Folk Festival, but it was something. I could gradually get comfortable with her being there and possibly get to the festival level of confidence. We have them at my house, I texted.

omg I would love to! ♥♥♥♥♥

Crisis averted! See, I could be the self-assured Filipino, my chest puffed out, and my chin held high. Maybe I was gaining that ever so important thing called confidence. I'd never felt so relieved in my life. Everything was falling into place, and I had the greatest girl behind me.

I'll see you at school? I can find you between third and fourth?

She replied with a kissy face. I smiled, holding the phone close to my heart.

After I savored the emotion, I rolled off the bed and got ready for my day. Downstairs, my grandmother was cooking. I could hear the sizzling as I entered the kitchen. The smell of seared pork filled the room. The rice cooker was full, and empty plates were scattered atop the counter.

I came up behind her and hugged her. "Good morning," I said. "How are you feeling?"

"Oh, you know," she said. "Getting ready to go back to the Philippines." Then she squeezed her lips together, and her body softened. I wasn't sure how she really felt about going back home. I suspected that she was sad, but there wasn't anything either of us could do. I was heartbroken. I'd just started getting to know her, all because of my own insecurity, and now she was leaving.

"It'll be OK," I assured. Whipping out my phone, I said, "We'll keep in touch. We can video chat."

"OK," she said with a tinge of excitement. Then, she pointed to a plate with her lips. "I made something for you." I looked over her shoulder—Spam, sunny-side up eggs, and rice. She always knew how to start the day right.

A sweet aroma tickled my nose when she lifted the lid of a medium-sized pot that was simmering on a burner. Spooning vegetable oil on the eggs with the spatula, my grandmother said, "I made some champorado." The chocolate-based porridge bubbled in front of me, the smell wafting up from the pot. Heaven had opened its registration period and offered a huge discount to get in.

My grandmother pointed at a plate. I took it into the living room to eat. Headline news was on, the volume turned up so my parents could hear from their bedroom. On the set, a far-right Republican was spouting the party's normal talking points—a wall to secure the border, discrimination against trans people, and how to control women's bodies. Watching it made me ill. I never thought anything could make champorado taste bad, but I was wrong—headline news did the trick. My grandmother hummed a soft hymn as she exited the kitchen and made the long trek upstairs. The anchor then said, "When we come back, we'll talk about the rise of white nationalism."

I turned off the news so I could relish in the remaining bites, and once I finished my meal, I went to the kitchen to rinse off my plate.

"Did you eat?" my father asked as he entered the kitchen. The water was running on top of the plate. "I just finished," I told him.

"Oh." Eyeing the pile of Spam and full cooker of rice, he said, "Want to bring some to school?"

I declined.

"You can have some for lunch," he offered.

Waving him off, I said, "I have to stay in shape for the dance."

"Oh," he responded and then grabbed a plate for himself. He sulked as he covered his plate; his only son was abandoning his mission to feed people.

"But thank you for offering," I said. I didn't want him to feel bad. He was just trying to be a good father. It was weird seeing this activist badass pout around the house. One day, I hoped to make him proud.

My father nodded, his eyes never making contact with mine.

Damnit!

"You know what?" I said. "I changed my mind. I could use the carbs." A wide smile grew on his face. "I'll take some to go."

My father grabbed some Pyrex and filled it with a heavy dose of eggs and rice. He then laid some Spam over the top. "Here you go," he said. "This should get you to dinnertime." He grabbed his plate and proceeded to the living room. Stopping mid-step, he said, "I'll see you at practice tonight?"

"I wouldn't miss it," I replied. "There aren't that many left." He smiled and then disappeared. In the living room, I could hear the television turn on, the volume set high and a talking head screaming at the host.

"—Trump can't just send federal investigators into downtown Portland," the voice said. "These marchers are peacefully protesting against racial injustice—"

In the car, pulling out of the driveway, I picked up my phone. "Group text to Walter and Dennis," I said into the receiver. "Any plans later? I can hang after school for a little while if you guys want." I swung the steering wheel around and shifted into drive. "Let me know. Send."

I drove to school in silence, alone with my thoughts. I was excited to see Bethany, to continue where we left off. I felt more and more comfortable with my dancing, and if the rehearsals went well, then maybe I could get to the point where she could come to the festival. The thought gave me a warm feeling. I just needed to keep remembering how awesome she was, and how she'd been so supportive and interested in my heritage.

I was so lost in thought, the next thing I knew I was pulling into the parking lot. When I saw the front of the school, the high I'd been feeling went away. Just like that. Suddenly, I was white knuckling the steering wheel until my fingers hurt. A group of football players was standing by the entrance, two of them tossing a football back and forth.

Nick was in the center of it all, his perfectly styled blonde hair covering his winning smile like a douchebag Zack Morris. He was larger than life and almost as tall. He looked like the head coach giving instruction, each player's attention solely on him.

What was he even saying to them?

I pulled into a spot and then looked around. There wasn't another entrance into the building. My stomach dropped. I would have to go through Nick.

Should I just wait until they leave? My nerves were telling me yes, but then Bethany got in my head. Her words were ringing over and over.

"You should stand up for yourself."

Sitting in the car with the engine humming, I twisted the key and the car silenced. I waited until the front of the school cleared out.

My phone buzzed. Walter.

I'm in.

Soon after, Dennis responded.

Me 2!

Can finally nail down plans!

A blitz of messages between the two of them followed, almost like we were back to normal. Going to the big dance. Only I wasn't going.

I'll see u guys later, I texted.

I entered the school, and as I walked down the hall, I saw that the homecoming committee had put up a bunch of new posters and flyers. Some had already been drawn on. I especially liked a row of movie posters that were added above our lockers. It all kind of made me wish I could go to the dance.

"There's only ONE homecoming dance!" one flyer screamed.

"Don't be left out!" another cried.

I chuckled. A lump formed in my throat. Today, I was going to tell Walter and Dennis that I wasn't going. As I got to my locker, I overheard Jackie, another girl from my class, talking with a friend about who they thought would be homecoming queen and king. One of them was holding a flier asking students to submit their nominations to the committee by Thursday.

Soon I was at my first class—English—and when I peered into the room, only a few students sat talking to one another. I entered and took my usual seat by the window, staring out into the parking lot, waiting for the class to start. I was filled with anxiety all through English, Health, and Algebra.

There was only a small window in between classes, so when the chance came, I grabbed my backpack and bolted out of the room like a racehorse out his gate. Sprinting down the science wing, I turned down the main walkway and then rushed to Bethany's locker. Walter and Dennis were in view. The two were standing in front of Walter's open locker, conversing.

I caught Walter's eye. He jerked his head up, dishing out a quick nod. "Heyo!" he said, but I breezed right by him and Dennis. "Where ya going?" Walter called after me.

Squeezing through a group of kids and twisting my upper body, I said, "I'll call you later!" After a couple steps forward, I stopped. "Wait, I got something for you." Then I pulled out the Spam breakfast from my backpack. "Here," I said, "from my dad."

Walter peeled off the lid, and I could see the joy on his face, followed by Dennis's. The two inhaled the aroma, their eyes closing and their smiles reaching the heavens. I spun back around on the ball of my foot, a classic dance move, and trudged through the row of bodies. A mess of students was congregating in every corner of the hall I passed.

"Are you dressing up?" one boy asked his friend. "I'm thinking about just wearing jeans and a blazer."

Then I rounded the corner.

"Who do you want to see as homecoming queen?"

"I hope Aspen gets nominated."

Turning the corner, I rammed into Nick.

When I crashed into him, the force from my body stopped, and I nearly lost myself under my footing. Nick then shoved me hard, a smile on his face so wide that it would distract anyone from noticing his shoulder crushing into me.

"That one was for the test!" he yelled.

I pressed on and was now several steps past him. My body had so much force there was no way he was going to stop me. If he was douchebag Zack Morris, I was A. C. Later!

Students began walking to their classes, disappearing into various classrooms as I made my way to Bethany's locker.

I rounded the corner and saw Bethany digging through her belongings. From where I was standing, she looked as beautiful as ever. She wore a turquoise tee with checkerboard suspenders over slick, black leggings tucked into leather Doc Martens. Her face, framed by her dark hair, was made up with heavy eyeliner and dark lipstick. I couldn't believe this amazing person was into me. Like *really* into me. Instantly, my anxiety turned to happiness.

Bethany pulled out a couple books and slid them into her backpack.

"Hey," I said.

Startled, Bethany stood upright. "Hi!" she said, her voice high and squeaky.

A student next to her closed her locker. Bethany turned and smiled.

"By-eee," the girl said and then left.

"Thanks for waiting for me," I said as I put my hand on her shoulder. "You look great!"

"Thanks," she said softly. Her smile was as big as a rainbow.

"So . . . how are you?" I asked, still unsure how she was feeling after my indecisiveness.

Bethany shrugged. "Good," she said, with a touch of uncertainty. "I'm excited to see you dance." Her gaze fell to the floor. "Even though it *is* only rehearsals."

Inside, my heart was slowly breaking.

"I know," I said in an apologetic voice. "I just need some time."

Her lips twisted, and she nodded. "I understand," she muttered. Her eyes still focused on the ground, she said, "Maybe I'll just go to the homecoming dance."

NOOOOOOOOOOOOOO!

Saliva formed in my mouth, and as I swallowed the bitterness, I nodded in agreement. It then got quiet and awkward, and I didn't know what to say at this point.

Then she smiled. "Please tell your grandma that I enjoyed meeting her."

"I will," I said.

Before I could say another word, Bethany moved in and kissed me. On the lips! It was like the world stopped and nothing mattered anymore. Not my embarrassing family, not my insecurities, not even Nick. There was only Bethany.

*[A three-minute montage of fireworks finales
blasts onto screen. Shots of New York,
London, Paris, and then Sydney.]*

[KATY PERRY sings "Firework" on the screen.]

*The kiss would win "Best Kiss" at the MTV
Movie & TV Awards, overtaking Chase Stokes
and Madelyn Cline's on-screen kiss.*

It was the best kiss I had ever had. OK, it was the only kiss I had ever had. Unexpected as it was, her lips felt like rose petals against mine. I puckered my lips even more as warmth rushed through my body, from my head all the way down to my toes. We made out for a nearly a minute. All the noise around us dissipated. We shared a kiss so long that it lasted into the next period. The hallways were now empty, and the two of us late for our next class.

"Ahem," someone behind me cleared her throat. Bethany was smiling at this point. When I didn't respond, the woman tapped me on the shoulder. It was a teacher, Miss Billingsworth. I spun gracefully on the ball of my foot to greet her. "The bell went off. The two of you need to get to class," she informed us.

"We're going," I said. Then I turned to face Bethany and smiled. "I'll see you later." She was beaming, a grin spread across her face. There was a certain glow to her. I pivoted and ran down the hallway to gym class.

When I entered the gym, instantly the teacher was in my face. "You're late!" he shouted, marching up to me. His body was built like a tree: thick on top and skinny on the bottom. His head was shaped like a rectangle, his jaw line square.

"Sorry," I said. "I was . . . uh—"

"You were what?" He was now only a few inches away from me. "If you don't have a pass excusing you, you're in a heap of trouble," he said. Then, he leaned in closer to me, examining my face. His attitude suddenly changed. It was softer, almost fatherly, definitely friendlier. "Are you OK?" My eyes narrowed. Moving his head from side to side, he asked, "Did someone punch you?" His voice was kind, caring. It was nothing I'd ever seen. "Son, you can tell me."

Son?

The gym teacher was part of the football coaching staff. He was very manly, rough around the edges. His new attitude freaked me out. I had no idea what was going on.

"What?" I asked.

"Are you OK?" he said again. "It looks like someone socked you a good one." He pointed at my lips.

What's on my lips? I thought.

"Who did this to you?"

Did what? Then it hit me. Bethany's dark lipstick.

With great concern, he said, "Does it hurt?"

Hm, I think I could take advantage of this, I thought. Rubbing my lips together, I mumbled, "Yeth, it does." I licked my lips gingerly, the taste of lipstick bitter against my tongue. Speaking with a lisp to show the false pain, I said, "Can I go to the nerf?"

Some of the students were watching us. They had stopped what they were doing and now were just staring to see what would happen. The gym teacher extended his arm, pointing to the gymnasium doors. "You're dismissed," he ordered. "Get that looked at."

I slowly turned to the kids that were watching us and smiled. Then I left. The morning had gone better than I had imagined. Before school I'd been sulking in bed, worried that Bethany hated me. When I saw her, we kissed, and it was magical. And now this? No gym class for me? I was flying high. I walked down the hall, smug and overconfident, like I was Nickhead without the racism. My head held high, I strutted to the bathroom to wipe off my lips. *This is what it feels like for things to go my way*, I thought.

With the halls empty, the school was super quiet. When I entered the bathroom, my phone buzzed. Auntie Marisol. Rosario sprained her ankle. She can no longer dance in the festival. Her understudy, Eleanor, will have to fill in.

And just like that, my world ended.

My heart sank, and all the excitement drained from my pores.

I had nothing against Eleanor, but Rosario and I had been dancing Tinikling together for years. She knew my next step before I even took it. We had become perfect partners. All the good that happened was for nothing.

Outside in the hallway, a faint ruckus of voices passed.

"I can't wait for the dance!" a squeaky voiced girl screamed.

"It's gonna be *so* fun!"

"Maybe we should get a limo!"

"I hope Landon asks me!"

All the excitement trickled in the bathroom enough for me to hear. It was as if the universe was giving me signs. *Maybe I should just not go to the festival.* It felt like the world wanted to end it, and this was its way of doing so, and that the homecoming dance was my next "dance move."

11

One text message had rocked my world. I reread it over and over, staring in disbelief as I started tearing up. Even as my body tried to collapse in on itself, I told myself that I needed to stay composed. I was at school, and this was not the place. Closing my eyes tightly, I thought, *It will be fine. Eleanor is fully capable of filling in. We've practiced the dance. She knows what she's doing.*

[JULIANNE HOUGH appears dressed in an oversized outfit.]

[Audience applauses.]

[JAMIE looks up to see what the commotion is about.]

JAMIE: *What is* Dancing with the Stars *champion Julianne Hough doing here?*

[JULIANNE takes her bow.]

JULIANNE: *I'm here to take Rosario's place.*

[In one swooping motion, JULIANNE crouches down, grabs hold of her pant legs, extends her body with full force, and yanks the outfit off to reveal a stunning, tight, partially see-through Filipino dance gown.

> *[Audience cheers.]*
>
> *Overhead, Bill Medley sings, "Now I've had the time of my life, no I've never felt like this before."*

I followed the imaginary tune, sliding from side to side. My head swayed with the music. With my eyes closed, I positioned myself and started to dance the salsa. One step forward, one step back. My arms started to swing. I was getting into a groove. Then, I would fake push Julianne Hough away, and slide to the right as I planted rice. Repeating the motion to my left, I would pull in my imaginary partner and complete our dance routine.

In my mind, Julianne Hough danced with me. Together, we danced flawlessly, a perfect routine. Though, in reality, I danced alone, free of any negativity. When I opened my eyes, a jock was standing behind me. He had emerged from the stall and saw what I had been hiding for years. When he looked at me through the bathroom mirror, our eyes met. A smile began to grow on his face. Lightheadedness hit me as my muscles tensed. I couldn't think clearly. What was going on? I'd slipped a little in the cafeteria, planting rice near Bethany, but this? This was a whole new level of embarrassment. I was mortified. My face suddenly became hot.

The jock, Alan, quickly turned his head to avoid eye contact. He stepped past me, walked up to the sink, and started washing his hands. His head kept down, subtly clearing his throat as he rubbed his palms together under the water.

I couldn't help but stare at him through the mirror, frozen, my heart palpitating in my chest. *What is he thinking?* I thought.

As he washed his hands, a smirk escaped. He straightened his lips, but then they curled back into a smile, this time wider. He was starting to lose it, but he kept it together.

My eyes blinked rapidly, and a grimace formed on my face. I started to breathe heavily, my eyes darting around the room as the water splashed against the stainless steel. I could feel my eyes start to water, so I blinked back the tears until he was finished. All the good feelings I'd had after kissing Bethany had been erased—just like that. Between the news of Rosario's injury and my secret coming out, I was done for.

Alan swiped some paper towels from the holder and wiped his hands. I felt like he was taking a long time, but he continued to wipe and said nothing. Then, he opened his mouth.

"That," he said, "was so ridiculous." His shoulders bounced, and his smile changed to laughter. "Dude, seriously," he mocked. "That was the funniest thing I have ever seen." Then, he mimicked me, dancing with a silly smile on his face. His posture was stiff, unrelaxed. Auntie Marisol would have had a field day with him. "I'm the dancing queen," he sang badly.

My body sunk into itself. "Sorry," I tried to explain, "I just got some bad news."

Alan ignored me, dancing in a circle in front of me. The area was small, so his circles shrank with every motion, and periodically, he bumped into the counter or the stall door.

"Please," I said. "I was only dancing because I got some terrible news."

He stopped his motion. Looking at me with narrowed eyes, he said, "So, you dance when you get bad news?"

Shrugging, I said, "I guess."

He tightened his lips and then sharply nodded. "If someone close to you died, you'd start shaking your hips at the funeral?"

I raised one shoulder and cocked my head. "Sure?"

Alan blinked. He was looking down at the tile floor. Then he said, "You're so ridiculous." He shook his head, shot the damp towels into the garbage can, and disappeared from the restroom.

I stood motionless, stunned at what had just happened.

"That wasn't so bad," I told myself.

I waited out the rest of the period, and when the bell for the next class rang, I made my way to the room where

Bethany's class was and positioned myself outside the door-way. Various students passed by, their books cradled in their arms or held in their hands. Smiling at each person that walked by, I stuck my head in to see Bethany packing up her belongings. When she exited, I pulled her off to the side.

"Hey!" she said.

"Do you want to go somewhere for lunch?"

Saint Patrick's had an open campus during lunch period. I never left during lunch; I never had a reason to. Both Walter and Dennis were hot lunch guys to the core. Ever since grade school, the three of us would buy hot lunches and eat whatever was on the menu. Our longest hot lunch streak was 218 days straight, but then Walter got the chick-enpox. It took me a while to get over it. We never came close again, only making it to something like seventy-one straight lunches.

"I'd love to," she said with a wide smile and went up on her tiptoes to kiss me. Just like that, the magic returned, soothing all my fears and worries and washing the bad luck away. She leaned in close, the masses of other students in the hallway forcing her body into mine. I didn't mind—it took my mind off Rosario and the incident with Alan.

We walked to my car. A couple other students were thinking the same thing and were rushing to leave the campus. I nodded to them as we made our way to the parking lot and jumped in the car to head to the mall's food court.

"How has your day been?" Bethany asked as she pulled the seatbelt over herself.

I let out a long, drawn out sigh. "Well," I began, shifting into drive and then pulling away, the school building in my rearview. "I got excused from gym class because your lip-stick looked like a bruise on my face."

Bethany covered her mouth with her hand. "Oops," she said cheerfully. "Sorry," she chuckled, looking down.

I smiled. "Don't apologize. It was worth it."

She was leaning to the side, laughing subtly as we drove down the road. Then she turned to me. "Yeah," she said, reaching for my hand. "It was."

We drove through an intersection and then stopped at a red light. Only a mile or two up and we would be there. A crowd of cars passed through, the lunch hour bringing out many nearby workers.

"But that's not even the highlight," I said, my eyes focused on a Bigfoot bumper sticker on the car in front of me. I shook my head. *Still couldn't believe it*, I thought. "My dance partner for Tinikling sprained her ankle."

"Tinikling?" she asked.

The light turned green, and we pressed through.

"Sorry, it's a dance in the Folk Festival."

"That's not good, is it?" she said.

I turned to her and just frowned. "No, it's not."

The mall was now in sight; the large building complex took up nearly four blocks. Cars were placed strategically in the parking lot, many lined along the outsides (the employees I presumed), the rest scattered within the short distance to the entrances. We drove up the long drive until we found ourselves at the entrance to the food court.

"I'm sure things will work out," she said, squeezing my hand gently, her reassuring touch made my body soften.

When we arrived, the area was filled with a combination of shoppers and workers. Mothers sat with their children in strollers while their husbands or boyfriends ordered food at one of the many selections. A hip, trendy couple sat with lattes and their two dogs, who were sitting patiently by their owners' chairs.

"Wow," Bethany said. "This place is packed." She pointed out the only available seat before glancing between it and the various food options.

"How about you save that seat, and then I go up first?" she offered.

"Sure." I trekked over to the table and plopped myself down to watch Bethany approach the Italian café's counter. While I was scoping out the available choices, I saw a group of punk rock teens step up next to her. They looked older, maybe college aged. They were loud and attention seeking.

I watched as they commanded the area, and suddenly I felt smothered. Bethany just looked at them and stepped aside to make room. It made me uncomfortable, because for a moment, it almost looked like they all belonged together, like they had more in common than Bethany and I.

Wouldn't she rather be with these guys? I thought. *They all dress the same.*

Before I could get myself wound up, Bethany returned with her food. "Oh my God, that was weird," she laughed. "Did you see that?"

"I did," I said, raising an eyebrow. My heart slowed to a pitter-patter, and I slid back to the table.

"All right," I said. "My turn." I stood and walked over to the Greek eatery. I scanned the menu. I couldn't decide between a gyro, another dish that looked like a gyro, or a third meal that looked like a gyro.

"What's the difference between the gyro and the other gyro?" I asked the cashier.

She craned her neck, reading the menu options. "One has lamb, the other is mixed with lamb and chicken."

"And the other gyro?" I asked.

"That one has faux lamb."

While I stood pondering my choice, the group of punk rock teens approached the counter. Suddenly, there was a strange voice in my right ear—it was the guy who was closest to Bethany. I think he asked me something.

"Sorry?" I said, still caught up in my choice of lamb.

"What're you doing with that cute piece of ass?" he asked, jerking his head toward Bethany at our table. She had her back to us as she ate her spaghetti, completely oblivious.

Lost in the thought of lamb, a little lamb, or fake lamb, I said, "What did you say?"

He bumped into me, leaning in close enough that I could smell his breath. "Why don't you stick to your own kind?"

"I . . . don't understand." I turned to look at him, and he spun away to face the menu. He didn't try to explain.

"You don't belong with that girl." He cocked his head and scoped out Bethany again. "You should really stick to your kind."

"She is my kind," I pointed out, my calm tone belying my racing heartbeat. "We're both in high school."

Leaning closer to me, he whispered, "Don't be a smart ass. You know what I mean."

I inhaled deeply, trying to settle myself as I stepped up to the cashier's till to order the regular gyro. My heart raced hard against the inside of my chest, and I tried to force myself to stay calm.

I've never been in a fight, I thought, *but since I had my first kiss today, I might as well have another first.*

Even though I sounded tough, I really wasn't, and I was hoping that he would just leave.

Suddenly, the three of them were gone.

"Regular gyro" the cashier said, distracting me from the punk rockers. "Eleven dollars."

I paid for my meal, and when I strolled back to the table, I realized that the boy was talking to Bethany. For the most part she seemed to be ignoring him, but he was persistent.

I took the seat across from Bethany.

"This is, um, my boyfriend, Jamie."

Boyfriend? Suddenly I was a feather about to float away. I could barely contain my smile. Until I saw the boy again, then I silently fumed.

She gestured to me and then turned to the punk rockers. "So, if you three would please leave, I'd like to enjoy a quiet meal with my boyfriend."

The boy who'd harassed me only minutes prior changed his attitude. "Oh," he said. "This is your boyfriend?" Then he stared at me, smirking devilishly.

Not wanting to start any trouble, I said, "Nice to meet you."

"Seriously, go," Bethany demanded and flicked her fingers. "Bye!"

The three boys left the area, their leader walking backward with an arrogant smile. I watched him go out of the corner of my eye.

"What losers." Bethany rolled her eyes and swallowed a bite of her meal before focusing her attention back on me.

I clenched my jaw, trying to hold back my anger.

Looking at my lunch, she tried to change the subject. "A gyro? That smells delicious."

I swallowed, my curiosity getting the best of me. "Do you know them?" I asked, and then I took a bite and chewed slowly.

"No," she grimaced. "I'm assuming they thought that since I kinda dress like them, I'd want to hang out with them." She paused for a moment, before saying emphatically, "And I don't."

The atmosphere in the mall changed. I could feel the eyes of anyone who walked by lingering on me. *Should I be with another Filipino?* I thought. Judging each person, I glared at anyone who fit the profile—older white men, white boys with crew cuts, any white male in general, it was the whole gyro conversation all over again—and sank farther down into my seat in an effort to become invisible. I felt tiny in the world that I'd spent so long trying to fit into. I felt vulnerable.

[Cut to a serious episode after a real-life tragedy. The plot's theme is dramatic, and after the show, the cast gives a public service announcement, preaching to the audience to speak up if you know someone in trouble.]

MAIN STAR: Don't sit back and say nothing.

[The cast eyes one another, nodding gently in somber agreement.]

MAIN STAR: *It could be too late.*

[Fade to black with white letters zipping onto the screen with the name of a fellow cast member.]

[Screen reads "Rest in Peace" and the dates of the actor's life.]

Suddenly I realized I was staring blankly at my gyro and hadn't said anything for too long. I snapped my head up and glanced at Bethany. She was smiling innocently in front of me. I shifted my focus onto her, not wanting to get pulled into a depression. "How's the gyro?" she asked.

"It's good," I said, trying to hide my salty attitude from her. I was still smarting from my exchange with the older boy, but I didn't want to let Bethany know what happened because I didn't want her to feel worse.

"It looks amazing!"

I shrugged. "It's OK."

"I'm so jelly," she said, glancing down at her own meal.

Unfortunately, I was in no mood to chat. My hands were shaking from what had just happened at the counter with the punk rocker. I was grinding my teeth and a slight pain formed in my stomach. I had lost my appetite. I sulked deep into my chair, not realizing that Bethany had started to eat my gyro.

When I noticed what was going on, she chewed faster with a wide, innocent smile on her face. She was trying to get away with it, and it made me laugh. Watching her eat my lunch relaxed me. I wanted to hold onto this moment forever. Just being with her brightened my day.

"Sorry," she giggled, wiping her face with her hand. "I couldn't resist."

I slowly began to come out of my funk, and Bethany's happiness hit me hard. Her lips still had a slight film of tzatziki sauce, and seeing it made me chuckle. Her mischievous action calmed me. I wanted to reach out and wipe the sauce from her lip, but she was still shaking from laughing.

Instead, I pointed to my lip. "You've got . . ." She quickly wiped her face and laughed even harder.

Here was this beautiful girl who actually wanted to spend time with me. She wanted to go to the homecoming dance—the biggest event of the year outside of the prom— and I made her feel bad about it. And for what? To hide my career as a Filipino dancer? A career that was ending anyway? Was I this much of an idiot?

Was Fely Franquelli a Filipino legend?

Stealing the gyro back, I took a bite and said, "I'm glad you enjoyed it."

We lapsed into silence as we ate, enjoying each other's company. She, lost in her own thoughts, and me, thinking about the Folk Festival and homecoming dance. The day was beginning to turn around.

I realized that this was the second time that Bethany had come to my rescue. First, with Nick in the classroom, and now this. The drive back to school was quiet. So quiet that I had to break the silence.

"Hey." I placed my hand on her knee and caressed it. She took my hand and put it in hers, and instantly my eyes found our clasped palms. "Back at the mall, when you said that those dudes wanted to hang out with you because you dressed alike?"

"Yeah?"

Biting the inside of my lip, I said, "How do you feel about that?"

Her eyes narrowed. She released my hand and rubbed her chin with her finger. "What do you mean?"

We approached an intersection, the light red. When I stopped the car, I said, "It just made me think about something he said." Then I looked at her. She was pursing her lips. *Did I offend her?*

"How so?"

The light then turned green. She pointed out the window. I followed her finger and then pushed down on the accelerator and zipped through. "One of the things he said to me in line was to stick to my own kind." I signaled for the next street. There was only a mile left until we were back at school.

"Then you made a comment," I said, "and I thought about our relationship." She bit her front teeth down on her bottom lip, a smile engaging me to continue. "How do you feel about being in a relationship with me?"

"You mean when I called you my boyfriend?" she playfully said.

This made me smile, and I felt warm inside. "Well . . . that, but also . . ." She pulled back and cocked her head to the side. "Like with someone who's not white," I said.

Her lips formed a circle, and her head fell back. "Oh," she said. "I think I see where you're going."

"I'm just curious," I said.

"Honestly, I never even thought about that," she confessed. "Huh." Her gaze turned down.

I could tell that she hadn't *ever* thought about it. Which was a good thing. She wasn't cynical like me or prejudiced like Nick. Both traits that affected other people.

I pulled into the parking lot, finding a spot at the end of a row, just near the practice football field, and turned off the engine.

"I don't look at you that way," she said. Then she smiled. "Is that bad?" Her face scrunched. "I don't want you to think I'm not aware of us being different. I know sometimes I take it for granted, but . . ."

I could tell she was worried how this would go. She seemed concerned she had offended me again.

Shaking my head, to make sure I wasn't making her feel uncomfortable, I said, "No! That's good!" I frowned and then lowered my head. "Unfortunately, I think about stuff like this all the time."

"You do?"

"All the time," I said.

Her head moved forward, her eyebrows lifting. "Wow," she uttered. "Maybe I *am* privileged."

"It's why it was so hard for me to talk about my family and the Folk Festival." She slowly nodded, and I could tell that I was connecting with her, getting her to understand what it was like to be me. A person of color. "When you're a minority, you notice stuff like this all the time. Like a superpower of some sort." This comment made her grin. "And with things the way they are . . . stuff like what happened at the mall, and with Nick, is always in my face."

Students began walking down to the football field. It looked like gym class, and the PE teacher had assigned a leisurely walk or run around the track. When I saw this, I knew that we were late for our next period.

Bethany sighed. "I understand what you're saying." She looked to the field and then her phone for the time. "But, we're not all like that."

I know, I thought. *But one bad asshole spoils the bunch.*

"You're right," I said, "and that's what I need to get over." Saying this out loud made it more real to me, almost like I was ready to change my thinking.

More and more students tromped to the field. The air between us softened.

Grazing her skin with my fingertips, I said, "So . . . boyfriend?" Then I smiled.

She bit her bottom lip while simultaneously smiling. "Well, only if you want to be," she teased. She pulled my hand into hers, caressing it.

I do! I do!

Shrugging, I tried to play it cool. I wanted to say, "I'll be anything for you," but instead, "A million times, yes!" came out with ambitious cheesiness. I quickly shook my head, then dropped it to my chest.

Ay nako! I thought. I did everything but give her two thumbs up.

Bethany lifted my chin with her finger, looked me in the eyes, and leaned in and kissed me. We kissed for several seconds, until the students flooding the field distracted us.

"We better get going," I said. "I'll see you tonight? My house?"

We exited the car and entered the school. The rest of the day was a blur, my mind thinking only about Bethany: from solidifying our relationship, to what she had said. Not all people *were* like that. I needed to trust that the majority of people weren't. As much as this idea freaked me out, I started to feel better about my life, my family, and my heritage.

12

After school, I was hanging with Walter and Dennis at a secondhand store looking for clothing for the homecoming dance. I still hadn't told them that the festival was on the same day, so I was kind of just waiting for the right time, sloppily flipping through clothes on the rack in front of me.

Shuffling through his own rack, Dennis pulled out a peach-colored retro tuxedo with matching bowtie and cummerbund. "What about this?" he asked. He held it up, examining it from all angles, even holding it up to his body. The sleeves ended at his forearms, the pants reaching just over his shins.

He looked funny standing there.

"Looks small," Walter said, moving his head from side to side. He turned to me. "It might fit you."

I stopped digging through clothing that had little meaning and stared at Walter, thinking that right now would be the best time to tell him.

"Wanna try it on?" Walter said, collecting the tux from Dennis.

Shaking my head, I said, "Not really. It looks more like a tux from *Dumb and Dumber* than something James Bond would wear."

Dennis held the tux higher, looking at it in the light. Walter's eyebrows crooked. "You're probably right."

"I don't know," said Dennis. "I kinda like it."

Walter continued digging through the rack, sliding garments across the metal beam. Outside, a pickup truck with a loud exhaust system drove through the parking lot. I looked out the window and saw a rusted-out truck with oversized wheels and two flags—an American flag and a yellow Gadsden flag, which read "don't tread on me"— attached to the bed, propped up and flailing in the slight breeze, driving off into the distance. My breathing instantly began to race. I only caught a glimpse of the driver, whose tattooed arm was hanging out the window. The bill of a baseball cap covered the man's eyes.

Don't tread on me? I thought, as the truck disappeared. *Then why are you treading on me?*

My heart hurt, and suddenly I became depressed. Seeing the truck made me think about Nick and Trump fanatics, and how the only comforting thing I had—the Folk Festival—was going to be taken away as well.

"What's wrong, dude?" asked Walter. "Aren't you excited?"

Tell him now! "Yeah, about that." I shrugged. "Dennis," I said. "You need to hear this too." Walter's hand let go of the shoulder of a tweed suit jacket and looked at me. Dennis was holding up a pair of black pants against his body, the legs super long, covering his shoes and spilling onto the floor. It looked like his lower body was melting.

"What's going on?" Walter said. "Is it about *her?*"

Her? I thought.

"Check his text messages," Walter semi-joked.

The section of the store we were in was empty of people, the only person within earshot working the cash register, which was a good distance away. But for some reason, I walked them to the corner of the store, where the bookshelves started and the clothing racks ended. I wasn't sure if I was buying time or if I was frazzled by the pickup I had just seen.

"Remember how I told you the Folk Festival was ending?"

Walter's head tilted, then he shrugged and nodded at the same time. "I don't remember that."

"It was at the football game," I said, reminding him. "I think you were yelling at the field or something."

"You didn't go to the last game with us," he said snidely.

"He's referring to—" started Dennis.

"I know."

Walter and I exchanged looks. Then he nodded, encouraging me to continue by rotating his hand in a circular motion.

"Anyway," I said. "I can't go to the homecoming dance because it's the same day as the festival."

Walter's eyes bulged. "You're not going?" He whipped his head toward Dennis, who stood with his eyebrows furrowed. "We've been waiting for this since last year."

"I know," I said, "but last year the festival fell on the next weekend."

"So don't go," said Walter.

Just then, a customer walked by us and stopped at the bookshelf. She bent down and pulled out a paperback. I pointed down the aisle, walking forward, slightly prodding the two ahead.

"Yeah," Dennis offered, hanging the pants over his forearm. "Come and hang out with us at the dance."

"I have to go to the festival. I'm dancing in it."

"But you just said it was the last one," said Walter.

"All the more reason for me to be there."

Walter sighed loudly, his eyes rolling as he shook his head. Then, with sitcom-perfect timing, Bethany texted, asking what time she should come to the house. Reading the message forced a wide smile. I was giddy inside, my soul dancing to the Filipino love song, "Paubaya," by Moira Dela Torre.

"Who's that?" asked Walter, his eyes glaring at my phone.

My eyes grew to the size of beachballs. All I could think about was Walter's feelings toward Bethany. "Um . . ."

"It's *her*," he said. "Isn't it?"

"Dude, c'mon!" I said. "It's getting old." He was pissing me off, and I could feel my temper flaring. "She's actually pretty wonderful."

"Whatever," Walter said, and then he walked away. I watched him go to the other end of the rack and flip through some clothes, never removing any of them.

"You got a problem, too?" I asked Dennis, my voice tired and flat.

Dennis turned his head toward Walter. Then he came back to me and said, "I think he's pissed because it seems like you're blowing us off for a girl."

I peered around him. Walter had moved around to the other side of the clothing rack. "I get it," I said. "But this is the last festival. I just wish he would understand that."

"I'm sure he does," said Dennis, "but he sees it as you blowing us off. Like we're not worth your time. At the game, the cafeteria, and now the dance." He turned to see where Walter was. "He's just bitter because we used to do everything together."

Fine. I get it.

Walter stood at the front door, spinning around slowly. When Dennis and I looked at him, he checked his phone. He was avoiding me.

"You know what?" I said. "It looks like he needs some time." I looked down the main aisle to the farthest point of the store. "I'm going to check out the knick-knacks."

"Sure," Dennis said, then stepped away and rummaged through the clothes to find the peach-colored tux. He set the black pants on top of the rack, pulled off the retro tux, held it up, and said, "I'm gonna see if they have this in a bigger size."

"Bigger size?" I asked. "It's a secondhand store."

Dennis ignored me and then walked to the counter. Walter joined him. I watched from where I was standing and texted Bethany. Heading home now. Will let you know when I get there.

She replied with a thumbs-up emoji.

When I got home, I saw my parents standing in the entry-way of the kitchen, staring out into the living room where my grandmother was. My mother was frowning, and my father was staring blankly into the room. I looked into the living room and saw my grandmother sitting on the couch, rocking back and forth as the television blasted out a loud voice. Some news anchor talking about a clash between far-right and far-left protestors in downtown. Again.

"What's going on?" I asked.

"Your grandmother is going back to the Philippines," my mother said. She stepped aside to make room, and I slith-ered in between them, watching my grandmother like she was an exotic animal at the zoo.

*[A large aquarium appears on screen,
with GRANDMA inside.]*

*[JAMIE and PARENTS stare into it, poking the
glass until GRANDMA acknowledges them.]*

"I know," I said. "You told me that already."

"Tonight."

What!

My first thought was to run to her, hug her, and thank her for being a part of our lives. Then I remembered that Bethany was coming over, and I realized that now might not be the best time, especially with so many emotions cir-culating in the room. Plus, I wasn't sure this was the right time to introduce my girlfriend to my family. My grand-mother was getting up there in age, and my parents were worried that if she died, they wouldn't be able to afford to send her body back home to be buried.

"She hasn't been feeling well," my mother said. "She's been coughing a lot, and her energy has been low."

My mind went to the park. When evening hit, the temperature had dropped. Was I the reason she was going back so soon? This seemed like a rash decision.

"I had to make a choice," said my father. "Her health is declining."

"It's for the best," my mother said.

My father teared up. I could feel his body quiver next to me. "She wants to be buried with my father." I reached my arm around him and pulled him in close. It was weird being the one taking care of someone who was such a badass. But here I was.

The television was now barking a commercial. Animated voices shouted out of the speakers.

"Why tonight?" I asked. "Won't tickets be the same tomorrow? Or after the festival?"

Shaking his head, my father said, "No. I looked, and it's too expensive to ship her body to the Philippines if something happens to her." He sniffled up some tears.

What was going on? First the Folk Festival. Now this? I felt like my world was crashing down.

Home yet? It was Bethany.

I typed out a reply, saying that I couldn't tonight. Family situation.

Boo! I was really looking forward to this!

I just can't.

OK. I hope everything's all right. See you at school?

"She doesn't want to be cremated," my mother interjected. "She was very adamant."

My grandmother was staring blankly at the television screen and smiling. I leaned out a little farther to see what was so funny—it was an ad with a cartoon fungus, fearing the wrath of foot ointment. When it ended, she started laughing, and I had to stop myself from joining in.

"She doesn't want to go back home," my mother argued, as my grandmother started coughing uncontrollably. It was so bad that she nearly threw up.

The way my mother was debating with herself told me how difficult it was to make this decision.

"Your father's afraid that if something happens to her, he will have no choice but to cremate her so we could afford to send her back." Then she reached for his hand, clutching hers into his.

I watched as my father eyed his mother, her body shifting on the couch as her mind drifted, lost in another world, another time, another life. My father swallowed hard. He and my mother exchanged glances, and then he sighed.

"When does she fly out?" I asked.

"Your father is going to drive her to the airport soon," my mother said. "In a few minutes." The conversation stopped suddenly, and my mother drew back into the kitchen to start cooking dinner.

"I canceled mahjong night," my father said.

Without mahjong and dance practice, the house felt cold and lonely. For once, I didn't mind. Honestly, the news of Rosario's sprained ankle had put a damper on my mood, and I didn't think I'd be of any use. Plus, all the other events that had occurred; it had been a weird day. And now this.

"I guessed you had," I said. "There aren't any tables set up, and there isn't any food out."

My father nodded and then disappeared as my mother made herself comfortable at the head of the table, marinating a batch of tenderized pork shoulder in a bowl of soy sauce, garlic, vinegar, and Sprite. The Sprite gave the meat a lemony taste. For years, I'd never been able to figure out what the secret ingredient in her kabobs was—until I saw her dumping an entire two liter of soda into the bowl.

Watching my mother made me think. With my grandmother leaving, who was going to help with the cooking? Who was going to—

"You should go with your father," she blurted, her hands massaging the meat. "Say goodbye to your grandmother."

"Yeah." I nodded. "It would be nice to say goodbye." I thought about how distant I'd been with her, not really getting to know her because she didn't speak English and I didn't want to speak Tagalog in the house.

There was noise above us. I looked up at the ceiling and followed the sound down the hallway. My father appeared from upstairs, carrying a large bag with more than enough space to get my grandmother across the world.

My grandmother stood to greet him. She was slow to rise, her hand catching the arm of the couch. I watched her maneuver gingerly through the living room. When she moved, her palm grazed the drywall with each step. She still looked young, despite her condition. That was one of the nice things about being Asian. We looked much younger than white people. At least, that was what Walter used to say. Yet another example of his privilege—he could just say things like that. At the time I hadn't really understood why it was wrong to say, and why he was wrong to comment on my having a "permanent tan." Thinking about that statement now, Walter was correct. I *did* have a permanent tan; it just came with a lifetime of prejudice. I wasn't sure it was worth it.

I rushed over to grab my grandmother's arm. She thanked me with a smile and then stood like a little child while her guardians determined her fate.

"Can she fly by herself?" I asked in English so my grandmother couldn't understand the conversation.

My father's lips pursed, and he nodded. "She has to."

I looked at him. "Why?" I asked. My father stopped and set the suitcase upright. "I mean, why don't you or Mom go with her?"

My mother and father stole looks at one another. I found the expressions odd, and when I turned to my mother, she was nodding. Then she looked away.

"We can't go back," he said, almost relieved. "I'm on a blacklist."

A blacklist! That's right! For being a badass! I was in awe of my father. He was a real-life hero.

"Plus, it's expensive to go," my mother added. "We'd have to buy a roundtrip ticket, give your dad some spending money, it's—"

"We're already sending money to the Philippines—and gifts," my father interrupted, looking up, his eyes darting across the ceiling, "your—"

"Your tuition," my mother interjected.

"OK," I said, walking my grandmother through the house. *All you needed to say was blacklist,* I thought. I felt like the second part was an excuse, but who was I to judge? I was full of them.

"Your father is going to just say she's handicapped and needs a wheelchair." Both of them eyed my grandmother. They knew she didn't understand what we were saying. Carefully, quietly, my mother confessed, "That way someone always has to escort her. They'll have to take her to her connecting flight."

"What about when she's on the plane?" I questioned.

"Someone will take her to her seat," my father said.

I knew she had made the twenty-plus-hour flight before, but it wasn't until now that I wondered how she really felt about it, and how she would be treated. I spoke perfect English and I was still tortured on the regular—how would she fare?

"Then what?" I asked.

Shrugging, my father said, "She sits on the plane." It was almost as if they hadn't thought that far ahead, only thinking about when she needed help. Like her emotions just paused or something.

"She's just going to sit there?" I inquired, perturbed by their lack of consideration. My father could hear it in my voice.

"What do you normally do when you're on a long flight?"

"I don't know," I said. "I've never been on one."

"Well, if you ever go to the Philippines, you'll know." My father licked his lips and started searching for his car keys. With the luggage still in hand, he said, "You read, or you sleep, or you watch the inflight movie."

Just like that, my grandmother's life was settled. She was going to watch the *Back to the Future* trilogy or something, and all would be fine. A car that zipped through history and a doctor with messed up hair and a long, white coat. More than likely, it wouldn't even have subtitles for her to follow.

[In this episode, the entire cast knows that one of the supporting actors is leaving the show to pursue blockbuster movies.]

[Instead of just saying that, producers write her character out of the series.]

[Viewers follow her career, as GRANDMA goes onto star in movies that are consistently given rave reviews.]

My mother continued to massage the pork, staining her hands a chocolate brown. "She doesn't want to go back, but if she died here, we wouldn't be able to send her home. This is our only choice," she said, glancing at my father. "There would be no way to afford to send her back otherwise. It would cost too much."

My grandmother just stood there silently. I wasn't sure how much of the conversation she had understood. I guessed very little, if any. She knew this time was coming, but she seemed more relaxed about it than me. It was probably why she cooked champorado: her way of saying goodbye.

My father found his keys on the kitchen counter. "Ready?" he asked. He then turned to my grandmother and, in Tagalog, said, "Do you have everything?"

Smiling, my grandmother nodded, and my family dished out hugs to one another. My grandmother and mother shared a quiet, intimate conversation, and then she waddled over to me and kissed my cheek softly. Her thick red lipstick smeared across my skin, and as she gathered her belongings and composed herself, I quickly wiped it off.

"I'll have dinner ready when you two return," my mother informed us.

"Hey," I said to my mother. She looked up, her eyes on the brink of tears. "Would you teach me how to make champorado sometime?"

"Sure, Jamie," she said, and then she looked back to her recipe. "Anything else?"

"Maybe some egg rolls?" I started to feel sad. All the times my mother and grandmother had made them, I'd never once participated. *Another missed opportunity*, I thought.

"Of course," she said.

The three of us piled into the car for the short drive to Portland International Airport. She would fly from there to Vancouver International in Canada, where she would connect to the flight to the Philippines. It would be a long journey for her.

"Are you excited about the festival?" my father asked me.

I shrugged, my eyes locked in front of me. "Did you hear about Rosario?"

He nodded. "Yeah, your Auntie Marisol called to tell us. She was concerned about how you would feel when you heard the news."

I shrugged again and said nothing.

"Don't you want to talk about it?" He checked the rearview and then signaled into the next lane. There were only a few cars scattered along the freeway. "It's the last festival."

I slowly turned my head toward my father. "I know," I said. "But I don't really want to talk about it. There's really no need to. And now with Rosario out, what's the point?"

In the back seat, my grandmother hummed to herself.

"I wouldn't have that attitude," he said. "Eleanor is a good dancer." We overtook another car and then signaled back into the right lane. "She deserves a shot at dancing in the festival, especially if this is going to be the last one."

"She's a good dancer, and she *does* deserve to be there," I agreed. I looked down into my lap and closed my eyes, choosing my next words carefully. "I know she'll do fine."

I thought about how many hours Rosario and I had put in dancing Tinikling over the years. Although Eleanor and I had practiced, it would probably be a good idea to get some more time in with her.

I opened my eyes and turned to my father as I said, "It's just that I wanted to make the last festival a memorable one."

"It will be," he said, glancing sideways at me, "but it will be up to *you* to make it memorable."

"I guess," I said.

He was right. It seemed that everything came down to me: dealing with Nick, not disappointing Walter and Dennis, being honest with Bethany. Again, I was full of excuses.

I snuck a peek at my father, remembering the story that my grandmother told me about him. How he was such a badass that he literally had to leave the Philippines for being on the government's blacklist. Now he couldn't even go back!

I closed my eyes and exhaled all the past cowardice and resentment toward my family and heritage out of my body and said, "Can I tell you something?"

"Of course," my father said.

I opened my eyes. "I've been getting picked on at school." Even though I was staring out the windshield, I could see my father whip his head toward me in my peripheral.

"Who's picking on you?" he said.

"Some racist named Nick."

"At your school?" His voice was loud and accusing.

Nodding, I said, "Yeah. He's been doing it for years."

"*Ay nako*," he said loudly.

"I'm gonna handle it," I said. "But I wanted to tell you about it, because he's one of the reasons why I never want to speak in Tagalog when we're out."

My heart was beating fast now, and I could feel the adrenaline inside like electricity flowing through my body, making it tingle. It was probably what Bethany felt every time she had to stand up for me.

Oh yeah, Bethany.

"My girlfriend, Bethany, is helping me come out of my shell," I said. "She's helping me stand up for myself."

"You have a girlfriend?" my father asked. A smile grew on his face. "I didn't know that. What is she like?"

"Well, she was going to come over tonight for rehearsal, but . . ."

My father slowly turned to me. "Oh," he said. "Tell her to come over the next time."

"I plan to. I can't wait for you to meet her."

A burst of laughter exploded from the back seat. My grandmother was looking out the window. I followed her eyes and saw that she was looking at giant, lit-up golden arches. Her humming changed tunes. She started to hum the McDonald's theme.

"Do you want to stop?" my father asked through the rearview.

"Can I get some French fries?" she asked.

My father looked at me. "Do you want anything?" Waving him off, I stared into the restaurant's windows as my father took the turn into the parking lot. I waited in the car while the two went into McDonald's. Through the large, glass window, my grandmother scanned the menu, her eyes wide and filled with excitement as she pointed at various menu items. She and my father conversed for a moment, laughing as if they were enjoying a mother/son moment like he'd had growing up. When it came time to order, he translated what my grandmother wanted to the cashier. It was an assembly line of words: my grandmother to my father to the cashier and back again.

Bethany had it right, I thought. America was about diversity, the freedom to be different. There was nothing more American than watching my non-English-speaking grandmother order French fries from McDonald's.

When they returned, they were both laughing, my grandmother saying how my father was offering fries to everyone in the restaurant. He shrugged innocently, and they shared a look.

We continued to the airport.

The smell of the fries made me hungry, and almost as if she knew what I was thinking, my grandmother said, "Jamie, have some of my fries."

I twisted my head around to see her outstretched hand between the front seats, offering me a fistful. "Thank you," I said, collecting them from her hand.

Soon after, my grandmother began humming the McDonald's theme song again. Her voice was louder this time around. When she got to the end of the tune, I muttered, "I'm loving it."

We reached the airport soon after.

My father popped the trunk, and I got out to grab her suitcase. He helped her out of the car, and together we walked to the terminal. Once she was checked in, I hugged her and told her that I loved her. She smiled and turned to my father.

I stepped back to give them space.

"I'll miss you," my father said, his voice cracking. He rubbed his eyes with the back of his wrist, wiping away the sudden buildup of tears.

"I'll miss you too," she said. "Thank you for being a great son." She paused, collecting herself. "And husband." Then she looked at me and smiled. "And a wonderful father to Jamie. It was nice to get to meet my grandson." Returning to my father, she said, "I wouldn't have been able to do that if you didn't bring me here, and I'm forever grateful for that."

By now I was tearing up. Seeing how happy and thankful she was to be a part of this family made me realize how grateful I was to be as well. I never wanted to take that for granted again.

I watched her until she disappeared beyond the gate, looking back one last time at her family, and then my father and I drove home. It was quiet at this time of night, the highway with only a few cars heading the opposite way.

"Did you know that the festival was going to end?" I asked, my body semi-tense and my arms crossed. My parents had been a part of the association since before I was born, and each of them, at one point or another, held various officer positions on the board. I asked because I really wanted to know.

"I didn't know that this year would be the last," he said, "but from the last few years, with attendance shrinking each festival, I knew it was coming to an end."

He looked at me, waiting for a response, but I didn't acknowledge him. Instead, I kept my head straight.

"When we first started the Folk Festival, with all the other associations, most of our group was filled with just Filipinos. Gradually, one Filipino would marry a white person, or a Mexican, or a Black person, and after a while, the association went from the Filipino Association to the Filipino-American Association. Kids grew up, they started moving away to start their own lives, and suddenly the association had to rebuild. It went from mostly Filipino people to a good mix of all races." He turned on his blinker to exit on the next ramp into Milwaukie. "And that's fine," he said. "This is America after all."

"America is about diversity," I said, and I started to feel better about things.

He got onto the off-ramp and slowed as we approached the stoplight. "That's right," he said. "It's about opportunity, and culture, and everything that you are made of."

I looked at him quizzically, my eyes narrowing. "What do you mean?"

"You're an American, but you look Filipino, and your culture is a mix of the two," he said. He drove through the intersection and turned on the next street. "To live a full life, you should embrace the two. Be American, but also be Filipino."

His advice gave me comfort. It was really the first time we had a heart to heart. Mainly because I usually avoided it.

My father pulled into our driveway and shut off the ignition. "I'm excited to meet Bethany," he said. "I hope she will love our food."

13

The school day was quiet.

My father's advice ran through my head for most of the morning. My confidence was as high as it had ever been.

Bethany and I texted throughout the day. Mostly little anecdotes. With my new established title—Bethany's boyfriend!—I felt on top of the world.

Can't wait for you to meet my family, I typed out.

Yeah?

Of course! I texted. Isn't that what you do in relationships? Winky face.

It is!!!! Then a care emoji. There was silence over several minutes, stretching out the conversation. Then: *So excited!*

The chitchat fizzled like text messages do, but then we had a short visit in between third and fourth period, which made the classes fly by in a blur.

"Oh my God," she said in excitement when we met in the hallway. "I forgot to tell you about a dream I had." She was so excited to talk that she could barely breathe, stopping periodically to inhale.

Students passed by, talking amongst themselves, their voices intermixing with one another. Leaning in closer to move away from the pitter-patter of footfalls, I couldn't help but wonder at this beautiful person actually being my girlfriend. That—

She grabbed my arm, squeezing my wrist. "You and I were having a picnic," shaking her head and smiling at the same time, "but it wasn't just in some ordinary patch of grass." She nearly buckled over, catching herself at the last second. "We were having a picnic in a field of teddy bears." Then she lost it, keeling over as if she'd heard the funniest thing ever. And maybe she had because I did the same.

A field of teddy bears? How would that even work?

We said our goodbyes, until later.

There was a pep rally scheduled for one o'clock, ahead of the big game against Barrington High in two days. It was a small school across town with mostly Black students.

I sat in class, waiting for it to end. When the bell rang, I texted Bethany about sitting next to her. Seeing the last text chain about her meeting my family made me feel warm inside.

Sure, she replied. I'll meet you in the hall by the main entrance.

Great, I texted. See you then.

Turning the corner, trudging down the main hallway, surrounded by a herd of bodies filtering toward the gym, I saw Bethany. She was mid-conversation with a boy, nearly twice her size, and the pair of them were laughing. He was animated, his hands bouncing in front of them like he was showing her a magic trick.

The boy looked familiar, but I didn't know his name. Bethany laughed, throwing her head back with one hand pressed to her chest. I squeezed through a line of students, found some clearance, and speed walked toward Bethany. People entered the gymnasium through the large doorway three at a time, and the hallway became less congested. I had a clear shot to Bethany and the other student. When I reached her, she cracked a smile.

"Hey!" She greeted me with a kiss. Turning to the boy, she said, "Sam, this is Jamie."

"Nice to meet you," he said. "I've heard a lot about you." We shook hands.

"Sam and I live near each other," she said. "He's also on the football team."

When she said this, I thought about the far-right rallies. "You are?" I asked. He nodded, smiling. "That's great."

"I'll chat with you later," she said to Sam, then grabbed my hand, and we entered the pep rally together. There were long streamers hanging from the rafters and balloons tied to the chairs lined up in front of a small stage at the center of the gym.

"If we hurry, we can grab those two," Bethany said, pointing to two seats in the back corner. I nodded in agreement.

As we found our way to the seats, I saw Walter and Dennis sitting toward the front with space in between them. It would be hard to miss them—Dennis was wearing a bright white suit coat in the shape of the number seven. The shoulders were the top line of the number, and the body slanted at an angle to form the seven. From where I was standing, it looked weird without the zeroes next to him. Just a big number in the front of the bleachers.

Walter's legs were spread apart, and Dennis was turned slightly sideways, casually sprawling out in the small area as he talked, pointing toward the small stage.

Walter shook his head periodically. He then slid out his phone and began texting. A second later, my phone buzzed.

Saved U a seat.

Thx, I answered quickly, but I'm sitting with Bethany. Room for both?

No response. Instead, Walter's head turned, and he started searching the audience for me. I watched for a moment, following Bethany the rest of the way to our seats.

Almost as soon as we sat down, the principal walked out onto the floor, over to a podium with a microphone that had been set up off to one side. The student body applauded, and the principal took his place. He cleared his throat and then scanned the crowd, ready to address the students and faculty.

"Welcome everyone," he announced. "Thank you all for coming to today's pep rally."

One student in the back screamed out, "We were forced to come!"

There was some laughter. A teacher then shushed him, and the giggles died down. The principal looked out in his direction before leaning into the microphone.

"Before we get started, I wanted to address some housekeeping items." His words slurred into something forgettable as I found myself touching Bethany's arm.

"So, is everything all right?" she said. "With your family?"

Oh!

"My grandmother went back home to the Philippines."

Bethany's eyes widened. "She did? When? Why?"

"I think after she met you, she couldn't take it anymore," I joked.

Bethany squeezed out a laugh. A couple students looked. Then her smile quickly transformed, her expression turning more serious. "Why did she go back?"

"She's getting old, and my parents were worried that if something happened to her here it would be too costly to send her back home." I paused and licked my lips before continuing. "Her health is fading, and she wants to be buried with her husband." Thinking about it made me blue.

Bethany placed her palm on her chest. "That's so sad but sweet at the same time," she said. "To be laid to rest with the love of her life."

Her words comforted me a little, and my mood brightened. She always had a way of looking at the positive things in life. I, on the other hand, was the opposite. You would have thought *I* would be the one wearing all black, and not the other way around.

"I never thought of it that way," I conceded, and she smiled glowingly at me, her own mood majorly improved.

The principal's words became clear again. "Now, let's bring up our student body president," he said.

Oh no.

"Nicolas Walker."

Most of the students rose to their feet, clapping loudly and whistling obnoxiously. The bleachers started bouncing, and I nearly fell over. Bethany plugged her ears.

Nick paraded onto the floor and waved to the students. He walked to one side and bowed. Then he strolled to the other side and blew kisses.

Gimme a break.

The principal gestured to the podium, his eyes flashing, almost as gaga over Nick as the girls in the audience. Nick nodded and took his position. The clapping was still going strong when Nick began to speak.

[Live audience cheers.]

[NICK is the new hunk in school that everyone fawns over. He slowly takes over all of JAMIE'S friends, places to hang out, and even makes himself comfortable with JAMIE'S family, to the point that JAMIE finds himself plotting against NICK. But no matter what JAMIE does, he can't escape the attention that NICK is getting.]

"Greetings, fellow Falcons," Nick said into the microphone.

One boy nearby whistled. The sound was piercing. A couple students laughed. One boy shushed.

I was just thinking, *Falc U!*

"My name is Nick Walker, and I'm very happy to represent all of you as your student body president."

"I love you, Nick!" a girl screamed out.

He blushed and then delivered a winning smile. "Thank you," he replied. "I love myself too." The first few rows burst out laughing.

I nearly threw up in my mouth, gagging on imaginary bile. *I love myself too,* I thought bitterly in a whiny voice.

"Now, back to the pep rally," Nick said to dying laughter. He paused, looked beside him to the row of chairs. Then he turned back. "I'm excited to be standing up here today to introduce the students who are nominated for homecoming queen and king." Students started kicking the bleachers to show their support. "This is an American tradition," he said, looking around the gym, smirking, "and the moment we have all been waiting for. But first, we have a special surprise for you."

Members of the football team began to trounce out to the empty chairs lined up behind Nick. He high-fived each player—first the second string, followed by the kicker and less popular players—whispering something in each of their ears. A couple nodded, others gave a thumbs up.

Bethany clapped when Sam went up.

The players took their seats, and music started blaring. When the music hit a certain spot, one by one, the quarterback, two running backs, and two wide receivers walked out and took their respective positions on the floor.

Once they were all stationed, they waited a beat, before breaking out into synchronized dance moves. A few of them were pretty good—for jocks—and as I watched, I recalled my first Folk Festival.

I'd been nervous, overwhelmed, and excited, all at the same time. Auntie Marisol had stood off to the side of the stage, silently critiquing us as we performed the routine for the first time in public. At the time I hadn't been sure I was ready, but as soon as I got up on stage and the music started, the dance moves I'd spent so long perfecting just flowed through me. It was just like I was in my basement, practicing for the giant wooden utensils and the barrel man. It was after that first festival that Auntie Marisol had started assigning me more dances. Watching the football players, it was possible that a few of them were good enough to catch Auntie Marisol's eyes.

Students around me cheered. A girl in front of me buckled over in laughter. Her friend next to her was filming the show, while others nearby were snapping pictures and posting them to social media.

The football players were now posing like a boy band, sending what they thought were sexy looks to the cheerleaders. I was distracted by the poses, not noticing two of the players had run off the stage and disappeared.

"Oh my God!" someone next to us said.

The once beloved dancing football squad did the unthinkable and pulled out a stuffed dummy wearing a Barrington High jersey. The quarterback and the star running back carried it to the center of the floor, putting it on display for all to see. The dummy hung from a noose tied to a wooden beam, and they raised it high above their shoulders—they were *proud* of it.

A mock lynching.

Of a football player whose number belonged to a Black student.

I found the principal, who was looking around at the other teachers. He then looked at Nick, who was smiling and pointing and winking at some of the other players. The principal stood up and yelled across the gym, but I couldn't hear what he was saying.

Many of the students cheered, and I felt sick to my stomach. I could only assume that they didn't realize how offensive their actions were until the principal and several teachers finally ran up to the front and started ordering the jocks to stop.

Some of the students still didn't realize what was going on.

"Boo!" a chorus of kids screamed as the school officials shut everything down. A football player sitting in one of the chairs was recording the event on his phone, as were many of the students.

The principal watched as a teacher escorted the QB and running back off the stage with the dummy. When they disappeared, he returned to the microphone.

Nick stepped aside, shrugging at the principal, shaking his head as if he disapproved. He then ducked out of the way, hiding his mouth with his hand.

"I deeply apologize for this," the principal said. "What the football team did was not sanctioned by the school and those responsible will be punished."

Although the principal addressed the entire crowd, I couldn't help but think he was speaking directly to me. I was certain he was only saving the school's reputation.

"This is not who we are as a school, and we will be looking into this matter," he continued, cutting a look to the football players. "Unfortunately, our planned event has been tarnished by the actions of a few. The homecoming nominees will be announced over the PA this afternoon."

He then walked off the stage in the direction of the dummy and its instigators. The janitor followed, as well as the vice principal. And just like that, the pep rally ended.

14

After school, I drove Bethany home in silence, still preoc-
cupied by the mock hanging at the pep rally. Between that,
the rise of white nationalism, and my recent interactions
with Nick, I was stuck wondering how many more people
like him were out there. It seemed as though racists were
pouring out of the woodwork—the football players, the
punk rocker at the food court—how many more would
there be?

I was insecure about my race, even judging people
based on their skin color out of paranoia. I spent a long
time being closed-minded like the football players, Nick,
and even those kids who got suspended. I only was able to
accept myself through the efforts of Bethany and my father.

I wondered, *Was I just as bad as them?*

The principal had done the right thing, that was for sure,
but I was curious if the football players would actually be
punished. The ones who'd marched in the rally were, but
the pressure from parents, activists, and the school board
had played a big part in the decision. Plus, I wasn't sure if
those players started. The question became whether *these*
players would be disciplined. I could see that happening,
but not until *after* the homecoming game. That was how
cynical I had become.

Bethany kept to herself, more distant than ever. She
looked confused—maybe conflicted—about something, and

she remained quiet almost all the way home. I thought we were mulling over the same thing, but I couldn't be sure.

My phone buzzed, and I dug it out to read a text, my eyes moving from my phone to the road. It was from Walter. Holy shit man, the pep rally!!

"Sorry," I said to Bethany. "It's Walter."

She waved me off. "No worries."

"I'm shook!" I said into my phone, using talk to text. WTF were they thinking? Walter's response read.

"That it was funny," I responded, starting to get upset. "That a fake public hanging would be popular. They thought it would be OK to mimic a lynching."

It was sort of funny.

"It wasn't at all," I said in a huff, then shoved my phone back into my pocket, determined to leave the conversation there.

Bethany looked over at me. "Everything OK?"

"Sorry," I said. "Walter's being . . ." and then I trailed off.

She nodded. "Want to talk about it?"

"He mentioned the public hanging," I said dismissively. "He thought it was," I raised one hand from the wheel and air quoted, "sort of funny."

"How disgusting," she said, screwing up her face.

Thinking about it made me ill. My heart started racing as I thought about how far backward the world had gone. How much hard work by previous leaders had been erased so quickly. Tears sprang unbidden to my eyes and I sniffed, reaching out to grab Bethany's hand.

"Let's not talk about it anymore."

A smile escaped the side of her mouth. "OK."

We drove the rest of the way in silence, and when we arrived, the house was empty. It was very quaint: a single-story home without a basement.

When we entered, I glanced around the living room, which was the size of my bedroom. A loveseat and recliner faced a television on a stand. A coffee table sat wedged in between. Photographs of Bethany and her mother at various places—amusement parks, waterfalls, and mountains—peppered a bookshelf and random end tables.

"Do you mind if I look at some of the pictures?" I asked.

She smiled and then shook her head. "No, of course not."

One of the photos showed Bethany dressed like a "normal" kid. Her makeup wasn't as dark and her hair was lighter—a dishwater brown rather than the jet black I'd become accustomed to.

My nose scrunched as I pulled the picture closer to me.

"Oh my God," she said, "those pics are from forever ago." She then picked up one of her and her mother at the Grand Canyon. "This was when we had money to go on road trips." She smiled and then examined the photograph for several seconds.

I could tell the pictures hadn't been disturbed in a while from the void in the dust left behind on the shelf.

"Now all the money she makes goes to my tuition."

"Then why go to Saint Patrick's?" I asked. "Why not public school?"

"It's where my dad went," she said. I wondered where her father was.

"After they divorced, part of the court agreement was that some of the alimony would go to send me there. I think it was his way to keep a little bit of control over her." She shrugged. "I don't mind it, though." Then she smiled. "If I didn't go, I wouldn't have met you."

This made me feel loved, and the butterflies returned. The only reason I went to private school was because my parents were Catholic—in the sense that a lot of Filipinos were Catholic.

"How old were you there?" I asked, pointing to a photograph of her standing in front of the Columbia River, up on Mitchell Point in the gorge. Behind the river was the state of Washington, just a short distance away from where she was standing.

"This one?" She tilted her head, considering. "I think I was twelve or something?" She shook her head. "I don't remember exactly what year it was. I remember we were out for a drive though." Bethany studied the photograph. "That drive out of Oregon is so pretty," she said wistfully.

"You look different."

She laughed. "You mean I'm not all gothed out?"

I chuckled. "Something like that."

Her amusement quickly dissipated. "This was taken right after my dad bailed. My mom was infamous for taking long drives to take her mind off him." She closed her eyes and turned her body away from me so that I wouldn't see her hurriedly brush away rapidly forming tears. Sniffling, she said, "Sorry."

"Don't apologize," I waved her off. "That must have been a tough time for you."

Bethany slowly nodded and grazed the dusty frame with her finger, leaving a clear path behind.

"Do you mind if I ask when your father left?"

Wiping her face with her palm, she said, "Not at all." She turned to me, her face wet and faintly reddened. "Almost ten years ago," she said. I frowned. "That's why there aren't any pictures of him displayed. I think she couldn't stand seeing him."

"I'm sorry to hear that," I responded. I thought about my father. I couldn't imagine my life without him. "What about you?" I asked. "Don't you miss him?"

Her lips pouted, and her head dropped sharply. "I did, but it was too hard for me. I couldn't get over the fact that one day he was here, and then the next day he was gone. Every time I saw pictures of him, I felt like," she looked toward the front door, "he would come home any minute. Like we were still a family."

Bethany swallowed hard and stepped to another picture of her and her mother in downtown Portland, next to the white stag sign. She smiled as she bent down to examine it more closely. "This was after we went to Voodoo Doughnuts," she said. Her lips twisted, and a slight smirk came out. "I love the Portland Cream the best."

"Who doesn't?" I asked. "They're the egg rolls of Voodoo's."

Bethany turned around and looked at a picture on the end table. "My mom's been great. She tries really hard to give us a good life," she said. "But now she basically works all the time."

In that moment, I could see how much her father being gone had affected her. Here I was, ashamed to be seen in public with my parents—their loud, Filipino voices and accents, and their brown-colored faces—taking them for granted each day. I felt like such a tool.

My eyes darted around the room to the pictures of Bethany at all different ages. "Can I ask a question?" She nodded, forcing a smile. "When did you go from the person in these pictures to how you are now?" I asked.

She looked down at herself—at the black and burgundy vintage dress she was sporting, with a summer neckline and see-through patchwork on the cuffs of her long sleeves, over knee-high socks and Chucks—then curtsied.

"You mean this?" she said. I nodded. She giggled, pressing her hand up to her lips to hide her smile. "You're going to laugh," she said. "I actually watched this documentary called *Goth Cruise*. It'd been out for a while. My dad was gone," she said, shaking her head and shrugging, "and my mom was always working, so I just watched and read anything I could get my hands on to distract me." She tucked her bottom lip under her teeth and chuckled. "Although I wasn't too heavy into the whole goth subculture, I loved the style. I still do."

"I love it too," I said, my eyes doing a once-over of her outfit.

"But I don't fit into the whole 'I'm depressed, woe is me' stereotype," she said. "Which was probably what those punk rock douches were expecting. I mean, I breakdance for God's sake." She shuffled quickly, dropped to the floor, squatted into a pose, and then returned to standing position.

It all happened so fast. I could tell she'd been doing this for a while because of her coordination. "Which I learned from watching another documentary called *Planet B-Boy*."

"What is *Planet B-Boy*?"

"It's about breakdancing and hip hop," she said. "I watched it on YouTube."

"So, you just watched it and taught yourself?"

"Pretty much," she said. "I mean, it took some practice, but after a while I got it down." The side of her lip furled. "I had all the time in the world. What else was I going to do?"

"That's so rad!" I said. "You're a natural." I pulled her into me and wrapped my arms around her.

Her lips pressed firmly into a straight line. The room became quiet and solemn. To break the heaviness settling over us, I said, "Do you want to hear a funny story?" intending to change the subject.

"Is it about your family? I love hearing about your family," she added. "Plus, you get so animated when you talk about them. It's super cute!"

I understood better now why she wanted to know all about my family. Her father was gone, and her only other family member was working all the time. She didn't have a family structure like mine. She must've been lonely.

"It is," I said. Bethany clapped with her fingertips. "You've heard of Michael Jordan, right?"

She blinked at me, confused. "The basketball player?"

"The one and only," I nodded.

"What about him?"

"Back in the day, when he and the Bulls were at their peak, my parents used to root for them. Although Portland had a team, Michael Jordan had international appeal. Portlanders loved their Trail Blazers, but his Airness, he was the showstopper. My parents loved watching him, especially my father; he was a huge Chicago Bulls fan. Apparently, watching the Bulls was like going to see a play or a movie. It wasn't a game, it was a show."

"I've heard," Bethany nodded slowly.

"When MJ played, my father never stopped talking about him. Even now, he compares today's players to him. 'Who's the greatest ever?'" Rolling my eyes, I said, "Anyway, my father would sometimes call the Philippines and talk about Jordan to all of his family. It was like they were here watching the Bulls with him. The popularity of the Bulls spread internationally, especially in Asia. I guess he pushed for that market or something. I don't know, maybe Nike did."

Bethany listened with great interest, her eyebrows raising high on her forehead. "Even I know who Michael Jordan is," she said, "and I never saw him play. Honestly, I couldn't care less about sports."

"I know, he's a legend," I nodded. "Anyway, my mother would get calls from relatives back home asking about Bulls merchandise."

"You mean your aunts and uncles wanted Jordan gear?"

"No," I said, shaking my head. "They wanted to know if *my* parents wanted Bulls gear."

"Really?"

"Yeah, MJ was that big," I laughed. "I mean, the whole team was huge. Again, I've never even seen him play; I just know what my father raved about." My train of thought shifted. "Let me back up for a moment. My mother would support her family back home by sending boxes of clothes and shoes to my relatives. She still does. They eat up American trends, name-brand clothing, and shoes—you name it, they want it. My parents would get these clothes from secondhand stores. Something about name-brand clothing sparks a flame with our relatives."

I could tell from the way Bethany was looking at me that I had her full attention. "As soon as any of us got new clothes, my mother would toss our old clothes into a box to ship to the Philippines," I chuckled to myself. "Most of the time, I didn't even have time to mourn."

"That's nice of her," Bethany said. "Sure, it sucks to not have that mourning period, but . . ." Then she shook her head, her expression sarcastic as she looked away.

"What?" I asked. "You don't mourn your clothes?"

She looked down at her attire. "I think they mourn for themselves," she said, and I laughed.

Once I'd composed myself, I continued. "Anyway, Bulls merchandise at the time, especially Jordan gear, was incredibly expensive. Actually, it still is, and it's just as popular. My parents couldn't afford that stuff. They still can't." I shrugged. "Every now and again, my relatives would send pictures of them wearing the clothing she'd sent. Different brands of Zara, Kenneth Cole, whatever. Unfortunately, none of it was authentic Bulls gear, which is what they really wanted."

"Naturally," Bethany said.

"So, you know what the Philippines did?"

Bethany shrugged. "What?"

"Companies started manufacturing knock-off Bulls clothing. My relatives would begin sending clothes to my parents. They'd get boxes in the mail out of nowhere. All sizes, some so large no one in our house could even wear them. Jerseys, sweatshirts, everything."

"That's awesome!" she said, before breaking into giggles. "The thought of a third world country getting the richest nation in the world up to speed is the funniest thing ever."

I raised my finger, and she got her amusement under control before I continued. "*But*, and this is a huge but, the clothing wasn't exactly accurate. Legally, the Filipino manufacturers would get sued if the shirts read 'Chicago Bulls.'"

Bethany pouted a little.

"They didn't want to pay for the licensing," I explained. "So, they read Chicago Buuls. B-U-U-L-S, instead of B-U-L-L-S."

Bethany laughed and grabbed my wrist. "That's not a thing—is it?"

"Seriously," I nodded. "It's much cheaper that way, so they just produced them reading Chicago Buuls."

"No way," she said. Then she buckled over in laughter. "Chicago Buuls."

"No buulshit."

She laughed even harder, right up to that point where she wasn't drawing in enough air to make any sounds. When she composed herself, she said, "Who would wear that?"

A dumbfounded expression formed on my face. A frown as wide as the Willamette River. Slowly, my thumb pointed to my chest. "This guy," I said.

Bethany burst into laughter. She pointed at me and said, "You?"

"What could I do?" I said. "I was a little kid. I didn't know how to dress myself." I couldn't even look at Bethany anymore, she was laughing so hard. "The clothes are somewhere in my house." She was absolutely losing it, about to fall over in her hysteria. "A lot of the clothes probably fit me now, they were so big back then." Bethany couldn't contain herself, keeling over to clutch her chest. "Are you OK?" I asked.

Nodding her head, her smile wide across her face, she pulled it together enough to say, "Chicago Buuls," before cracking again.

I could tell she was happy—very different from where she was earlier, which made me happy.

"You need to wear a Buuls shirt to school," she said, her tone back to being light and teasing.

"What? And risk getting beat up?"

"Oh, c'mon!"

"No way," I shook my head.

Her mouth dropped into a pout as she batted her eyelashes at me. "For me?" she said in a soft voice, and I flushed at how cute she was. I dropped my chin, and when I looked up at her, she was only an inch away from me. We leaned into each other and kissed.

"Jamie?"

"Yeah?"

"I need to tell you something."

I looked at her under half-lidded eyes. "What is it?"

"You remember Sam?" she said.

"Yeah, the dude you were talking to."

"He asked me to go to the dance with him, as friends." She bit down on her bottom lip, her jaw jutting out in the process. "I told him about your festival, that you couldn't go with me." The side of my lip curled up. "Would you be all right with that?"

I didn't respond. I screwed my eyes shut and opened my mouth to speak, but nothing came out. It was like I couldn't speak the language, like my grandmother attempting to converse in English. A moan left my mouth, then a wordless whisper. Eventually I stopped trying and sighed heavily before falling silent again.

"Do you mind if I go with him?" Her nerves were obvious, her eyes not meeting mine. "I'd love for you to take me, but I know you have the festival."

Inside, I was heartbroken. *Of course, I want to take you,* I thought to myself. *It's just the Folk Festival is a magical event for me. It's the one place I can be with friends and dance Filipino routines, at the same time. Instead of being this scrawny kid who everyone laughs at, people look at me like Michael friggin' Jordan! I wouldn't be surprised if there were shirts in the Philippines with my face on it—ones that read Jamie Saantiago because they couldn't use my name legally!*

Bethany stared at me with raised eyebrows. "What do you say?"

Dropping my head, I said, "Of course you can go to homecoming with Sam if you want to, but I've been thinking, and I'd love for you to go to the Folk Festival with me. That is, if you want to."

> *LIVE AUDIENCE: Woo!*
>
> *[Cue cheer prompt.]*

15

The house was setup for rehearsal—the tables were a maze and the karaoke system lured potential singers in with its instrumental siren song—and my mother and father were in the kitchen preparing food.

Bethany and I entered the house; we were met with the sounds of vegetable oil sizzling against a bass line from Queen. The strong stench of *patis* circled the air. I instantly thought about my grandmother, wondering if she'd made it home all right.

Maybe I should video call her or something, see how she's doing, I thought. I turned to look at Bethany. *Maybe she wants to call too. She didn't get a chance to say goodbye.*

I came back to the present when the karaoke system started cheering.

Bethany sniffed the air, and her face crumpled. "What is that?" she asked. "It smells like fish, but stronger."

"It's *patis*," I said. "Basically, fish sauce."

"Pah-teece," Bethany repeated. "Pah-teece."

"It's used to season foods."

The buzz around the house felt right. Normal. Like I belonged. The idea had sounded crazy to me, but here I was, bringing my girlfriend into my once secret life, about to introduce her to the family.

Bethany took in the room, her gaze moving to each table. "Wow," she muttered.

"Filipinos don't mess around," I said and smiled. Not the embarrassed smile I used to give out like Halloween candy, but a genuine one. Like an "invitation only" smile.

> *[In this scene, JAMIE finally gets over his insecurity.]*
>
> *[Live audience cheers.]*
>
> *[A series changer based on network threats of cancelation, fan forum discussions, and falling ratings where the producers take a shot at going in a different direction.]*
>
> *NARRATOR: Does it work? You'll have to wait until the Nielsen ratings come out.*

"Hi," my father said, exiting the kitchen with an oven mitt on one hand and tongs in the other. His long sleeves were rolled up to his forearms. "You must be Bethany."

She nodded and smiled. "I am," she said. "It's nice to meet you, Mister Santiago."

His face jerked back, his smile knotting into a frown. "Please, call me Claudio," he said.

Claudio, I thought and smiled.

"Thank you, Claudio. It's very nice to meet you."

I melted when I saw them interact, finally feeling comfortable with my worlds coming together.

Etta James was now playing in the living room, the tune humming "At Last," and all I could think was how perfect it all was.

There was a loud pop in the kitchen. My father spun his head around. "That's the rice cooker," he said. Turning back to Bethany, he asked, "Have you eaten?"

Bethany shook her head. "I haven't, but I'm good right now. Thank you.

"You sure?" he asked. Then, "Mah *me!*"

"What!"

A quick pain struck my heart but didn't stay long and disappeared when I saw that Bethany wasn't running for dear life. The instrumental song was fading, applause ringing throughout the house. Next, a Rod Stewart song played.

"*Si* Jamie."

"What!"

"Just come here!" His face turned red. When he looked back to Bethany, he said, "We're cooking for the guests and," pointing to me with his lips, "Jamie's dancing group."

My mother appeared, her forehead glistening and the faint stench of pork was shooting out of her pores. Her eyes flashed with excitement when she saw Bethany.

"Oh, hi," she said. She glossed over Bethany with her eyes. "It's so nice to meet you."

"You, too," replied Bethany. "I'm excited to be here. To finally watch Jamie dance."

My father's face lit up. "Are you going to the Folk Festival?"

We looked at each other and smiled. "I am," she said.

"OK," my father said. "Well, we have to finish cooking before everyone comes."

"Do you need any help?" I asked.

"No, we're almost done," he said.

My parents disappeared into the kitchen, and I heard pans shifting around and lids clanking together. Aromas of vinegar and garlic wafted through the room and then dissipated.

"Your parents are awesome," she said to me, and then walked a couple more steps into the house. She scanned the living room, her gaze stopping on random things. Her attention drifted to the multi-tiered Capiz shell pendant light fixture in the corner of the living room. They were popular in the Philippines, and even I had to admit that they were quite pretty when the lights were on. A soft glow would shine through the shells, projecting a light display into the room.

"That is so cool." She walked up to the fixture, gently caressing the shells with her fingertips. "So soft and fragile," she said.

On the floor, lined up in a row, were various pairs of *tsinelas* and shoes. She stole a look and then glanced toward me. "Should I take my shoes off?"

"No, you don't have to." I quickly waved her off, lifting my own foot and wiggling it at her to show her my shoes. "Especially not tonight when people will be here." She nodded, a faint smile passing across her face.

Above me was the word "*mabuhay*" stretched across the wall in large lettering. I could see Bethany's lips mouthing the word to herself. She pointed to it, raising an eyebrow in an unspoken question.

"It means 'live.'"

"May boo hay," she said.

"It's pronounced mah-boo-hi," I gently corrected her, smiling at her attempt.

"Mah-boo-hi," she said. She repeated it again. "Mah-boo-hi. That's pretty." Then she whispered, "Pah-teece."

The television blasted a Justin Timberlake tune, and the upbeat melody ran through me. I faux planted rice and Bethany tried to dance with me. We laughed at ourselves as we fell into each other's arms. We stared into each other's eyes and kissed when the oven door slammed shut and the microwave beeped.

"Let's go up to my room," I suggested. "It'll be quieter."

We walked upstairs to my bedroom—my sanctuary, my safe space.

A couple of weeks ago, I would have died if someone like Bethany saw my room. It was everything I'd been hiding for years, like digging up an old time-capsule with your high school friends twenty years later and seeing how ridiculous some of the items were. Now I was almost eager to show her. Excited.

Reaching for the door handle, I said, "Don't laugh at my room."

"You're silly," she said, shaking her head.

"I'm serious. It's super embarrassing."

"*Mabuhay*," she said.

Live.

I swung open the door and there it was: my dancing attire. It was on a hanger on the closet doorknob. It was the first thing I saw upon entering, and it was the first thing Bethany saw, too.

"That's a cool shirt," she said.

The barong hung stoically, with purpose. Its fabric was clean and bright.

Bethany grazed the shirt with her palm. "It's super soft," she said.

"Yeah," I said. Underneath us, the audience cheered. "It's made from organza fabric."

"Organza?"

I shrugged. "The fabric is very breathable. It allows air to get in and out so you don't sweat as much."

Her eyes brushed across my desk. The coconut shells were stacked on top of one another. "For the festival?" she asked, picking one up. She pulled the thick rubber band and then examined it closely. She picked up another, held one in each hand, and then flipped them around, inspecting the entire prop.

"The coconut dance," I said.

She sat on the edge of the bed, scanned the room to see the photographs from different years, and then placed her hands together. "I'm glad you told me about this," she said. "Just being a dancer myself," her two hands pressing against her chest, "it's nice . . ."

I felt the same. It was . . . nice. My heart shimmied inside, a ping of happiness shooting up my spine.

"And the fact that you're good, too!" she teased, her small hand knuckling my leg softly.

"Well, I didn't learn it from a documentary," I said, confessing. "I'm not *that* talented."

She glanced around the room, her interest still peaked as her eyes perused the pictures and then sharply focused on my toy jeepney on the small bookshelf. Its bright colors, bedazzled so customers would ride, stood out against the white bedroom wall. She pointed, her eyebrows lowering.

"It's a jeepney," I said. "Like a taxi in the Philippines." I picked it up, the metal heavy in my hand, and showed it to her. She grazed her fingers over it. "My cousin mailed it to me."

"That's cool."

"I have a few of them somewhere," I said, looking around the room.

She patted the bed next to her, and I sat beside her. "So, what kind of dances will I see tonight?"

Downstairs, a chorus of voices began parading around the house. People were slowly trickling in as far as I could tell.

"Well, I think I told you about planting rice," I said.

"Yaass," she whistled, and then leaned sideways with a teapot spout and flare.

"Then there's the coconut dance," I gestured to the rubber band shell prop in front of me. "That's where we hit the shells together in rhythm." I smiled, never having believed that I would be confessing my secret. And to my girlfriend no doubt.

I couldn't help myself—I leaned in and kissed her, the memory of our first kiss traveling through my body up to my brain. My hand ruffled her hair, and I suddenly got warm. When I moved back, she said, "What was that for?"

Shrugging, I replied, "Just wanted to kiss you."

A man started singing Adele; his voice screeched throughout the house. It was overbearing and unpleasant.

"And then Tinikling, where me and Rosario . . . well, now Eleanor," I said, a flash of bitterness hitting me, "dance in between bamboo sticks as they're slid into each other."

Bethany's eyes furrowed. "Bamboo?"

"Yeah," I drew out the word. "It's actually pretty cool."

"Why not Rosario?" she asked with uncertainty.

Downstairs, the voice belted out the chorus of "Hello" and, as much as I loved this song, right now I wished it was called "Goodbye."

"She sprained her ankle," I said. "So now I'm dancing with Eleanor, her understudy."

"Oh, yeah," she said. "I remember. Is that bad though?"

Bad? I thought. It was like when Shemp replaced Curly in the Three Stooges. It wasn't *bad*, it just wasn't the same. If this was a sitcom, it would be exactly like that.

I shrugged deeply. "It's not bad, I guess." My lips twisted sideways. "It's just that Rosario and I have been dancing Tinikling for years. We've always practiced together, sometimes daily," I said. "We knew each other's strengths and weaknesses. When she shined, I didn't. Where I excelled, she didn't. It was the perfect partnership." My eyes suddenly began to water. I sniffled. "This last dance won't mean the same thing." Swallowing hard, I said, "It just sucks."

"That happens," she said, and then she reached her hand out and placed it on my thigh.

Below the sound of applause rang throughout. The guests' voices were getting louder, and it sounded like a party was going on downstairs.

I looked toward the door. "Sounds like everyone is showing up," I said. Then, my heart started racing in excitement, anxious about the night.

"Just the three dances?" she confirmed. "Planting rice, coconut dance, and Tiniking?"

"Tinik*ling*," I corrected.

"Tinikling," she said. "Gotcha." Her gaze darted around the room. She didn't say anything, just looked around.

I suspected she was taking it all in, like I'd done when I first started dancing. It was a lot to consume, and Bethany, full of questions, was digesting all the information. Watching her filled my soul.

"Maybe we should," I began and then checked my phone for the time. "Never mind. We have a little bit of time." Her attention found me, and her smile was wide. "Anything you want to know?"

"Everything," she said. "I'm just fascinated with it."

I told her when I first started. My first experience as a Filipino dancer was coconuts, with planting rice soon after. Auntie Marisol positioned me behind Patricia, who would be my planting rice partner for the rest of my tenure in the troupe. Patricia was one year younger than me and the daughter of a friend of my parents. Other kids lined up next to us. There were eight in total. The coach moved her students accordingly, and once she had her dancers in the correct formation, she moved to the front of the room.

"Now, watch and follow me," she ordered. Then she started dancing the routine, counting aloud with each step.

"One and two and three and four," she sung. "Five and six and seven and eight." Her movements were quick and immaculate; she was graceful across the carpet. She slid across the floor, tilting her body when necessary. "And repeat. One and two and three and four. Five and six and seven and eight. One and two and three and four."

Her back was toward us, and she expected us to follow her lead. Eventually, we did.

"Five. Six. Seven," she'd counted. "Everyone."

Though it took multiple attempts, we managed to learn the dance in one evening. At the time, I didn't know what my parents had gotten me involved in. For them, it was just a means to play mahjong with their friends.

The ruckus downstairs was getting louder, and the karaoke was blasting Bruce Springsteen. A heavy accent started singing, "Born in the USA."

I demonstrated the dance in the small pathway between my bed and the desk. Bethany stood up and began to mimic my dance movements, adding in her own groove from her breakdancing background.

Then, as we were getting close, our bodies bopping to our own internal dance beat, there was a loud knock on the door.

"Jamie," my father said. "It's time to rehearse."

16

When we came downstairs, the house was filled with the usual characters—dancers, the mahjong enthusiasts, and random visitors positioned in a different place than the last time the dancing troupe rehearsed.

"Jamie," Uncle John Carlo said. He was sitting on the couch, mowing down some egg rolls that were spread onto a plate—handfuls at a time, just throwing them down. If he had any more, he could package them and sell them as Lincoln Logs: Mansion Edition.

"Hi, Uncle John," I said. "This is Bethany." He held up an egg roll, smiling while chewing at the same time.

"Nice to meet you," Bethany said. He nodded without saying a word, so we moved on. Turning to her, I whispered, "I think he's related to one of the dancers, but I'm really not sure."

She smiled.

This was the first time I didn't feel embarrassed or ashamed around Filipinos—or "white" like I used to feel.

Suddenly, my father came out of the kitchen holding a tray filled with barbecue-pork kabobs. His lips were pressed together, his forehead creased, as he dodged people left and right to set the kabobs on the corner of the long table of food.

He arranged the kabobs nicely, lining them up in rows, and then turned to Bethany. "Want to eat?" Before she could answer, he pointed to the table. "There's *pancit*, adobo, chicken curry, bar—"

"Uncle Claudio!" Althea called out, examining the karaoke microphone like it was a spaceship from another planet. "How do you get this thing to work?"

"Oh," he chuckled, and then disappeared to attend to his guest. Soon after, Bette Midler was playing on the television.

In the kitchen, my mother and Auntie Bea Joy were screaming over the hum of the microwave. Something about Manny Pacquiao transitioning out of boxing and into politics.

"*Anak ng id-jut*," my mother said, laughing.

"*Diba?*"

I couldn't help but laugh. "Welcome to the Santiago house," I said.

> *[Cut to introduction of MTV's THE REAL WORLD (PHILIPPINES), where a bunch of strangers live together in the same house and viewers decide which cast members they will fall in love with.]*
>
> NARRATOR: What will happen when Filipinos stop being nice and start getting REAL?

Bethany's eyes widened, a faint smile plastered across her face as she took in the setting. I wasn't sure what she was thinking, but I couldn't possibly translate everything and sum it up in a reasonable amount of time.

Bethany grabbed a plate, piled one of each type of food, and we headed downstairs to rehearsal.

We stepped into the basement, the room filled with dancers, and Eleanor approached us. After a quick introduction, Bethany made her way to the side of the room and took a seat on a folding chair. I watched as she popped a piece of kabob meat into her mouth and examined the decorations in the room. She stood to get a closer look, and my attention returned to my dance partner.

"I hope I can fill Rosario's shoes," Eleanor said. She was overly cautious, knowing full well how important this festival was. She wasn't as tall as Rosario, not as agile looking, but there wasn't much I could do now. "I know how good of a dancer you are, and I'm confident that you'll guide me to greatness."

I was flattered, but I didn't want to break what little confidence she had. In a solemn tone, I said, "You'll do fine, you know the routine. Plus, we've practiced this together before." She nodded. "I've been doing this for a long time, so you have nothing to worry about. But if you'd like, maybe we can get together and practice."

"I'd love that," she said. "Learn from the master." She winked.

Auntie Marisol interrupted our moment when she asked for our attention at the front of the room. "All right everyone," she clapped her hands together, raising her voice. "Come together!"

Bethany found her seat and watched, stuffing her face with Filipino food.

The dancers came to attention, lining up in front of our longtime coach. She waited until she had everyone's ears. "This will be our last practice before the festival. I have some prior engagements already scheduled, and then the night before the festival I will be helping set up at the venue. Dancers who are not first stringers are expected to be there, which means Arturo, Corbin, Jasmine, Tessa, and Anthony," she pointed to various backups and lesser-used dancers. There was a collective groan from the group. "I'm sorry," Auntie Marisol said, "but I cannot have the first stringers getting hurt before their dances. We already lost—"

A clunking sound made its way down the stairs. It was a steady pace, very slow. I spun my head around to see what the commotion was about. The rest of the group followed soon after, curious about the mystery person.

Ca-clunk, ca-clunk, ca-clunk.

Arturo rushed to the sound.

Ca-clunk, ca-clunk, ca-clunk.

Suddenly, there were two rubber feet nearing the bottom of the stairs. Two long aluminum stems appeared. Attached was an injured Rosario.

Arturo assisted her the rest of the way down, collecting a crutch with one hand while guiding Rosario with the other.

At first sight, my mood brightened. I was excited to see her. "Rosario!" I exclaimed. "It's so great to see you."

Rosario was stumbling, walking with a hobble until she reached the solid floor. A few of the dancers clapped. The applause brought a smile to her face. "Thank you, everyone," Rosario said. "I'm very sorry I can't dance at the festival, but I wanted to come to show my support."

The applause increased. I moved over to her and gave her a hug. "Thanks for coming," I said, before turning to address Eleanor. "And don't worry, you're in good hands."

Eleanor blushed. "I'll do my best."

Rosario's eyebrows lifted. "Let me know if you need any pointers, or at least," gesturing to me with her lips, "help dealing with this one."

The three of us shared a laugh. Then I shook my head. I glanced at Bethany, who was staring with an endearing look on her face.

Auntie Marisol said, "Let's get dancing. There is no more time to waste."

Above us, karaoke and clicking ivory filled the void. The beat to a Whitney Houston song came on and an out of key voice began singing.

Corbin turned on the music. The first of the dancers took their place.

While the younger dancers took to the floor, I helped Rosario over to where Bethany was sitting and introduced them.

"This is the one and only Rosario," I said.

"Thank you," Rosario smiled, "but I don't know about one and only." She laughed at the notion. Then her body deflated, and she stole a quick look at the dancing. I could tell she was still sad about having to miss the festival.

She came back to Bethany. "It's nice to finally meet you," she said. Tilting her head toward me, she added, "He told me a little bit about you."

"You too," Bethany said, in between bites. "All good things." Rosario gave me a look. I nodded. "He said that you two are the perfect partners." Bethany continued to compliment her in an effort to raise her spirits. "You know what the other is thinking," she said. "That's what makes you so great together."

Bethany was proud of us—of *me*—and she wanted everyone to know it. Hearing it convinced me that I'd made the right decision to invite her. Now I couldn't imagine dancing in the last festival without her in attendance.

Rosario's eyes closed softly. She dropped her chin and said, "Well, we *were* perfect partners. Unfortunately, I can't dance, and the show must go on." She feigned a smile. "Stupid ankle," she said.

I looked at Rosario, smiling. "Eleanor and I will represent."

"Damn right," she nodded decisively. We fist bumped, and when we pulled back our hands, our fists opened and our fingers spread apart.

Behind us, the music played while Auntie Marisol instructed the dancers. "Posture!" she screamed.

I'm going to miss that voice, I thought.

"Jamie said you're going to the festival?" Rosario asked Bethany, who nodded as she swallowed a bite of *pancit.* "Wanna sit together?"

"That would be great," Bethany answered, her hand across her mouth as she chewed.

The dance ended, and the rest of the troupe cheered. I spun around and clapped with them. The youngsters took their bow, and Anthony and Corbin set up the space for the next routine.

This dance involved mostly Filipinas, with two Filipinos serving as chaperones, staying on the outskirts of the routine, for the most part. It was called Itik-Itik. Each dancer mimicked duck movements: flapping their wings with their elbows and splashing water onto each other and themselves as they glided across the floor. It was slightly comical, and in the end, a couple "ducks" attracted "mates"—the two males on the outside looking in.

I turned to Bethany, who was mesmerized by the dance. She never blinked; her plate lay forgotten on her lap. Rosario had slunk down into the chair next to her, her crutches resting against the wall. While Bethany was lost in the dance, I retrieved the barrel man, holding it behind my back as I returned to the two. As the dancers moved around the floor, Bethany picked up an egg roll and took a bite.

While her hand was still in the air, I said, "Bethany."

Her eyes found me. I showed her the barrel man.

"Oh God," Rosario laughed.

Bethany studied Rosario, narrowed her eyes, and then returned to me. Chewing the egg roll, she asked, "What is—"

I slid off the barrel so the barrel man's egg roll was staring at Bethany's egg roll.

Bethany burst out laughing, spraying me with a mushy light-brown colored glob of ground pork and carrots.

Rosario rolled her eyes, and I keeled over in laughter.

The music ended, and the coach said, "Planting rice dancers! Take your places."

Had the time already passed that quickly? I composed myself and walked to the center of the room.

"You better walk away," Bethany said, laughing.

I took my position at the back of the formation, glanced at Bethany, and smiled. The dance included all ages, with the younger planters at the front of the line.

"Music please!" Auntie Marisol demanded.

As I slid across the floor, dropping invisible rice onto the ground, I counted the steps in my head, softly singing the lyrics that I'd made up when I first began dancing. "Planting rice is never fun, never fun, never fun. Planting rice is never fun, I'm so hungry."

I repeated the lyrics until the dance moved into the next phase of the routine. "When I dance, I look so cool, look so cool, look so cool. When I dance, I look so cool, I'm so awesome."

"Very good!" our coach said and clapped her hands. "Next dancers." I returned to Bethany and Rosario and sat on the empty chair next to them.

"What were you singing there?" Bethany asked. Her plate had dwindled to a few scraps and silverware.

"For me to keep on pace, I invented lyrics," I said. "I sing the words to the tune of 'London Bridge is Falling Down.'"

Bethany smiled, and I blushed just thinking about everything that had happened since I'd met her. *Really* met her.

[Cut to a thought bubble . . .]

[A montage of memories of BETHANY and JAMIE throughout the series flashes onto the screen until it is covered in nothing but white thought bubbles to indicate how many memories the two have shared.]

[Thought bubbles disappear one by one.]

The troupe continued in front of us. When the dancers finished, Auntie Marisol had the Pandanggo dancers perform. A few minutes later, she called for the coconut dancers to take their positions.

I jumped off the chair, grabbed my coconut shells, and secured them to my body.

Rosario clapped, and Bethany cheered, "Yay!"

I danced the routine flawlessly, like I'd done in the past many times before, periodically glancing in Bethany's direction. She never wavered, her eyes always focused on me, watching my every step. When we finished, the girls ushered out the wooden blocks, and Corbin and Anthony carried in the bamboo poles.

Bethany's eyes widened. "Tinikling?"

I nodded. "This is it," I said.

Rosario sighed, her head dropping as the kids took their positions on the floor. "I can't believe I'm going to miss this," she said.

Eleanor stepped in between the poles, bending her legs then stretching them out.

Bethany set the plate onto the floor and stood up. "I want to get close and watch," she said. "This dance sounds so cool."

"Jamie," Auntie Marisol called out.

"Sorry," I replied, then joined Eleanor.

In the center, waiting for the music to start—the kids in their positions with their hands grasping the ends of the poles—I exhaled deeply, blowing out the slight nerves that had always struck before I performed this dance in particular.

"I'm so nervous," whispered Eleanor.

Nodding as I exhaled, I said, "You'll be fine. Just follow my lead." She nodded slowly. "You got this!"

The music started, and the girls tapped the poles onto the wooden blocks. The sounds of clanking and swooshing increased as my feet jumped out of the way at the right time.

I stared at the floor, the poles sliding in and out, our feet blurring as they moved quickly on rhythm. I spun around, and as I turned, my gaze fell upon Bethany, who was moving her legs along with us, memorizing the cadence and routine like a student in class.

The sight distracted me for a moment, and I nearly tripped over myself, the bamboo clipping my ankle. A collective "ooh" rang out, but I managed to stay upright and got back on track.

But then, Eleanor tripped up herself, and the bamboo slid into her toes.

Was she watching me? I thought. *Inexperience?*

She winced, and the poles slowed to a point that we could rejoin with little error.

I eyed Eleanor. "You OK?"

"Yes," she muttered. "Still trying to get used to the speed."

We continued until we'd built to a moderate pace—*clank, clank, swoosh*—and when the song cut, I jumped off to the side and bent over to catch my breath. I rubbed my ankle, but it only hurt a little bit.

Eleanor subtly limped to the side where Rosario and Bethany were sitting and rubbed her toes. Rosario bent over and comforted her, telling her that it would take time and to keep her head up.

"You did great!" Bethany said to Eleanor.

The party upstairs was in full swing when Auntie Marisol dismissed rehearsal.

The four of us—me, Bethany, Rosario, and Eleanor—sat for a minute, catching our breaths and tending to our battle wounds.

Rosario was giving Eleanor some pointers. "The key is to kick your feet higher than normal," she said. "Even if you've cleared by an inch."

Eleanor nodded as she stretched her toes, periodically rubbing them.

"Yeah," I said. "I used to think I looked funny, but nothing's worse than those poles hitting you."

A couple of the younger kids stayed back to chitchat or reset the basement to how it was before practice.

Eleanor's phone buzzed. She looked at the text. "Sorry," she apologized. "That's Ryan. He's on his way to pick me up. I should get going." She used one of the chairs to prop herself up and put on her shoes.

"Since we have the next couple days off," I said, "maybe we can get together and practice?" I looked at Rosario and Bethany. "Or maybe just hang out and go over things?"

Nodding, her smile widening, Eleanor said, "That would definitely work for me." She circled the group with her eyes. "I'll bring Ryan. Maybe we can grab food."

"Should work for me," said Rosario.

"Anyway, I should get going." Eleanor waved and walked up the stairs and out of the basement.

"I should go too," said Rosario. "Just let me know what the plans are."

I walked with her to the top of the stairs, said I would text her, and returned to the basement where Bethany and I continued to hang out.

"That was *so* much fun," she said.

It sounded like the guests were having a blast. I could hear their footfalls moving along the ceiling.

Bethany was hyped up. She couldn't keep still and danced alone next to me.

"Do you want to dance with the poles?" I asked.

She nodded, her lips slowly parting. "Can I?"

Mariel and Angeline were in the corner, showing each other videos or memes on their phones. Giggling to themselves, Angeline held her phone's screen so the two could watch together.

"Angeline, Mariel, can you two come over here for a second?"

"Sure, Uncle Jamie," said Mariel.

They hustled over in an instant.

"Bethany would like to dance with the bamboo. Do you mind?"

"Of course not," said Angeline.

Bethany and I took positions in the center of the poles, our bodies facing together.

"Just look at it like jumping rope," I said. "They'll tap twice up and down, then slide into the center." She looked down in front of us, at our feet. "We'll first jump up and down, then when the poles slide together, we'll jump on the outside."

The tip of Bethany's tongue poked out of her mouth, and she eyed the poles for a moment.

"And then repeat it for a couple of times." She nodded automatically, as if she was taking it all in. "With your dancing skills," I said, "you won't have a problem." She raised her chin, her eyes large and flashing. "Just follow my lead."

I turned to each girl. "Let's start off slow," I instructed, "and then go faster on my command."

Clank, and we jumped up.

Clank, and we jumped up.

Swoosh, and our legs jumped out, missing the sliding poles.

When the girls returned the bamboo to their original positions, our feet came back to the center.

Clank, clank, swoosh.

Clank, clank, swoosh.

And we repeated the process. "Faster," I said.

And the girls went faster, this time at double the speed.

Continuing the simple motion, jumping up and down and then leaping with our legs spread out, I felt like Bruce Lee teaching his martial arts to Americans. I wasn't sure if my teaching Americans would be frowned upon as well. I hoped to God there wasn't a curse that would end up killing me before the festival ended.

The thought made me chuckle, but I remained focused, not wanting to ruin it for Bethany, or risk the bamboo crashing into my ankle. Again.

"I'm going to do the full routine in bits and pieces," I said, the poles striking one another and sliding into each other with a loud bang. "Just watch and get the moves and timing down."

Bethany jumped in tempo, her feet matching the flow of the poles and the speed they were traveling. Up and down, watching as I danced the first sequence. After a few rotations, the *clank, clank, swoosh* of the bamboo at a consistent pace, Bethany followed my motions.

Clank, clank, swoosh.

Clank, clank, swoosh.

Of course, she was a natural. "Perfect posture!" I joked, channeling Auntie Marisol even though Bethany didn't understand it. She just kept going.

It only took her a few attempts to get the routine down, her natural dance ability taking over as she followed the beat. Soon after, she was adding in the rest of the moves and dancing along with me. Nothing against Rosario and Eleanor, but Bethany was nailing it.

We danced for hours, the guests yelling back and forth in Taglish and the karaoke game roaring in the living room. Eventually, Bethany mastered the steps.

> *[Cut to a montage of JAMIE and BETHANY dancing the routines in different clothes and in different times of the day to show how far they'd come as a dance team.]*

"I can't believe how fun that was," she said, as we positioned the empty chairs against the wall. Mariel and Angeline told Bethany she was great and then disappeared up the stairs.

We were finally alone.

"I can see why the Folk Festival ending is a big deal for you," she said. "It must be difficult."

Pursing my lips, I nodded. I was catching my breath when her face turned serious.

"You probably don't want to hear this, but I think your lack of being proud of your heritage caused the festival to end," said Bethany.

My eyes narrowed. "What do you mean?"

"The interest might have waned, but when you're ashamed of your heritage, and you're not out there promoting it, why would anyone want to be a part of what you're doing?"

Wow, I thought. I slid down into my seat. What Bethany said made sense. All the kids out there like me essentially ended the Folk Festival.

She nodded toward the bamboo poles resting in the center of the room. "You should be encouraging people to come see you dance," she said. "It's amazing."

Bethany. Smart. Pretty. Confident. *Right.*

17

With a couple of days left until the Folk Festival, I invited
Eleanor over to practice. She brought Ryan over, and I also
invited Rosario (who declined since her ankle was still sore)
and, of course, Bethany.

I'd only met Ryan once, at the festival last year, but he
seemed like a nice dude.

They all showed up at the same time, which was perfect for me, as I was just sitting on the couch waiting for
them, watching my father sing a near flawless rendition of
Michael Jackson's "Beat It."

He'd gone through different phases of Michael Jackson's
career—pre-surgery, post-surgery, *hee hee*, and then wacko—
before company arrived.

"Oh, hi," my father said.

The three of them entered, and each said hello in their
own upbeat way.

"Mah *me!*" he said. Then he addressed the group. "Come
in, come in." He waved each person in as each made him or
herself comfortable in the living room.

"What?" my mother called down from their bedroom.

"*Si* Jamie!"

"What?"

"Just come down here!" He smiled, the microphone in
hand. "Have you eaten?"

"We're going to practice a little," I said, my eyes going from my father to Eleanor and back.

"Yeah," said Ryan, "then we're going to get *halo-halo.*"

Footsteps tromped down the stairs. My mother soon appeared. "Oh, hi," she said gleefully. "What're you doing here?"

I repeated what I'd told my father about getting some practice time in with Eleanor. "And then there's this food cart downtown that serves halo-halo."

"I can make halo-halo," my father said. Then he and my mother quickly exchanged words in Tagalog. He gave me the microphone to hold. "Jamie, go get me some—"

"Dah *dee!*" screamed my mother. "They're going to practice first!"

I couldn't help but laugh and be grateful that they were my parents.

"What's halo-halo?" asked Bethany.

I knew she would want to know. Always asking questions. I smiled.

"You'll find out," I said with a slight tease in my voice. I handed back the microphone to my father. He pushed some buttons and Journey began playing.

"It's only the most delicious Filipino dessert you'll ever taste," said Ryan.

My eyes narrowed, my neck jerking to the side to convey my disagreement. "I think champorado would have something to say about that," I replied.

My father's voice rang next to us, singing the first lyric to "Separate Ways."

"Pfft!"

"What're you guys talking about?" asked Bethany. "I'm so fascinated."

After a bit more trash talking, we ventured downstairs. The bamboo poles were still in the same position. While Eleanor and I practiced, Ryan and Bethany worked the bamboo.

"All right," I instructed. "You know the routine. The easiest thing to do, aside from kicking your legs up high, is to always look through the poles so your eyes don't follow them. Otherwise, you'll get tripped up."

"Ahh," Eleanor said. She nodded. "That makes perfect sense."

Behind me, I could hear Bethany whisper to herself, "Look through the poles."

"Ready?"

We danced the routine several times until we made it through without mistakes.

After that, we hopped into the car and hit up the food cart. I ordered for Bethany, building her the perfect halo-halo.

"Here you go," I said, holding a rainbow-colored sundae-looking dessert. "Custom designed by yours truly."

Bethany's mouth dropped open. "It's so pretty," she said, reaching for it. She glanced at mine. "What did you get? The same?" I nodded and took in a spoonful. "What's in it?" she asked, rotating it in the air so she could see all the colors mixed together.

Swallowing, I said, "Well, there's shaved ice, evaporated milk, some sugar, raspberry jelly, jackfruit, leche flan, and gummy worms."

Bethany laughed silently, her mouth forming a circle for a few seconds. "This looks amazing."

"You're in luck," Ryan said. "This is usually a summer dessert," looking back at the food cart, "but they sell it year round."

"Cheers," I said, and we tapped our cups.

All of us took our respective bites, enjoying the lazy evening. The sun was going to set soon, and the air felt cool. As I sat there, I thought about the festival. All the years I'd danced in it, never wanting to share it with anyone. Now? All I wanted to do was share it with people. Bethany's comment really struck a chord with me. *I can't believe I was so embarrassed about something that made me so happy*, I thought. Before I could feel sad about everything, Eleanor cleared her throat.

"I appreciate the help today," she said, then took down a spoonful. My lips pressed tightly, I nodded. "Rosario was also a big help. We talked last night, so I feel pretty good about everything."

"You're going to be awesome," said Bethany. She slid in a bite and then turned to me. "This is fantastic."

"Told you," said Ryan.

Shaking my head, I said, "Don't even start." I laughed, and the four of us enjoyed the remaining sunlight.

"What is a . . . what was it called? Champorado?" asked Bethany.

18

When I got to my locker, Walter and Dennis were waiting for me. Since Bethany, we had only hung out sporadically. With the upcoming festival, and Walter's attitude toward her, I just wasn't in the mood—but my locker was only a couple lockers down from both of theirs, so it was impossible to avoid them.

"Not hanging out with Bethany?" Walter said accusingly.

The comment bothered me, but at least he was using her name. He must have lightened up, or Dennis had talked to him. Dennis, excited about the homecoming dance, wore a slick black tuxedo in preparation of the James Bond themed party. There was only one day left, and he could hardly wait. He'd always been the guy who went all out, so this surprised literally nobody.

I looked Dennis up and down and smiled. "Double Oh Seven, huh?"

Dennis nodded, then formed a gun shape with his hands and mimed blowing smoke away from the barrel. "Don't you forget it," he said with a grin.

"Those the pants from the Salvation Army?" I asked. The pants were a perfect fit on him: slender down his legs and cuffed right on top of his shiny black shoes.

"Yeah," he said, nodding. "Had to get them tailored at the bottom." I was reminded how my grandmother could have fixed them. "But they turned out great."

"Well?" asked Walter, short and to the point.

Ignoring him, I said to Dennis, "Who are you taking to the dance?"

"No one," he shook his head. "Going stag."

My shoulders sank. "Double oh no."

"Our choice," he shrugged.

Switching my attention to Walter, I said, "No date as well?" Walter then punched my shoulder. Super hard. "Ow!" I wailed. "What was that for?"

"Seriously, you gonna just ditch us for your girlfriend?" he demanded.

I dropped my gaze to the floor, unable to meet his eyes. In a soft voice, I said, "I've got the Folk Festival."

"You've had the festival every year for how long?" Walter said. "Nine, ten years?" His eyes crossed to Dennis, who nodded. "But this is the first year we've hardly seen you." He swallowed, his Adam's apple rolling down and then back up. "What's the difference this year?"

I glanced up to see that his gaze was locked on me, so much so that I turned away again. He soon got the picture.

"That's what I thought," he chuckled to himself amusingly, which quickly turned to annoyance. "You've been ditching us for *her*, haven't you?"

The statement pissed me off. Why did he even care? Was he jealous because I had a girlfriend? I thought he'd be happy for me. *Aren't you supposed to be happy for your friends?* I thought.

"Why do you care what I've been doing?" I asked.

Walter ignored me and barreled on, his tone accusatory. "This entire time, you've been telling us you've been busy with the festival." Through gritted teeth, he continued, "You haven't been that busy. You've been lying about spending time with that freak."

Freak?

Walter pursed his lips. "Haven't you?"

Freak!?

Freak!!!?

I rushed him, and in a sudden burst, slammed him against my locker. People around us stopped to stare. This was the most violent I had ever been with anyone. I couldn't believe how quickly I'd snapped. All the confidence I'd built in the last few days, from Bethany, from my father, exploded out of me.

Where was all this anger when Nickhead was around?

"Don't talk about her like that!" I snapped, pushing Walter back against the locker. He was much taller than me, but the anger inside snapped out of me and onto him. I was surprised at how fast he'd stumbled.

We stared each other down as my chest rose and fell rapidly. My arms were shaking, but I wasn't about to let him go. "Don't ever talk about her like that again," I said, spitting when the words came out. "Understand?" I was breathing so heavily that I almost hyperventilated.

Walter nodded slowly. He glared at me, his eyes never leaving mine. After a few moments, I looked away, my focus darting around the area, at the frightened looks of the students next to us.

Dennis then intervened. "Chill out, he was just joking."

"Oh, just joking," I said, losing it. My voice carried to those around us, and I stared down a watching student, who quickly turned and buried his head in his locker.

Who was this Jamie? I thought. I kind of like him.

Returning my attention to my friends, I said, "Just like the football team *joked* with the students about hanging a Black kid?"

Walter's head jerked back in surprise. "What?" he said. "What does *that* have to do with anything?"

"We're talking about Bethany," Dennis said. He looked confused.

I turned my gaze toward him. "So *you* think she's a freak too?" The fury was building. Suddenly, I was becoming one of those extremists, infuriated by any little comment. I was worried I would start picketing every cause that bothered me on the internet. *#boycottbesties!*

"No," Dennis said. "I don't." He backed away from me and slid close to Walter. Gesturing to both he and Walter with his thumb, he said, "And Walter doesn't either."

Walter's demeanor softened. "What does Bethany have to do with what the football team did?"

The reports about the pep rally incident had traveled in record time around the school. In a written statement, the principal delivered a one-week detention to the responsible parties beginning *after* the homecoming activities, which hardly surprised me. "We take these matters very seriously and do not condone any ill will toward our fellow human beings." *Blah, blah, blah.* "Although the players involved participated in a horrible display of poor taste, it was not their intent to bring hatred into Saint Patrick's." The memo was written to show that the school had a zero-tolerance policy. Well, zero unless you were the first-string football team and just said you were joking. It was white privilege at its finest.

The school did bring in a counselor to hold open sessions with anyone who wanted it. The principal, supported by the coaches, mandated that the football players see the counselor once per week to stay active on the team roster.

It was something, but I still didn't think it was enough. Would they even track the players' attendance? And if they did attend, would the sessions be legit? I was still cynical toward those who'd showed their biased sides, including Walter, who was now staring at me under half-lidded eyes.

"Do you think I'm racist?" Walter asked softly.

"Like I told you before, I think you're privileged." I'd calmed slightly, my voice dropping, so I was no longer bordering on shouting at him. "You said yourself that you thought the pep rally incident was sort of funny." Shaking my head, I continued, "It wasn't funny at all. Period. It was offensive. It was disturbing. Not to mention cruel. Had the opposing quarterback been white, this would have never even happened."

"What wouldn't have happened?" Walter said. "Those stupid jocks still would have done it." I looked at him skeptically. He leaned into me, waiting for an answer.

"Quit defending their actions," I scoffed. "You're implying that those jocks are ignorant, that they didn't know what they were doing." Pointing my finger at him, I said, "They knew exactly what they were doing and knew exactly what message they were sending." I shook my head, rolling my eyes.

[Season 7, Episode 4: Muslim family moves in next door after a real-life stereotyping incident made national news.]

[Entire CAST is on screen.]

[The FATHER gathers all the kids together to deliver a key lesson on accepting every person, no matter his or her race, religion, sex, and so on and so on.]

FATHER: Muslims are just like any other group of people. All people have the potential to do good or bad things, regardless of race.

I could feel my muscles tensing and my anger rising once more. "The jocks did the unthinkable. Well, I guess anything is possible in today's world, and once they got in trouble," air quoting when I said the word "trouble," "they back pedaled and said that it was just a joke."

Both Walter and Dennis stood listening to my soap box speech. First period was nearing, and students were collecting the books they needed for class around us, but I didn't care.

"Their whiteness got them out of real trouble. The principal is allowing them to play in the homecoming game, go to the dance, and serve their sentence after it's said and done." Gritting my teeth, I said, "And you essentially tried the same thing to get out of trouble. You've disapproved of Bethany ever since I told you I liked her, and now that you're finally caught," I said, doing air quotes again, "you're saying it was just a joke."

Walter slowly nodded. "You know what?" he said. "I'm not making any excuses, and you've known me for a long time, so I'll let you judge if I'm a bad person or not. But what the football team did and me thinking Bethany is weird or different are two different things. Whether you see that or not is on you." Then he turned away from me and started moving things around in his locker.

I ignored him and opened my locker. *She's not a freak*, I thought, sneaking a look at Walter. *Why can't you just like her?*

I slammed the locker and walked away, passing my two friends without saying a word. Behind me, Dennis said, "Bye!" but I blocked him out and headed down the hall. It had cleared a bit as students found their classrooms, and I was relieved that there were fewer people around after my outburst.

I marched over to Bethany's locker. She pulled me in and kissed me passionately.

"I've had so much fun with you lately," she said. "Ever since I learned Tinikling, I've been dancing the routine in my living room." She shrugged. "It wasn't the same. I had to line up some blankets as the poles." Smiling, she said, "But still." Hearing this tugged at my heartstrings, pulling me in all directions, and I felt like floating away.

"I'm glad to hear," I said. "I brought something for you. You ready?"

She looked toward me and nodded. Slowly, one by one, I unbuttoned my shirt. I couldn't look her in the eyes because I would start laughing. When the buttons were unfastened, I opened my shirt to display, in all its glory, a choppily drawn bull. A scribbly font above the bull read: "Chicago Buuls."

Bethany's eyes widened. Her mouth dropped and the most endearing laugh escaped her, her smile so wide her eyes almost completely disappeared. She was laughing so hard that she could barely draw a breath, and I couldn't help but join her. It was a moment so epic we missed the start of class.

19

We're doing Shari's for lunch, Dennis texted. U should join.

Busy, I whipped back. I was still salty about the conversation with Walter. I'd been thinking about it for most of the morning.

With the first two classes in the books, I entered the room for third period math and sauntered by the teacher, plopping into the desk by the window. It was my usual spot in every class. Kids were peppered around, chitchatting amongst each other.

"Good morning, Jamie," the teacher said.

"Morning," I replied, quickly making eye contact with her, only to return my gaze to my desk. Behind me, a girl was talking about an after-homecoming party.

"I heard Roderick's parents are going to be out of town," she said to her friends.

"That sounds fun. I wonder who all is going."

My phone buzzed again.

Dude, we've known each other since kindergarten, he replied. Don't U at least think this deserves a conversation?

My heart racing, I sighed, and my shoulders dropped. Did Walter put you up to this? I typed. Why didn't he ask?

No.

"OK, class," the teacher said aloud. "Let's take our seats."

A shuffle of shoes scattered behind me, desks rattling and repositioning, students filing into their respective places.

Class is starting. I gotta go, I texted.

We'll be there at lunch if you wanna join.

The teacher began class, but all I could think about was my friendship with Walter. Dennis and I were rarely on bad terms; he was just his own dude who generally let things slide, so I knew that this text message was more than trying to get me to talk to Walter. It was about mending our friendship.

I thought about the times we'd spent together. We were essentially joined at the hip. There was one time when Dennis and I had bet Walter that he couldn't wear whipped cream on his nose for the entire day. He accepted and almost made it through every class, bargaining with those teachers who asked him to wipe his face, saying that it was a bet and that he would offer a percentage to each teacher if they let it slide. None of the teachers wanted to be involved in a bribe, so they had either made him sit in the back of the classroom or, in one instance, outside in the hall. That was until social studies, the second to last class of the day, where upon seeing him the teacher did nothing but point to the principal's office. Walter argued and delivered his case like a trial attorney, but eventually gave in and just wiped his nose. It was a big win for Dennis and me—five whole dollars!

As the teacher discussed Algebra, I texted back that I would meet them. He blitzed back a thumbs up, and I sat through the rest of the class disinterested.

At the first chance, when the teacher was writing something on the board, I texted Bethany about my lunch plans.

Sounds like a good idea, she replied. It would be nice for you to spend time with them.☺

Tonight, though? I asked. I have a surprise for you. I added a winky face for good measure.

She replied with a row of hearts. Then, C you.

I slid back into my seat. For the rest of class I continued to reminisce about our friendship. Like the time Walter went on a road trip with my family to California. He didn't wear socks the entire trip. My father kept saying, "*Bastos,*" waving his hand rapidly in front of his nose. After a while, he couldn't take the smell any longer. He tossed Walter's shoes out the window somewhere along Highway 101.

There was also the time we rode the bus to Multnomah Falls. The trip took forever, but it was super fun, and we never even considered calling his parents. When we returned, his father was pacing in the kitchen and had called everyone looking for us, including my parents. I was supposed to stay the night, but his father was so upset that he drove me home after midnight and told my parents what had happened.

I continued to remember the fun times, and the next couple periods flew by.

At Shari's, the diner was packed. The clanking of silverware against plates rang in the air. Servers shouted across the room, dancing in between the aisles to drop off orders or refill drinks. The smell of freshly brewed coffee circulated the room.

"Order up!" a cook screamed, then continued preparing the next few orders.

I scanned the restaurant and saw Walter and Dennis sitting at a round table near the back. I entered the dining room and took an empty seat at the table. Dennis, still sporting his sleek, black tuxedo, greeted me with a wide grin.

Walter just sat, staring blankly into the menu, slightly standoffish and aloof.

"Hey, Walter," I said.

"Sup," he said matter-of-factly but didn't make eye contact.

Instantly, I started to sweat. He was going to make this difficult and awkward, and I wondered if this was a mistake.

Then, Walter's eyes found me. "No girlfriend?" he asked.

"Nope," I said, shaking my head. "I came to hang out with you guys."

Dennis was looking around the restaurant. Only two servers were on the floor, both tending to customers. A buildup of plates rested on the ledge, waiting to be served.

"I wonder if someone called in," he said, standing to look around. His gaze darted toward the front, where the lobby and cash register were. A small crowd had formed at the entryway, waiting to be seated.

"I'll be back," Dennis said. "I'm gonna try to find a waitress."

We only had an hour for lunch, and at this rate, we'd miss the next period, possibly the one after that.

Dennis was gone, leaving me and Walter alone. I couldn't help but think this was Dennis's plan from the beginning. I'd been to Shari's a hundred times before, so I knew what I was ordering. Walter, though, just sat with his eyes locked onto the plastic-coated menu, flipping the heavy pages back and forth. The menu never changed, so I figured he was stalling on purpose.

"I wish you'd give Bethany a chance," I said, finally. Walter looked up at me, his eyebrows creasing.

"Why?"

"She's super cool," I replied. "Once you get to know her, you'll see that."

Dennis walked by with a family of four behind him. He pulled out a chair and the mother took it. Then the rest of the family followed, and Dennis disappeared, back to the front of the diner. Walter and I watched him, and then our eyes found each other.

I shrugged, and he chuckled. Instantly I could feel the tension lighten. Walter must have felt the same, because his demeanor changed, softening into the person I'd grown up with.

Why are we even arguing about this? I thought.

"Look," he said. "I'm sorry for calling Bethany a freak. I'm sure she's awesome. It's just when you started hanging out with her, I felt like you abandoned us. Like you were trying to hide her from—" Distracted, his eyes drifted to the side, and I followed.

We spotted Dennis gesturing to a table and smiling. A couple took their seats.

Walter and I exchanged looks. He laughed. "And you left me with this one." Dennis returned to the table. "What're you doing?" Walter asked.

Dennis's hands flew up, his shoulder shrugging so hard he nearly fell backward. "I went up to the front to see if there was a waitress around," he said, his attention finding the entryway. "But when I got there," gesturing to the couple he'd just sat, "they all thought I worked here."

I nodded toward Dennis's attire. He looked down—his tuxedo.

"Oh my God," he said, the info dawning on him. "They think I'm the host."

"Maybe that's why we can't get any service," Walter said. He looked around. Both servers were tending to customers. "They must be short-staffed."

Shaking his head, Dennis said, "I'll be back." Then he was gone, in search of an employee of any kind to take our order.

"I didn't mean to," I said. "It's just—"

"I get it," Walter said. "A new relationship." He pursed his lips, nodding as his eyes drifted slowly away. Then he returned to me. "That doesn't even bother me anymore." His head tilted to the side, then sharply returned. "I mean, it did at first, but what really hurt," his eyes burying into mine, "is that you think I'm racist." There was a distraught look on his face. "We've known each other forever."

My chest sank. I felt awful. "You're right," I said. "The rise of white nationalism has gotten to me, making me look at everyone differently. It's not fair, and I'm really sorry. It's just been hard lately. I feel like the world is going backward."

Nodding slowly, Walter said, "I understand that. It's easy for me because I look like everyone else." He glanced around the room. I did the same. Dennis was nowhere to be found.

Then, Walter said, "I didn't think what the football team did was funny like 'ha-ha' funny. I meant funny in the sense that I can't believe that people are like this." The side of his lip curled up. "You know? I mean, those players who were suspended for going to a white supremacist rally. That's insane!"

As I was listening to him, I started to think about what Bethany had said about the festival—how people like me contributed to it ending because I wasn't proud of my heritage, and that I should be, because that was what America was about.

"I've acted immaturely," Walter confessed, "but I'm not like *that*."

"I know," I said, smiling. "I'm so sorry for thinking the worst of you. I took it out on everyone, when really the problem was my insecurity. I did the same with you. Instead of talking to you, I just lumped you in."

"And I'm sorry I didn't give Bethany a chance. I was punishing her because I was mad at you for abandoning us."

"Apology accepted," I said.

"Same."

We shared a laugh. It felt genuine, like how things had been between us in the past.

I unbuttoned my shirt. "Check it," I said, displaying the cartoonish drawing. Walter buckled over in laughter. "Epic."

"I think I still have mine somewhere. It was so big when your mom gave it to me, I just put it somewhere," said Walter.

And just like that, we were back to being friends—at least on the surface. Then, Dennis returned with both hands full of food. He placed the spread on the table, dishing out random items that he'd selected.

"We haven't ordered yet," Walter said, the menu still in his hand.

"Yeah," I said. "What is all this?"

Dennis whipped his head toward the kitchen, where a cook was laying down plates of food on the shelf.

"Since I was seating people, the cook thought I worked here. He called me the new guy," chuckling aloud, "so he told me to take the food because the servers were busy," he explained. "So don't ask and just eat."

We did, and the three of us were back to our old selves.

20

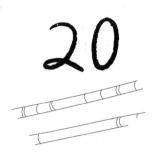

That evening, after school, my father was singing a Dean Martin tune on the karaoke machine, and my mother was upstairs watching television. Other than that, the house was quiet—almost uncomfortably so. There wasn't the usual smell of Filipino food emanating from the kitchen like I was used to. I missed the sound of my grandmother humming in between sizzling egg rolls. I missed her in general.

I felt good about the reconciliation with Walter, and Dennis's stunt with the food came with a price. Literally. We had to split the big bill three ways, which I hated at first but then added it to my list of memories with them. *The time when we . . .*

As my father belted out his latest hit, and I waited for Bethany to come over, I texted Rosario. How's your ankle?

It's getting better. I'm walking without crutches now. Another line came onto my phone. But just barely.

The television grew louder, and I looked up to see my father waving to invisible fans. He turned right, waved, and then turned left, spinning on one foot, and then bowed.

Not enough to dance at the festival, she added.

My father blew kisses to someone, singing the next line without missing a beat.

Volare, oh oh,
E cantare, oh oh oh oh,
Nel blu, dipinto di blu

Another text came in. But I'm sure Eleanor will be great.
I know. It just sucks that you can't dance in the last festival.
Right?

My father was swaying left to right, moving the microphone from one hand to the other, while waving his free hand with each exchange. He did this for several stanzas.
But you're right, I texted. Eleanor will be great. We've practiced a bunch. She's no Rosario, but still!

The fake applause startled me. The score appeared on the screen, and just like that, all the scores that had been replaced during the mahjong nights were back to reading my father's initials. He studied the number pad on the microphone and punched in a number. Tony Bennett. He sang a few lines, swaying side to side whenever the lyrics changed.

I better get going, Rosario typed. But I'll see you at the festival.

The doorbell rang. My eyes shot to the door, and I texted Rosario goodbye. Sliding my phone in my pocket, I stood from the couch.

My father paused his song, the screen frozen with lyrics sprawled across the middle.

"Just Bethany," I said, and then started for the door.

"Oh," he said, handing me the microphone. "I'll warm up some food." He scampered to the kitchen.

Bethany entered and we kissed. She looked at the microphone. "Are we singing?" Stepping in, she noticed the lyrics paused on the screen.

"I never bother with people that I hate, that's why this chick is a tramp."

The old Jamie would have been embarrassed, insecure, and ready to make excuses. He would have run out of there, leaving nothing but a cutout outline of him in the wall.

Now, I just laughed, and said, "Yep. You know how my family is."

"Awesome," she said. "I wanna sing too." She curled her bottom lip under her top teeth. "I wanted to sing before, but we were busy dancing." Inside I smiled, my soul anxiously awaiting the last festival jubilee.

The microwave beeped in the kitchen, and the door opened and closed. My father reentered the living room with a plate filled to the brim with Filipino food—a pyramid formed with a base of white rice and topped with chicken adobo. Egg rolls lined the perimeter like decorative logs outside in a yard.

"Have you eaten?" my father asked.

Bethany's eyes flashed wide, and they sparkled when she saw the plate. Rubbing her hands, she said, "No. I figured you'd offer me something." Her eyes shrank as she smiled with her teeth.

She took a whiff of the steaming adobo, the soy sauce smell circulating in the air.

"This smells so good," she said, and then sat down on the sofa. She turned to me and said, "Will you sing a song for me?"

Before I could answer, my father said, "Yeah, Jamie can sing." He took the space next to Bethany. She popped an egg roll into her mouth, nodding at the same time.

"Let me just look for a song," I said. I thought about what song I could sing, where my voice wouldn't sound too flat, and without the high notes that made my voice squeal.

Bethany balanced the plate of food on her knees and clapped quietly. "I can't wait," she said.

I scrolled through the large catalog of titles, passing by songs that I thought I could nail, and kept searching for that perfect tune.

[JAMIE'S singing voice suddenly transforms into CLAY AIKEN'S smooth-sounding voice. He sings the lyrics loudly, hitting the high notes with ease.]

[Camera zooms in as JAMIE belts out the long notes. Before JAMIE finishes the live audience applauds.]

[Camera zooms onto audience, to people tearing up from how beautifully JAMIE sings.]

[The ratings are huge, leading to JAMIE signing a multi-series deal with all the major networks.]

But it isn't a sitcom, I thought, and I can't sing for the life of me.

I took forever searching, so long that the system auto-selected a song and started playing "I'm Too Sexy" by Right Said Fred.

My father leapt to the floor and started to dance, and Bethany began giggling. As for me, I almost threw up in my mouth. Of the many songs the karaoke machine offered, why this one? Why on earth? I wasn't too sexy for anything!

The song's introduction was nearing its end, and I could sense the lyrics were going to begin. As comfortable as I'd become around Bethany, I couldn't bear to sing this song. Not one word of it. Mainly because I was a skinny kid who'd reached his growth potential in the sixth grade. So instead of embarrassing myself, I pushed the end button, and the song finished abruptly. The built-in audience booed, and my score rang up as a zero.

Pointing to the screen, Bethany laughed, "You got a zero!"

"Give me that," my father said, swiping the gadget from my hand. He then dialed in his go-to song and took his position in front of the television.

I sat down, exhaled internally. I looked at them, and each was in their own happy world, blissfully enjoying what life brought them. No matter how embarrassing it was. My vision turned to the big sign on the wall that read "Mabuhay." *Live.*

The music began and my father slowly started to shake his hips. He wasn't coordinated to say the least, his upper body moving much faster than his lower. He looked like he was desperately trying to keep a hula hoop around his waist. And he was losing the battle.

Watching him made me happy. The fact that this badass who'd gotten blacklisted from the Philippines was busting a move solidified my feelings about myself for good. Suddenly my confidence returned.

Then, the lyrics to the Spice Girls' "Wannabe" kicked on, and instantly my father transformed into Scary Spice. "Yo, I'll tell you what I want, what I really, really want . . ."

Bethany began to howl in enjoyment. Her plate almost fell off her lap. She caught it just in time, snagged an egg roll, and shoved it into her mouth. She moved from side to side, dancing along to the song while my father screamed out the lyrics. I just shook my head, my face broadening into a deep smile.

Bethany placed the plate on the end table before sidling up next to my father. When the opportunity presented itself, she joined in on the lyrics. Their voices combined were nothing to hoot and holler about; rather, seeing them was what made it worthwhile. Sometimes she didn't even sing the correct lyrics, but she didn't care. She was having a great time.

They sang like no one was watching, neither caring what anyone thought. I stood, and like I did when I danced Tinikling, I waited for the right moment and jumped in. The three of us sang the rest of the song like beagles baying in the night—loud, screeching, and awful to listen to.

When the song and subsequent applause ended, the score registered a perfect one hundred. My father stepped aside and gestured with his hand to Bethany. I did the same. He said, "We did it. A perfect score."

Bethany, joking along, said, "It was all you two. I was just here for moral support." She chuckled to herself, utterly filled with happiness. Watching her be herself made her so attractive to me. She was as beautiful as ever. "That was so much fun!" she said.

The telephone then rang. My father meandered to the phone and answered. "Hello?" He listened for a second. "Oh, how are you?" my dad, in Tagalog, said into the receiver. "What's going on?"

I used this opportunity to have Bethany for myself. Gesturing to the staircase, I pointed with my lips. "Let's go upstairs."

My father's voice carried up the staircase. He rattled off a string of Tagalog words, falling out at almost a hundred miles per hour. Then, he screamed, "Mah me!"

Above us, my mother yelled back. "What?"

"Pick up the phone. It's Mel!"

"Who?"

"Si Mel!"

We reached the top of the stairs and to my left, my mother picked up the phone. "Hello! Oh, *kumusta ka?*"

I felt the need to translate. "She said, 'How are you?'" Bethany nodded, and when we entered my bedroom, my laptop's screen was flipped up.

I looked at my phone. "OK," I said. "Perfect timing."

"For what?" Bethany asked.

"I set up a video chat with my grandmother." Bethany's eyes widened. "I figured you didn't get a chance to say goodbye."

Her palm grazed my forearm, and her mouth drifted open. "That's so sweet," she said.

"It's tomorrow morning in the Philippines," I said. "My mother arranged a call with my uncle." I pulled up the program and dialed. "Hopefully this works."

The video engaged, and soon after, my grandmother's face appeared. She looked fragile, her face worn and tired looking but in good spirits. It looked like she had lost weight, her neck a rail covered in wrinkles. Her lips were splattered with maroon-colored lipstick. Dabs of pinkish rouge filled her cheeks. The video was grainy for a moment, until it straightened into a crisper picture.

When I saw her, I felt complete, like my life was at peace. I wasn't sure if I'd ever see her again after we'd dropped her off at the airport, and I didn't want that to be my last memory of her. I just looked at her and smiled.

"Hi, Jamie," she said when she saw me. Her voice was brittle, and her face lit up. Then she turned to Bethany and smiled.

Bethany waved.

Exchanging glances to Bethany and my grandmother, I said, "Do you remember Bethany?"

My grandmother nodded, her gaze moving to Bethany.

"What did you say?" Bethany asked.

"I asked her if she remembered you," I muttered out the side of my mouth. "She did," I confirmed. Bethany tapped my wrist, giddy at what'd just happened.

I spoke to my grandmother in Tagalog, translating every sentence to Bethany.

She leaned over, whispered, "Ask her how she likes being back home."

I translated, and my grandmother cried. Then she answered, her voice frail and crackling. After a second, she started coughing.

While my grandmother composed herself, I translated, "She wasn't happy at first, but when she saw her other kids, and visited my grandfather's grave, she knew that it was the right choice."

Bethany's palm found her chest, and she swooned. "That's the sweetest thing I've ever heard."

My grandmother looked blankly into the camera, her eyes empty, almost hollow. It looked like she was in pain or hadn't been doing well. "How are you feeling?" I asked.

"OK," she answered. She held her closed fist up to her mouth, about to cough, but instead cleared her throat. "I'm staying with your Uncle Romulus," she said.

Uncle Romulus poked his head into the picture, smiled, and then waved. "*Kumusta*," he said.

I said hello back, and then translated for Bethany.

"Are you excited about the festival?" my grandmother asked.

"I am," I said. "It'll be nice to get up on stage one more time."

"It's too bad it's ending," she said. Her eyes moved to Bethany. "But now you can focus on something else," and then she smiled.

I looked at Bethany, and then back to my grandmother. "I sure can."

Bethany sat smiling. "What just happened?"

Turning my body to face her, I said, "She approves of you."

Bethany's body lifted, and her eyes beamed.

My grandmother started coughing uncontrollably. When she recovered, she yawned. She started getting sleepy, and Uncle Romulus kept having to pop in and out, to the point that he said that she needed to lie down. It was only around ten in the morning there.

I updated Bethany on what was happening. When it was time to hang up, I felt a pain in my heart, knowing that I would probably never see her again.

We said our goodbyes, and then suddenly, my grandmother's face disappeared from the screen—and from my life.

Bethany and I sat holding hands for a few beats. She leaned over and placed her head on my shoulder, and we continued to stare at the blank screen.

"How are you feeling about everything?" she asked.

"Honestly?" I said. She nodded, her cheek rubbing up and down my shoulder. "I feel excited, but sad. Like it's one of my favorite times of the year, but I'm finally at the point where I'm accepting it."

"Lots of emotions," she said. "I can imagine."

"Yeah."

"Yeah."

We said nothing, and I was content to sit there like that, but then there was a knock on the door. My mother poked her head in.

"Jamie," she said. "We're going to meet your Uncle Mel."

"What's going on?" I asked.

"He found a mahjong set at a new Filipino grocery store in Gladstone," she said. "He's there now guarding it so no one buys it until your father can check it out."

I shook my head, squeezing out a chuckle. "I think we're good," I said, looking at Bethany, who sat with crooked eyebrows.

"OK," my mother said. "We'll be home later." And then she was out.

I looked at Bethany, translated the dialogue. She laughed. "Your dad is so funny and so cool now that I think about it," she said. "Now I know where you get it from."

We kissed. For a long time. When we finally took a break, I asked what she wanted to do.

"I'd really love to dance Tinikling," she said.

"Yeah?"

"If that's OK with you."

Of course, it's OK with me. I love Tinikling. It's what I've tried to perfect my entire dancing career.

"That sounds awesome," I said and then cocked my head. "But we'll have to improvise." Her eyes narrowed. "C'mon, I'll show you."

We took the two flights of stairs to the basement. The bamboo poles were still in their position, perfectly spread apart and set atop the wooden blocks.

"Since there isn't anyone to hold the sticks," I said, grabbing the ends and spreading my arms way out until the opposite ends of the bamboo pointed at each other. "I'll have to work one side while you dance in the center." I showed her what I meant by clanking the bamboo up and down and then sliding them together. The opposite ends pointed sharply toward each other, only to turn away when I swooshed them together.

"Ah," she said, as I continued the motion.

I pointed to the center with my lips. "Whenever you're ready," I said.

I continued the pace until she leapt into the center, her feet instantly jumping to avoid the swoosh. She straightened out her body, danced the routine that I'd taught her, and spun around so her back was facing me.

"Wow," I said. "Showoff." I picked up the pace, the bamboo roaring like nearby thunder, and Bethany spun back around, her feet dodging the poles like she'd been dancing Tinikling for years.

She was incredible to watch. Adrenaline rushed through me as I banged the poles faster and faster.

Clank, clank, swoosh.

Clank, clank, swoosh.

I became more excited, watching my two worlds mesh so easily in one place.

[This episode would be the season finale. The show would go into summer reruns, only to return for the new season with a recap of events until now.]

NARRATOR: *Did CLAUDIO find a new mahjong set?*

Will JAMIE and BETHANY'S relationship go to the next level?

Whatever happened to NICK?

And how will the final Folk Festival go?

Find out on the final season of LOVE, DANCE & EGG ROLLS.

21

Today was the big day. The Folk Festival. The *last* Folk Festival.

Bethany and I walked into the venue ahead of schedule. There was no requirement on when to arrive, so long as we arrived before our performance. Many dancers drove in with their families, so they could experience the festival together. I, on the other hand, always wanted to arrive at the festival early enough to get a feel for the room before anyone else arrived. The emptiness of the auditorium added to the mystique, and I craved the nostalgia.

The stage in the large auditorium was decorated like years past, with the respective countries' flags hanging across a black backdrop. The backdrop just touched the floor, and the flags appeared to be floating against the pitch-dark landscape.

"Holy, moly," Bethany said. She turned her head slowly toward me, her mouth opening at the same time.

The darkness made the flags standout, bright and commanding as they looked suspended in midair. It was dead quiet, adding to the magic of the Folk Festival.

"Pretty rad, huh?"

Folding chairs were lined up in rows, spanning half the auditorium. The seating capacity was around one thousand, but last year's attendance only registered at four to five hundred.

"It looks like one of those documentaries on famous dance groups," she said. "Where it's the best teams in the world competing for one trophy." Then she squinted at me. "Are you famous?" She smiled and playfully jabbed my shoulder.

I shrugged, thinking how attendees would treat us after each performance. "I guess it depends on who you ask," I said.

"Too bad it's the same day as homecoming," she said. "I bet a lot of people would love to see this."

The words saddened me at first, thinking back to Bethany's comment about people like me ending the festival. If I'd only promoted it to the kids at school, then maybe we could have bought another year.

"Shoulda, woulda, coulda," I said in a sad voice.

"I'm sorry," she comforted. "I didn't mean to make you feel bad." Then she pulled me to her and looked me straight in the eyes. "I'm very proud of you," she said. "You've really come a long way since we started going out." She closed her eyes, nodded.

"Thanks," I said. "You're a big part of the reason for that."

Bethany took in the room. "This is so amazing. It's so big!" She looked up to the rafters, admiring the room's height. "I think I would get nervous if I were up there." She wandered up to the front of the stage. Placing her hands flat on top of the platform, she rolled her head backward and looked straight up to the ceiling. She then shrieked and lowered her chin sharply to her chest. "Whoa," she said. "That just gave me the heebie-jeebies." She then looked at me.

"Do you want to get up on stage?" I asked. "I mean, but not look up." Then I smiled.

"Can I?"

Nodding, I led Bethany to the side where the staircase led up to the top. She grazed her fingers across the thick skirting. "This is so smooth," she said.

"It's nice and thick so you can't see underneath." I pinched the material with my fingers, and then we continued to the stairs.

"It almost feels like satin," she mused.

On the stage, Bethany stood in the center, staring out into the empty seating. "You can barely see the chairs," she said. Her head moved from side to side. "It looks like a giant black hole."

"That's the nice thing." Pointing to the first row of chairs, I said, "They're far away enough that they don't feel like they're in the same room." Then I pointed toward the back and then up to the rafters. "To be honest, it's one of the only ways I can perform. If I could see their faces—like actually see them and not just shadows or when the spotlight hits them—I think I would freak out." Then I remembered Bethany at the game. "I'm not like you," I said. "How you can just bust it in front of a thousand people."

"You mean like this?" Then she shuffled her legs, stopping as her face danced into a smile.

"Exactly," I said. I still couldn't believe this super awesome girl was into me. "The people who put this together do a nice job of blending the colors so that everything looks the same," I said. "I think it helps us focus more on what we're doing."

Bethany walked to the front of the platform and then squinted her eyes to see. "I guess I can see that," she responded. "I can't wait to watch you dance for real, not just in practice." She then spun around and kissed me gently, right there in the middle of the stage. Butterflies rose in my stomach, just as they had the first time we had kissed.

"Jamie!" My father's voice startled me. I couldn't see where he was in the dark room until he approached the stage. "Myra needs you at the booth."

"Hi, Claudio," Bethany said.

"Hello," my father replied.

"Where's Mom?" I asked.

"She's helping with the food," he said, whipping his head behind him, his lips leading the way. Then, he turned to Bethany. "Are you excited to see Jamie dance?"

Nodding, she said, "I sure am."

"He's been dancing since he was a child." Then my father slid to his side, bending his body at his waist. "He's a good rice planter."

I was no longer embarrassed. Instead, I just laughed, and Bethany joined in.

"What does Myra need me for?"

"She has the schedule of performances."

Bethany glanced at me. "The schedule of performances?"

"The schedule's important," I said. "It displays, *on paper*, the order of dances and their associated troupes." Bethany's mouth opened in acknowledgement, and she nodded slowly. "Rumors on who would close out the show generally began a few months prior, but no one knows the true order until now."

"So, this will determine who closes out the *final* Folk Festival?"

"It sure does," my father nodded. "The Filipino Dancing Troupe has closed out the festival the most times." He looked at me and winked. "I'm sure this time will be no different."

"There's only one way to find out."

"Well, then let's go find Myra," Bethany said brightly.

The three of us walked off the stage and made our way down the hallway toward the booths. Slowly the building started to fill with volunteers.

I stared at the decorations in the hallway, remembering all the other times I'd performed. Between each dance, I'd visit with my fellow dancers from other countries, striking up conversation and tasting their countries' food. It was wonderful, and now, I got to share it with Bethany.

I snuck a look at her, reached for her hand, and clutched it in mine.

"How do they decide which dance ends the show?" Bethany questioned.

"The committee is made up of members who represent different countries," my father explained. "The members consider each dance, the complexity of the dance, and the tenure of the dancers performing."

"Auntie Marisol sits on the committee," I chimed in. "She's the only coach to do so. There was a big outcry over it from the other dance coaches, but none of them did anything about it. So, naturally, she pushes her dancers and campaigns for our positions during the festival." I shrugged.

"Like a lobbyist?"

Smiling, I said, "Something like that."

"Wow, she must really care about you guys."

She did, and I realized how much I'd miss her. I almost teared up at the thought. We turned the corner and saw a row of tables pushed up against one wall. Members of different countries were talking amongst themselves as they set up their booths, taping up posters and dropping leaflets and fun facts onto their displays.

"Claudio!" Simultaneously, the three of us spun around. "Claudio!" the voice said again.

"Oh, hi!" my father said. He turned to me. "You remember Chit?"

"Of course, I remember Chit," I said, and I did . . . this time. "He was my confirmation sponsor." I glanced at Bethany. She didn't need to know that my mother had to tell me who he was.

To me and Bethany, my father said, "Go on." Then he walked the opposite way toward his friend.

The members of the Vietnamese table were taping up fun facts about their country. One of the girls spotted me and then smiled.

"Xin chào," she said. "Hello."

I nodded. "Hi."

"Your dresses are so beautiful," Bethany complimented them.

The girls bowed. "Thank you," one said.

"What are they made from?" Bethany, as always, was full of questions and always wanting to learn something. It was one of the traits that I found most attractive about her.

The girl walked around from the back of the table to greet us. She curtsied and then twisted her knees to make the dress twirl. "This is what you call an *áo dài*. It means long shirt."

"It's very nice," Bethany said. "Can I feel it?" She then cut a look to me. "Is that weird to ask?"

I shrugged hard, almost causing my shoulders to cramp.

The Vietnamese girl laughed and then nodded. "It is traditionally made from silk, but nowadays, any material will suffice." She raised the hem and held it up for Bethany.

Bethany softly rubbed her palm over the material. "This is so nice," she said. Her head sank into her shoulders, and a smile beamed from her. Then she watched as the other girl unpacked a box. "Well, thank you," Bethany said. "I don't want to keep you from decorating your booth."

The girl smiled, her lips tight and pointy.

Bethany and I continued down the aisle, passing various tables—Polynesia, Korea, and Japan. Some were completely bare, while others were decked out like they were participating in a contest. We reached the India table, and Bethany stopped and started reading the pamphlets that the representatives had laid out.

"Hello, Jamie," Miksa said. He danced in the India troupe and was good from what I could remember. I just nodded. Addressing Bethany, he asked, "And who might this be?"

"Hi," Bethany said, extending her hand to shake his. "I'm Bethany. I'm with him," she said, nodding her head in my direction.

"Nice to meet you," Miksa said. Turning to me, he asked, "Did you see the schedule?"

I shook my head. "I was just making my way to our booth."

With a slightly sour tone, he said, "I'll save you the time." He slid a piece of paper toward me.

Another member of the India table, Ashaki, appeared holding an aluminum tray with steam rising off the top. The aroma began to tickle my nose—samosas.

Bethany inhaled. "That smells delicious."

"Thank you," Ashaki said. "They're vegetable samosas." She placed the tray on the table. "We like to give our guests a little taste of home," she bragged. "We're the only booth that offers food." Her eyes rolled toward me. "All the others force you to walk to the dedicated food court." Then she looked at me and laughed. "Just teasing you, Jamie." She turned to Bethany, whose gaze was moving from me to them and back.

"I know you are," I said, and then I became sad, because it was the last time I'd have these exchanges in this setting.

"Can I try one?" Bethany asked.

Ashaki nodded. "Yes, of course. Be careful, it's hot."

Bethany took one and then blew on the hot samosa to cool it before biting into it. Chewing, she said, "Oh my goodness. This is wonderful." She closed her eyes and savored the taste. "It's a joygasm in my mouth!"

While she was eating, I read the list, searching for key words only. Pagtatanim. Maglalatik. Tinikling. And then I saw it. In writing. My jaw dropped, and a smile formed on my face.

"Congrats," Miksa said.

"What's going on?" Bethany asked, and I showed her the lineup. Tinikling was closing the festival. The *last* festival. Not only that, the Philippines had the second to last dance as well. "This is awesome!" She pulled me in for a hug.

We said our goodbyes and continued walking down the aisle, passing various countries, until we reached the booth belonging to the Philippines. At that moment, nobody was there. I searched around, looking down the aisle but to no avail.

Stretched across the table, from one side to the other, was the country's flag. Its simple design—royal blue, scarlet red, and the white triangle with the yellow stars and sun— was a nice touch. It was impressive, to say the least, far more so than the rest of the booths.

Bethany traced her finger around the sun and its rays. "What a beautiful flag."

I nodded. "I hope you don't want me to explain the design to you," I said, smiling. "Because I can't." She turned to look at me, the corners of her mouth turning up. "I know, I know. I'm a horrible Filipino."

"You're not horrible," she said. Then she closed her eyes. "I can't remember if I learned about the flag for my paper."

That's right, I thought. *The Spanish-American War.* I immediately remembered paella. I felt warm inside, loved.

She squeezed her lips together, opening her eyes. "I can't remember," she said. Then her eyes bulged at me. "I'm just surprised how little you know about your culture."

Just then, Rosario limped over. She was carrying a stack of paper, placing the sheets on the edge of the table. I was surprised to see her.

"The three stars represent the three main islands of the Philippines," Rosario explained. She reached over the table and pointed at each star. "Luzon, Visayas, and Mindanao, and the eight rays of the sun represent," looking up to the ceiling, "I think, the first eight provinces?" She eyed me, seeking an answer.

Shaking my head, I said, "I'm not sure. If they do, I know one is Manila, the capital of the Philippines."

"That's so interesting," Bethany nodded.

"Sorry," Rosario said. "I should know this. I guess I'm not *as* horrible as Jamie." We shared a laugh.

"Are you manning the booth?" I asked.

Rosario nodded. "Just for a little bit," she said, pursing her lips. "Until Myra comes back. She had to run to the store to get some tape."

"Gotcha," I said. The halls were filling with more and more people, the time nearing the festival's opening. I took a quick glance and then returned to Rosario. "Have you seen Eleanor?"

"I haven't," she said. "I called her last night. Just wanted to see how she was holding up." Rosario unpacked a small box, and I rushed to grab the contents. They were postcards of various sights in the Philippines—the Chocolate Hills, San Agustin Church, Mayon Volcano, and Puerto Princesa River. The sights made me smile. They were so beautiful, and deep down I kicked myself because I had never once wanted to visit the Philippines.

Maybe I could go one day to visit my grandmother.

"She seemed excited about the festival," Rosario said. "I'm sure she'll be here soon."

I nodded. Stacking the postcards in neat little piles, I asked if there was anything she needed help with.

Rosario shook her head. "Nope," she said. "That should be it." She sat down in the chair behind the table. "Now, I just sit until either Myra comes back or Auntie Marisol shows up." She flashed us a smile, before saying to Bethany, "I'll come find you when I get in there."

We walked away, down the hall toward the auditorium. When we turned the corner, Walter, Dennis, Sam, and two of his teammates were standing at the other end of the hall, lazily looking in all directions until they spotted us. I couldn't believe what I was seeing.

Sam waved, tapped Walter's shoulder, and the small group of students approached us.

"What're you doing here?" I asked.

Before Walter could speak, Bethany stepped up to Sam and hugged him. "Sam!" said Bethany gleefully.

The two embraced and then separated. Walter said, "We figured homecoming wouldn't be the same without you there." He shrugged.

I looked at Dennis, who had to be disappointed in the decision. He was wearing normal street clothes, after all. "Even you?" I asked.

Nodding, Dennis said, "Yeah. There's always next year, and since this is the last festival, we," eyeing the other students, "thought we should at least check out one of these."

"Since you'd been doing it for a while," added Walter.

Bethany's eyebrows creased. "I'm surprised you're here," she said to Sam.

"Well," he replied, "when you turned me down for the dance," scoping me up and down playfully, "I didn't really have a reason to go." He tilted his head to his shoulder. "And no one wants to go without a date. That's lame."

I smirked, my gaze finding Walter and Dennis.

"Same," said Dennis. He looked away, observing a shadow or spiderweb on the ceiling.

A muscular teammate with a blonde crewcut nodded. "Plus, we don't agree with what those players did at the rally. I thought the school should have been harsher on them." His voice was deep. Sympathetic in tone. "And those dudes who got busted going to the white supremacist rally? Screw them."

All three football players pinched out apologetic smiles.

Crewcut then craned his head toward me. "Jamie, I hope you don't think we're," addressing his teammates with his thumb, "all like that."

I did, I thought, *but now I don't.*

Shaking my head, I smiled. "I appreciate you saying that."

22

The festival was starting! Dancers were taking their positions; the crowd of people were sinking into their seats.

I hung out with Bethany to watch the first dance: a Korean folk dance called *Hallyangmu*. The three performers told life stories of Korean nobles during the Joseon Kingdom through dance, using paper fans as props, each wearing a flowing outfit. It was mesmerizing.

The audience clapped for the Korean dancing troupe on stage known as Kor-eography. The troupe insisted on stressing the first syllable to get the full effect, but oftentimes the announcer never did so it just sounded like "choreography." Most people didn't get it, but it was too late to change its name now.

Bethany watched with starry eyes, clapping when the dancers did something extraordinary.

I was getting nervous sitting there, a combination of emotions rushed through me—jitters, excitement, anxiety. Leaning into her, I whispered, "I'm going to find my troupe." She nodded without addressing me, still in awe at the dance routine. "I'll find you later," I said.

I quickly glanced around the dark auditorium, but I couldn't find where Walter, Dennis, and the three jocks were sitting. I'd have to try and find them later. After they left us earlier, I hadn't seen them again, but I did get a text saying that they'd found the designated food court. Were they still eating?

For the rest of *Hallyangmu*, and during the entire next dance, I found myself under the stage, watching the crowd of faces after each routine. I peeled back the curtain sporadically waiting for my turn to come. It was difficult to see without enough lighting, but every so often, the spotlight would circle through the audience and give me a clear view.

My best friends sat a few rows from the front. Dennis was filming the performance, and it looked like Walter was snapping photos, holding up the phone and aiming, and then slipping it into his pocket randomly. A smile formed on my lips. I felt happy. All my worlds were together, and none of them stressed me out.

This was the first time I'd counted faces, heads really, and seeing people as individuals rather than as a collective audience was a completely different sensation. It was almost more personal, as if each person was coming to see just me.

A small bout of sadness hit me as I remembered that this would be my final festival. Would it be memorable without Rosario?

I saw Bethany in the front row, cheering on each dancer like she was their one and only fan. I then looked to my best friends. I answered my own question—yes, it would be the best Folk Festival ever!

My parents and Chit paraded down the aisle, snagging the end seats in the first row. As the lights slowly dimmed, Rosario found the seat next to Bethany. Seeing Rosario as a spectator instead of a performer was unusual to me—it didn't seem natural. It didn't help that there were empty seats peppered in the mix.

I had danced these numbers a million times, and I knew each routine back to front, but for some reason, this new perspective was starting to affect my psyche. Add to it the fact that the attendance was half of what it was the previous year, and the individual faces came more into focus. When I started to really think about everything, the nerves slowly rushed in. In years past, when the crowd was full, from wall to wall, the blend of faces appeared emotionless and distant. It was much easier to perform in front of a full house than a select few.

Then, the announcer introduced the next dance—planting rice. His voice circulated throughout the auditorium, "Please put your hands together for the Filipino Dancing Troupe as they dance Pagtatanim."

When I heard the troupe's name, I ran out to where the stairs were and joined my group for our final planting rice performance. The audience clapped, and when I had a chance, I reminded my fellow dancers of something. "This is our final performance together," I said. "Let's make it count." A few of them nodded.

The music started, and the dancers marched onto the stage. Hearing the audience quelled my emotions. After touching the platform and settling into my comfort zone, the nerves dissipated. When the time came to fall into the zone whole heartedly, I chanted, "Planting rice is never fun, never fun, never fun. Planting rice is never fun, I'm so hungry."

Collectively, the Filipino Dancing Troupe twisted to the other side, and then slid in the opposite direction. All of us, at once, began to sing, "When I dance, I look so cool, look so cool, look so cool. When I dance, I look so cool, I'm so awesome."

Hearing this forced out a chuckle, and when I started to laugh, almost uncontrollably, the rest of the troupe joined. It was not as serious as it usually was, or how I'd built it up in my head.

Even though it was the last planting rice dance, I felt an odd calm pass through my body. Like a Hall of Famer playing in an exhibition game, it didn't matter if I messed up or blew it completely. It was almost like rehearsal—just a fun time with my Filipino friends.

It was then that I started to feel young again, innocent, as if I'd just started dancing. The nerves were gone, and the feeling of being the star performer entered my body and my very soul. I used the new-found feeling to my advantage, harnessing the positivity to enhance my performance.

There was a roar from the audience. My eyes caught Bethany, and although she was shadowed, I could tell that she was snapping photos of the dance troupe.

A voice that sounded like Sam's screamed, followed by Walter and Dennis.

I turned my foot, spinning in a half circle, and then slid across the stage. "I'm so hungry," I sang. In a groove, the troupe planted rice across the entire platform. The final part started playing. When the chord struck, and the time was right, the entire group of dancers sang out loud, "I'm so awesome!"

We chanted this at each opportunity, and by the end of the planting rice routine, several audience members were singing along. The music stopped, and we posed until the crowd began clapping. Bethany jumped from her seat, and my father started whistling. He screamed something, but the clapping drowned out the words. The crowd rose into a standing ovation—it was the biggest reaction of the evening so far.

I felt important, desired, and when I saw Bethany clapping and screaming her heart out, and Walter and Dennis enjoying themselves, I became emotional. But more importantly, I felt like I belonged.

We set the tone for the rest of the night. The organizers had made the correct call in having the Filipino Dancing Troupe close out the festival.

Walking off the stage, I brushed against Miksa, whose Hindu Hype was waiting in the wings to go on next. "Good performance," he said.

"Good luck." I continued walking, and when the lights flickered on for the short break, I went to find Bethany.

She wore a wide smile and looked at me with abundant affection. "That was so amazing," she said, leaning in to hug me. I was sweating from the dance, and my clothing was sticking to my skin, but she didn't seem to care. "I'm so proud of you."

Catching my breath, I said, "I just want to thank you for everything." Her head jerked slightly back, surprised at the statement. "You taught me how to accept myself." She looked at me with adoring eyes. "And I'm a better person because of it." This was the most confident I had been with my dancing, as well as with myself, and it was all because of her.

"That's so sweet," she said. "You're welcome."

The announcer came on and said a few words about the Indian troupe. "Coming up in five minutes, we'll continue with the next dancing troupe, Hindu Hype. Five minutes." He set the mike in its stand and stepped off the stage.

"I'm gonna grab something to drink and dry off before the coconut dance." Licking the salty saliva from my lips, I said, "It's coming up soon."

"Do you want me to come with?" she asked, her head moving from the stage to me and back.

I shook my head and waved her off. "No, you don't have to. Just in case I'm not back in time for the next performance." She just nodded. "I'll see you in a little while."

"OK," she said and sat back in her chair next to Rosario. I headed toward the hall. The short break was concluding, and the scarce audience was shuffling back into the auditorium to watch the Indian troupe.

"That was so wonderful," a woman said to me as I passed.

"Great performance."

"Good job!"

A couple people patted me on the shoulder.

"Can I take a picture with you?" one man said. Complying with his request, I posed for a selfie. This triggered another picture, and another, and soon after, I was signing programs as people shuffled back into the auditorium.

This was what the Folk Festival was: a means to celebrate different cultures and traditions and give those who weren't exposed a taste of diversity. It was exactly what Bethany defined America as being. I had learned so much about myself from her, and instantly, I teared up.

"Are you all right?" a woman asked.

Wiping my eyes, I said, "Yes." I nodded. "This is the last festival and it's really setting in now." Sniffling, I said, "Thank you all for coming. You have no idea how much it means."

The woman smiled. She gathered those who were milling around, and we took one big picture. The woman, calling the attention of each person, said, "On three, we say, 'We're so awesome.'" People positioned themselves to squeeze into the frame of the camera's lens.

"One, two, three." In unison, the gathering called out, "We're so awesome!" Laughter rolled through everyone. After the photo, the small group returned to the performances.

Within seconds, the aisle was nearly empty. Eleanor was chatting with Ashaki at the India booth. As they spoke, Ashaki offered Eleanor some samosas. She accepted gracefully and popped one into her mouth.

Just then, my father appeared with Chit. "Jamie, you remember Chit?"

"Hello," Chit said. "You dance well."

"Thank you."

My father turned to his friend. "Jamie has two more dances tonight."

"Oh, I can't wait to see the other dances."

"He is also in Maglalatik and Tinikling," my father bragged.

Chit's face lit up, and periodically, he looked at me with a smile. They continued to converse for a while, alone in their own little universe. It felt nice to have a father who was proud of me.

All of a sudden I was extremely thirsty. "I have to get some water," I told them. My father nodded. Before they could return to the auditorium, I said to my confirmation sponsor, "*Salamat.*"

I looked down the hall to find Eleanor, but she was already gone. When the doors to the main room opened, I could hear applause. The Indian troupe was putting on a good show, I guessed. I continued down the hall, nearing their booth. Ashaki's face brightened when she saw me.

"Hi, Jamie," she said. "How's it going?"

"I saw Eleanor over here. Do you know where she went?"

Her head swiveled from left to right. "She went that way." She pointed down the hall, away from where all the action was. "She got a phone call." Then, she said, "Do you want a samosa?"

"No, I just came out for some water. Thank you, though." Then I disappeared from the table, in search of my partner.

I searched for a while, without any luck. Where was she? I hoped she was all right. Ashaki said something about a phone call?

I could hear the music softly through the doors, and I had to return because the coconut dance was nearing, and I needed to get ready.

The dancers in my troupe prepared behind the stage, sliding on their coconuts and positioning them for maximum impact. Roger practiced his moves off to the side, jumping off one leg and striking the shell at the same time.

He nodded when he saw me.

"Have you seen Eleanor?"

He shook his head and continued warming up.

I sighed heavily, taking a quick look around the venue. Where was she?

The Korean troupe went up again, the members' second dance of the night.

I slipped on the shells, closed my eyes, and conducted my own ritual, meditating away the negative vibes and instilling in myself the belief that everything would go as planned.

Here we are, I thought, pacing back and forth in a straight line. *The final coconut dance.* Blowing out a stream of air in front of me, I looked at my getup, the coconut shells strapped to my body and limbs. *Strike 'em hard, strike 'em loud, and strike 'em proud.* It was a short chant that I'd invented a few years back.

The coconut dance was more advanced than planting rice, so it needed a little more pre-game preparation. For Tinikling, I had an entire ritual, which involved disappearing and being alone for a good portion of time beforehand.

[Cue a montage that starts from when JAMIE first begins dancing and culminates to the present time.]

NARRATOR: *Sweeps week? An anniversary like the one hundredth episode? The end of the series? Spoiler alert. It's the end!*

My eyes opened wide. It was time to bash some coconut shells!

23

My barong shirt looked sharp around my body, and the fabric felt cool on my skin. Coconuts had ended as expected—a flawless performance by the troupe.

The finale was coming, and I needed to mentally prepare. Eleanor was still nowhere to be found. Was she nervous? She'd nailed the dance at practice. Where was she?

Of the five dances that the Filipino Dancing Troupe was performing, it was the only one she was dancing in. I guessed that she was somewhere prepping herself for the finale. After all, this was her first time dancing Tinikling in public.

As much as it should have, Eleanor's absence didn't bother me. I had my own pre-game ritual, and it required complete privacy. I had no time to worry about anyone else. Pacing behind the stage, I pumped myself up for the big one. I told myself positive sayings, ones that I'd memorized during my tenure as a dancer. It was how I stayed connected. How I stayed true to learning my craft.

"Nobody cares if you can't dance well. Just get up and dance. Great dancers are great because of their passion."
– Martha Graham

"You dance love, and you dance joy, and you dance dreams."
– Gene Kelly

"When you dance, you can enjoy the luxury of being you."

– Paulo Coelho

I meditated the bad vibes away and breathed in and out, slowly and deeply.

Earlier in the festival, I'd nailed planting rice and the coconut dance with a graceful ease. Auntie Marisol was impressed with my performance. She called it perfection. Now, there was only one dance left before Tinikling.

I watched several of the female members dance Pandanggo, a Filipino folk dance that used candles as its main attraction. The troupe members held candles in their hands and balanced them on top of their heads. Then the girls mimicked juggling, their palms rotating in circles to give the illusion that they were tossing the candles up into the air. Each of the dancers had a different colored gown. Together, as they danced in circular patterns, the performers looked like a kaleidoscope. The routine was very slow and mesmerizing. It was the calm before the storm that was Tinikling, the perfect setup for the grand finale.

When a couple of the girls nearly dropped their candles—a collective "ooh" came from the crowd—the dancers' quick motions were the only thing that prevented a disaster. The dancers returned to form, and the crowd cheered loudly, clapping for several seconds. For the auditorium being at half capacity, it sounded as if there was a full house.

As I watched the girls dance, I realized something. There was still no sign of Eleanor. Suddenly, my heart hurt. Where could she be? I was starting to grow concerned. I started to panic, looking around but seeing nothing due to the darkness in the room. The dancers only had a few minutes left before the main event.

"Where is she?" I took another second to look around, but to no avail. Searching around the area I found myself underneath the stage, peeking through the long curtain that covered the stage's platform.

Walter was off toward the side of the aisle, snapping pictures from different angles. Bethany was sitting in the front row, her attention locked on the dancers and their movements. "Pssst," I stage-whispered. The music was too loud, and the clapping drowned out my attempt. "Bethany!" I said. Nothing. I waved my hand in a circle, and after a few circles, she spotted me. She smiled and then waved.

I mouthed the words, "I can't find Eleanor."

"What?" She cupped her hand around her ear, tilting her head toward me. "I can't hear you," she said, her finger pointing to her ear.

"I can't find Eleanor!" I repeated.

The music was now only seconds from the end. I could feel their dance steps above me. They were circling, and I knew that in a very short time they would be finished, and the stage would be mine and Eleanor's. That was, if I could find her.

Bethany shook her head and shrugged.

I sighed, looking next to flag down Walter, so I could have him relay the message. But he was gone, back in his seat. I dropped my head sharply.

The song stopped, and the audience clapped robustly. Bethany took the opportunity to dash over to me, kneeling on the ground beside me.

"I can't find Eleanor," I said again.

The lights in the auditorium brightened.

Bethany looked around for a moment and then pointed toward the entrance. Eleanor didn't look right, her fingertips scratching her forehead when she arrived.

"There you are," I said in a worry. Her face looked flushed, patches of redness around her cheeks. "Are you OK?"

She shook her head. "I . . . uh . . ." then she turned away, distracted by something. "Sorry," she said, returning to me. "Ryan was in a car accident."

"What?" Bethany said. "Is he all right?"

The girls tramped off the platform, down the stairs, and out of sight. The MC took his position and thanked the dancers.

"C'mon," I said, waiving the two under the stage so we could go to the back to talk in private. The three of us snaked through the large metal structure until we were behind the stage.

"That was the Pandanggo dance," the announcer said, the applause dying out as he spoke. "Weren't they wonderful?"

The crowd clapped.

"Now, what happened?" I asked.

"Ryan was in a car accident on his way here," Eleanor said. "He was rushed to the hospital, but I don't think it's serious."

The crowd was still ecstatic, cheering with everything they had in them.

"We are going to take our final break before the grand finale," the announcer said.

Tinikling was next, and the girls who operated the bamboo poles ran onto the stage to take their positions. They set up the wooden blocks and wiped down the platform where Eleanor and I would be dancing. A couple boys from the troupe brought out the poles and placed them in front of the girls.

Eleanor pouted, her chin lowering. "I have to go see him," she said. "I'm sorry, but I can't go on."

"What do you mean?" My stomach dropped, and it began to hurt. *The final dance and there wasn't going to be a final dance?* I thought. I was mortified.

Bethany's eyes widened. "You can't dance Tinikling?"

Eleanor grimaced and shook her head. "I have to go check on him."

I looked up to the rafters, seeking an answer that didn't exist. "What am I going to do?" I asked rhetorically as my heart started racing. I was starting to panic, more than I ever had in my life. Every possibility passed through my head at once.

First, the Folk Festival was on the same day as homecoming. I finally got the girl, and I couldn't take her to the dance.

Second, Rosario went down. My longtime partner would have to sit out.

And third, Eleanor's boyfriend got into a car accident. Thank God he was OK.

I started to regret coming.

Maybe I should have just taken Bethany to homecoming, I thought.

Just then, Bethany started scheming. "What if I filled in?"

> *[BETHANY, wearing a black leather jacket and oversized sunglasses, rides onto set on a motorcycle twice her size to the song "Bad to the Bone."]*
>
> *BETHANY (looking at JAMIE): Did someone call a backup dancer?*
>
> *[BETHANY winks into the camera.]*

"Oh my God," I said. "You know the routine. We practiced it a bunch of times. But . . ." We both looked down at her wardrobe. She was dressed in full goth garb. "You can't wear that."

"What choice do we have?" she said.

Eleanor looked at Bethany and eyed her up and down. "We're about the same size. You're a little smaller, but . . . here, trade clothes with me."

"Are you sure?" Bethany asked.

"Yeah, but we have to hurry," Eleanor said. "There isn't much time."

I turned around so the two could undress and exchange clothing.

Above us, the announcer walked up to the microphone. His voice rang clear through the auditorium. "Are you ready for the grand finale?" he said. "This year's Folk Festival will conclude with the Filipino Dancing Troupe performing the dance, Tinikling."

Bethany emerged from behind me. She looked stunning in traditional Filipino attire.

"What do you think?" Bethany asked. She twirled, bending her knees and dipping down to the floor.

"Wow! You look fantastic." And she did. Her goth makeup complemented the Filipina gown.

Eleanor, on the other hand, looked like a girl who tried to get a job at Hot Topic and failed. The clothes just didn't look or fit right, but she didn't care. "Thank you," I said to Eleanor. "Tell Ryan to get well." She smiled and was gone.

"I can't believe you're going to do this," I said. "And not—"

Bethany's frown stopped me in midsentence. She looked at me, then to the rest of the dancers in my troupe, who were all lounging around behind the stage, some feet away from us.

"What's wrong?"

Her lips parted slowly. "I can't dance with you," she said, looking down at herself and then to me.

"Why?"

Clapping began to die down. The announcer cleared his throat. "We would like to thank you for your support," the voice echoed into the auditorium.

"This is a Folk Festival," Bethany stressed. "Put together by a bunch of Asian organizations. For Asian people!"

"What?" At first, I didn't understand. I shook my head.

"What're they going to think about a white girl dancing in their festival?"

I spotted a few members of the dancing troupe, then several more. And it dawned on me. She was right. I was so caught up in the nostalgia of the last festival. To go out in style.

What was I going to do?

The auditorium was nearly quiet, a couple whispers here and there, waiting for the finale.

An idea then hit me.

"I know," I said. I quickly gathered the Filipino dancers that were nearby and told them the plan. Each of them had his or her own excitement brewing.

I returned to Bethany. "What's going on?" she asked.

"You'll see."

"We could not have put this event on without you," the MC said. The crowd clapped again. "Now, without further ado, please put your hands together for the Tinikling dance, performed by members of the Filipino Dancing Troupe."

Bethany stole a look behind her, the Filipino dancers lining up one by one. She slowly turned to me, her mouth dropping open as her lips curled into a smile.

At this moment, my heart was filled with joy, and I remembered how close we'd become in such a short period of time.

[Cut to the "wedding special," where the entire episode's storyline is only two minutes in length but stretches out due to all the unnecessary montages and flashbacks.]

[The time BETHANY showed up the opposing team's cheerleader in breakdancing. The time JAMIE was so nervous talking to her in the cafeteria. The time she first met JAMIE'S family. And the time she learned how to dance Tinikling.]

It was like we were at our very own homecoming dance. Our eyes locked on one another as thunderous applause broke out. Smiling, I said, "Ready?"

"Let's do it."

Together, we looked behind us.

Bethany and I then walked out onto the stage, hand in hand. The dancing troupe followed. The crowd was on its feet, cheering and clapping. One woman, who must have taken a picture with me earlier, screamed, "You're so awesome!" Some of the people in the audience laughed. It was like a dream.

The girls who worked the bamboo sticks kneeled, and Bethany and I walked to our respective positions. The dancers crowded behind us, forming a semi-circle and curling out onto the sides of the bamboo.

"Jamie! Jamie! Jamie!" Dennis chanted, attempting to get the crowd involved.

A couple people followed suit, but for the most part, the loud smacking of the bamboo quieted them.

The poles reached their sweet spot, the perfect velocity for the dance to begin.

Clank, clank, swoosh.

Clank, clank, swoosh.

Bethany winked.

In my head, I heard the intro to "Bad to the Bone." Nodding, I mouthed, "We got this!" When she responded with a sly smile, we started the routine, just like we'd practiced in my basement.

The dancers each did his or her own thing: a couple planted rice, some did moves from a dance that didn't make the festival, two dancers performed a combo coconut dance and hip-hop routine, and the Pandanggo girls danced together. All of them having fun.

Clank, clank, swoosh.

Clank, clank, swoosh.

I could dance each step with my eyes closed, but this was all still new to Bethany. Part of being a great dancer was making your partner better. I wasn't going to let her down.

"You're doing great!" I said over the music. She nodded and copied my every movement.

The girls working the sticks moved the bamboo faster and faster. I watched Bethany move her feet in between the poles, kicking up when she needed to avoid contacting the bamboo. She was a natural.

Around us, the dancers did their thing. The music picked up, and so did the movement of the bamboo sticks. I watched as Bethany danced her heart out, raising her knees high and stepping in between the sliding poles like she was running on hot coals.

The audience began clapping.

Clank, clank, swoosh!

Clank, clank, swoosh!

The music suddenly became faster, and the girls continued their assault of the bamboo. The crowd gasped, mesmerized by our effort. They were quiet. The only noise in the auditorium was the bamboo striking the boards, sliding across them and into each other with a loud smack.

Bethany and I spun around in a one-eighty, our backs toward each other and our feet stepping in and out of the poles in unison.

Clank, clank, swoosh!

Clank, clank, swoosh!

"And turn in three, two . . ." I shouted.

After a measure, we turned around to face each other, our legs copying each other like a pair of synchronized swimmers.

Clank, clank, swoosh!

Clank, clank, swoosh!

The music sped up again, and the girls matched the velocity of the beat. I was getting tired, the sweat pouring down my forehead as I jumped and stepped, and then stepped and jumped.

Bethany's eyes were facing down, looking through the bamboo as they passed underneath us. I paced my breaths with the sounds—in, in, out; in, in, out—until the song started to slow.

Clank, clank, swoosh!

Clank, clank, swoosh!

Clank, clank . . . "Ugh!"

Bethany mistimed the bamboo, and the pole crashed into her foot, causing her to trip. She fell to the side.

My eyes widened, and I screamed, "Bethany!" I jumped to the side, the poles still moving and the music still blasting. Kneeling beside her, I said, "Are you all right?"

She was rubbing her foot and laughing so much her face had turned beet red. She stood and then bowed. I shook my head and bowed with her. The dancers around us all bowed as well.

Some of the audience clapped, while others just stared in amazement.

Walter, Dennis, Sam, and the players were standing and clapping. Sam whistled.

There was still a minute left in the routine, and the girls were still tapping in chorus. Some of the troupe started cheering us on, encouraging us to continue. I waited for the right time, to jump back in. Bethany did the same, and together, we finished the routine until the song began to fade out. Soon after, the dance was over.

It was silent for a second, and when the lights turned on, the audience jumped from their seats and clapped so loudly that the noise pierced my ears. We jumped off to the side and bowed again, our hands clasped together. I released her hand and then pointed to her so the crowd would applaud her and her alone. I looked out into the mass of faces, and the people in attendance were staring at me. But instead of their eyes making me feel insecure, even with a misstep, they were cheering me on, cheering *us* on, and this made me feel like I'd done something remarkable, something special.

Bethany grabbed my barong, pulled me into her, and kissed me.

"Are you OK?" I asked.

Smiling, she nodded. "Yeah," she said. "I started watching the hip-hop dance around us and just got distracted." She shrugged.

Of course, I thought.

"I thought you were perfect," I said. And we held each other until the clapping died down.

At that moment, we were the only ones in the room, on the stage. This was our homecoming, the biggest dance of the school year.

The final Folk Festival was officially over. Even with all the mishaps, it was the best one yet. Thinking back at everything in my life, I realized something: I no longer had to imagine this being a sitcom. It *was* a sitcom, *my* sitcom. I had the same issues, the same family problems, and the same friend problems.

24

I was still drunk from the festival, the feeling of euphoria from the night before still tingling throughout my body. A spark of joy passed through me.

Someone had filmed the performances and posted them on social media, tagging the association, which then tagged the dancers, until the dances had been viewed hundreds of times. The footage was perfectly produced, almost as if someone had full access to the stage.

Bethany texted. We had planned to spend the day together, our first as a couple without the heaviness of the festival lingering over me.

OK, I texted, I'll see you soon ☺, then slid the phone into my pocket and watched the Tinikling dance for the umpteenth time that morning.

"Jamie!" my father called up to me, his voice excited. "Jamie!"

I slid off the bed and headed downstairs. He was standing in front of the television, the local news running a story on the Folk Festival.

"What is this?" I asked, a smile growing on my face.

"That's you," he said, pursing his lips toward the screen. "Mah *me!*"

"What?" she screamed from the kitchen.

"*Si* Jamie!"

"What?"

"Get in here!"

The voiceover was speaking over the footage, the same video that was posted online. In the corner of the screen, it read "Courtesy of Marisol Domingo".

My heart exploded with happiness. Auntie Marisol cared so much about us that she'd taped every performance and blasted it on social media. She'd campaigned for her dancers to close the show, and now my face was plastered on the local news—and Bethany's!

My mother soon arrived, and when she saw me and Bethany dancing, she pointed, "You're famous!" and hugged me.

Not an ounce of embarrassment was there. No fear of what people would think when they saw this. There was nothing.

Instead, I found the story online and shared it with Bethany, Walter, and Dennis.

Watching it now! Bethany replied. So cool!

The anchor then appeared on the screen, watching the remaining seconds of the video before it disappeared. He turned to the camera. "What a fun time," he said. "Well, that's all for *Good Morning, Portland*. *Meet the Press* starts now." The political program's familiar theme started, and my father took his regular spot on the couch.

Wow! A text from Walter said. Looks awsum! Dots danced across the screen. Sam said sum more of the jocks were seen at the white supremacist rally downtown.

What?

Ya, he typed.

More suspensions? I typed.

idk, texted Walter.

How did they find out?

Video, Walter responded. Some of em wore their letterman jackets. LOLZ

Wow, I thought.

Walter typed, And you wont guess who else was there? More dots, then nothing . . . Nick!!!!

What!? I responded, not believing what I was reading.

ROFL, typed Walter. I know right?

Are you kidding?

SMH. Then Walter switched gears. Will chek out link.

My mother returned to the kitchen, but before entering, she said, "Come in here when you get a chance."

I nodded without addressing her, typing away at my phone's keypad, responding to Walter. Gotta go. Bethany is coming over but I have to get something done beforehand. See you at school?

Thumbs up, typed Walter. Then, Nick LOLZ.

On the television, the host started the show by saying, "How has the rise of white nationalism hit our local communities? On the panel today is . . ."

I disappeared into the kitchen. My mother was sitting in her usual spot, the table pushed up against the wall, the memory of my grandmother lingering nearby.

Splayed across the tabletop were random ingredients—cocoa, sweet rice, and dark chocolate chips among them. I whipped my head to the stove, a large pan sat atop the burner, slowly boiling water, a plastic ladle nearby. It was happening, and I couldn't be more excited.

My gaze found my mother, who was smirking impishly. "You asked if I would teach you how to make *champorado*," she said. Then she pointed to the empty chair with her lips. I took the seat with the excitement of a kid playing musical chairs, pumping my fist underneath the tablecloth.

"We have to wait for the water to boil, then we'll add the rice," she said. "Then when it's stirred enough, we'll add the cocoa, then the sugar, and chips." With each ingredient, she nodded. My eyes grazed the tabletop as she said each item, committing the steps to memory until it was time.

"We have bacon bits?" I asked.

"In the fridge."

Behind me, two panelists were calling out Portland by name, saying how federal police had been guarding the courthouse downtown for the thirtieth night in a row.

I shook my head, thinking about the students in school suspended for rallying with white supremacists, then the pep rally, and then Nick, and I felt nothing. Like that was America. If you wanted to be a racist, a Nickhead, it was your right.

"Your father told me about your bully," my mother said, as we waited for the water to boil. My eyebrows twisted like a worm across my forehead. Almost like she was reading my mind. "Do you want to talk about it?"

"Not really," I said, and I didn't. Not because it bothered me, but because it *didn't* bother me anymore. I was legitimately over it, but also, I had a feeling that Nick had his own trouble coming. Brimming with confidence, I uttered, "He's not worth my time." Then I pinched my lips together and shook my head.

Just then, the water bubbled enough for me to hear, and I stood and dumped the rice into the pot. It sizzled a bit, then settled onto the bottom. I stirred and stirred until it thickened, then followed the rest of the steps until it cooled into a chocolatey porridge. I inhaled the cocoa and closed my eyes. My grandmother's smile appeared, and I teared up.

The doorbell rang. Bethany.

I prepared two bowls, dripping pieces of bacon on the top, and set them on the table. Then I ran to the door and opened it. My mother, dressed in her robe, escaped upstairs to change.

The host on television was wrangling in his guests, who were talking over each other, trying to get their respective points across.

Bethany, wearing a white T-shirt with a Chinese symbol on the front and a checkered skirt that fell just above her knees, smiled. Then her nostrils flared, and she said, "It smells like a chocolate bar exploded."

"It did," I said, gesturing for her to come in. "I made something for you." We walked hand in hand to the kitchen, passing my father whose eyes were glued to the screen.

"Hi, Claudio," Bethany said.

My father, as if he had just awoken from a trance, turned to address her. "Oh, hi," he said, his voice jubilant. "Have you eaten?" His eyes drifted toward me. "Jamie made champorado."

"I can tell," she said, inhaling the aroma that was filtering throughout the house.

We entered the kitchen and sat at the table. The champorado was still hot, smoke rising from the top.

"What is that?" she said, squinting to get a better look. "Bacon?"

"Yeah. The saltiness balances out the sweetness," I said. "Kind of like how we are as a couple—I'm always salty, and you're always sweet." And then I smiled.

"Not anymore," she said, and then moved my hair away from my face and looked at me. She kissed me, and all was good in the world. "You've really changed, and I love that about you." The aroma then got the best of her, and she looked down toward the bowl. "I don't have to try this to know it's better than halo-halo, right?"

"It's the best," I said. "But don't trust me. Just try it. You'll see why it's my favorite Filipino dessert ever." She took a bite, savored it for a second, and then swallowed. I watched her, thinking that if there was ever a chance to lock this girl down for life, it was now. "My grandmother used to make it all the time."

As if she'd discovered gold, Bethany's face brightened. "Oh my God," she said. "This is delicious." She swallowed. "So much better than halo-halo."

"Right?" I said. "I'm glad you like it." I took a bite of my own. We enjoyed the meal together, without saying a word. It was then that I thought about everything—my grandmother, school, my parents, my life, and how I was going to live it going forward. I snuck a look at Bethany, quiet in her own delicious reverie, and smiled. I had her to thank for it.

"So, now that the festival is over," Bethany said, her spoon suspended in the air with a scoop of champorado, "what are your plans now?"

I shrugged, sliding a spoonful into my mouth. Chewing, I thought about the question. Then, after I swallowed, I said, "I don't know. Maybe join the Filipino-American Association." I placed the spoon down into the bowl. "Who knows?" I said. "Maybe I can help build interest in the festival? I mean, it got some good coverage. People seemed to like it." Bethany placed her hand on top of mine. I looked at her and said, "Probably go to some of these school events."

Bethany, nodding, said, "Yeah, prom might be fun to go to." She smiled.

"If I joined the association, would you want to become a member, too?"

"I would love to," she said. Her smile was so big right now, and I could tell that she felt right at home with me. "That would be so much fun."

> NARRATOR: Will there be a spinoff focused on JAMIE and BETHANY'S life after? Perhaps a story about their future, how the festival returned, how they graduated from college, then got married, and finally had children?

My phone buzzed. Walter. Great story! Then, check it.

A link came up on my screen.

"Who's that?" Bethany asked.

"Walter," I said. Then I remembered. "I forgot to tell you. Nick was caught at one of those white supremacist rallies downtown!"

Bethany's eyes widened. "Really?"

Nodding, I showed her the text chain between Walter and me. She squinted to read, periodically breaking into a smile, and when she got to the bottom, she clicked on the link that Walter had sent.

"What's this?" she asked. Together, we looked.

25

The video of the dances was seen by nearly every student. Walter created a Facebook page, and soon after, the shares racked up in the hundreds. I was tagged in each post, some from faculty but most from students, so I saw the extent of the coverage firsthand. The page had almost six hundred likes. When Bethany and I scrolled through the posts, we saw that many students had posted different passages, pictures, and videos.

"Hey, Jamie!" one girl posted. "Awesome performance." A video was attached of her dancing alongside the news story, mimicking our moves in Tinikling. She had a hundred plus reactions.

Another post was by a different student, this one named Emily. The post said, "Your dancing inspired me to come out, show my talent. When I was a child, my mother enrolled me in sewing classes. This was the first thing I ever made." She was in a photograph, holding up a thick blanket. Bethany and I exchanged looks. What was happening? Emily was smiling wide, the perfectly sewn blanket covering much of the photo.

Wow!

Another student posted a picture, standing in ballet's fourth position, his feet crossed and facing in opposite directions, his knees softly bent downwards. He was physically fit. "I've been in ballet for most of my life," he said in his post. "The balance helps me in baseball. I've never told anyone about this." A second photo was posted of him posing in *demi-pointe*. Then a third of him *en pointe*.

This is incredible!

Bethany leaned into me, resting her head on my shoulder. I couldn't help but smile. The likes were increasing by the second. The page likes multiplying.

A text came through. Walter. Bethany straightened her upper body, and we checked the message: Dude! Nick. Got. Suspended LOLLOL

My mouth dropped open. I was stunned. Mister Popularity. Suspended.

Bethany started giggling uncontrollably. And then so did I. As Bethany regained her composure, I channeled my father. What would he do? I pulled up the never-ending text thread between Nick and I and stared at the subtly racist comments he'd sent me.

Tarantado! I typed and returned to Bethany.

Her eyebrows creased. "What was that?" she asked.

"Just calling Nick an asshole." We laughed again.

Eventually, we continued through the page. A new post jumped onto the feed. It was a video of a student standing in front of a white canvas. "*Estamos orgullosos de ti* Jamie. *Мы гордимся вами, Джейми. Nous sommes fiers de toi* Jamie. *Wir sind stolz auf dich*, Jamie." Then she smiled. "I speak five different languages," she boasted. "Six, if you count sign language." Then she signed the statement. In the comments, she wrote, "We're proud of you, Jamie."

I couldn't describe how delighted I was. It was nice to know that there were other students with similar interests outside of school. Knowing that some of them were also embarrassed of their hidden talents made me feel like I was a normal kid. Not a minority, not a Filipino, but an American.

A post from Sam: "Seeing you out there dancing was awesome," he wrote. "Do me a favor. Take care of Bethany for me."

A gang of cheerleaders posted a video. The head cheer-leader, Gabby, was holding a crown. Into the camera, she said, "On behalf of all the students at Saint Patrick's, we'd like to name you Folk Festival King." Then she pushed the crown into the camera's lens as if I was right there with them. "We'll make it official at school."

A random post said, "Jamie. I just want you to know that I am an outstanding chess wizard. I can beat anyone in three moves or less."

I couldn't believe what I was reading. Bethany leaned in and hugged me. I scrolled down the tens of posts that had occurred overnight. Many had gone unnoticed due to the large number. People had sent messages. They'd posted pictures of themselves doing outstanding things.

Then, a small, skinny boy stood in a frame of a video, frozen with the play button in the center. Bethany tapped the screen, and the boy came to life. Behind him was an easel. "Jamie. When I see you in school, I want to give you something." He held up the picture. Both Bethany and I leaned into the phone. It was a drawing of Bethany and me dancing Tinikling. The picture was in full color; it hit each detail with precision. "I've been drawing my whole life," he explained. Looking down over the illustration, he pointed at the bamboo sticks. "I wasn't sure how long the sticks were. I wanted to make it as realistic as possible, matching the ratios." He shrugged. "Anyway, I hope you like it."

"How cool is that?" Bethany said, her eyes gazing up at me.

My mouth dropped open. It was the neatest thing any-one had ever done for me. "It's incredible." I was in awe.

Where am I? I thought.

The boy smiled. A second passed. He set down the pic-ture on his bed. "I'm going to art school in California," he said. "It's always been my dream."

I shook my head in disbelief, watching as Bethany swiped slowly through the posts. There were congratulatory declarations, several shoutouts, and other pictures. We finally found the first post. It was timestamped just an hour or so after the final dance at the festival.

It was from Walter. A video.

He stood frozen in the middle of his living room. Smiling. The large triangle in the center of the video begging for me to push it. So, I did.

"Jamie," he said. "I'm sorry the festival ended, and even sorrier that it's taken this long for me to finally see it in person." He nodded. I could tell he was getting emotional. "And Bethany, I'm sure you're there watching this with him. I'm sorry I didn't approve of you in the beginning. You're pretty awesome, just like Jamie said." He raised his one shoulder. "I should have believed him."

A tear started to build in my eye.

"I wanted to create this page to immortalize the Folk Festival so you can always relive it. And from all the posts..." *How did he know there would be so many?* I chuckled at the thought. ". . . I can tell that if it weren't for homecoming, most of the student body would've been at the festival. So, I hope you enjoy and hold onto this as a keepsake for when you need it."

Bethany squeezed my hand tightly. My eyes instantly found it.

Then, Walter smiled mischievously. "Oh, and one more thing," he said. He slowly lifted the bottom of his sweatshirt until I could no longer see his face. The intro to the Michael Jordan era Bulls starting lineup started playing through the phone's speakers. Underneath was a white T-shirt with a cartoon bull drawn on it. It read "Chicago Buuls."

Bethany started laughing like she had when I'd first told her about it. So much so, she nearly fell off the bed. Luckily, I was still holding onto her hand.

Snorting, Bethany said, "Buuls." She continued to laugh to the point that her eyes were watery, and her cheeks were red. I basked in the moment with Bethany for a while, staring at the video with the shirt frozen on the screen.

For years, I was hiding something that turned out to be popular. All because of my self-doubt and the fact that I was ashamed of my heritage.

As we sat there bathed in happiness, Bethany in her thoughts, and I in my own, I realized something. I realized that I had everything that I could ever ask for.

Love.

Dance.

And egg rolls.

Acknowledgements

I've always wanted to write this story. It's loosely based on my own life—an American born Filipino kid who danced in Filipino folk festivals. I acted very similarly to the way that Jamie did: I rejected my heritage even though I loved dancing.

Now, this was many years ago (in the early to mid-80s), when the world wasn't so politically correct. Off-color jokes were accepted by some people, and back then, we didn't seem to have the PC police looking over our shoulders.

This could be the reason why my bully rose to such a prominent position in my life. Simply put, he could get away with it, because, for the most part, he was just "joking."

It could also be the reason why it took me forever and a day to write this book. It took a long time for me to overcome the color of my skin, and since I was born and raised around white culture, it was easier to just assimilate.

It wasn't until recently that I accepted my race and ethnicity (I'm in my 40s—think about that), which was how this story came to life.

But I couldn't have written it without the help and spirit of so many people. Namely, my wife, Bonnie (pssst . . . Jamie and Bethany = Jason and Bonnie), for never seeing me as a brown-skinned, insecure Filipino kid, but rather as a soulmate, spouse, and best friend. She's often told me to get more involved with my heritage via the Filipino-American Association, going back to the Philippines, and even learning to speak Tagalog. (I also can't speak the language. Shhh!) She's learned to cook chicken adobo, barbecue-pork kabobs, and egg rolls. So much better than I could ever do! I really don't know where I would be without her.

Additionally, a special thanks to my parents, my grandmother, my family, and the Filipino community, both back home in the Midwest (Iowa/Illinois), in Portland, and all over the world, who I've had the great fortune of getting to know via this wonderful thing called the internet. The entire staff (editing and otherwise) at Ooligan Press, for turning this book into what it is. First, they took a chance on a mediocre writer with a big idea. And second, they brought so many great ideas and helped me write the best story I possibly could. They gave me confidence that I could actually write this book.

And finally, I want to thank the Filipino-American dancing group back in my hometown. I never thought I'd actually like dancing coconuts, planting rice, and Tinikling, but with their support and friendship, they all made it an enjoyable experience. It's something that I will cherish forever.

Resources

Stop the Bullying

stopaapihate.org

stopbullying.gov

stompoutbullying.org

thehopeline.com/topics/bullying

youthempowerment.com/being-bullied

Join the Filipino Community

fanhsoregon.wordpress.com/links-locations

filamvancouver.org/fil-am-community-resources

filipinocc.org

filipinoculturalschool.org

nafconusa.org

fylpro.org

Jason's Family Recipe for Egg Rolls

Ingredients

- Frozen egg roll wrappers (I specifically use the Wei-Chuan brand because of how light and crispy they are)
- Ground pork*
- Shredded carrots
- Shredded lettuce (or cabbage)
- Chopped white onion
- Salt and/or pepper (to taste)
- Sesame oil
- Soy sauce
- One beaten egg (used to seal the egg rolls)

*Vegetarians can omit the pork if needed, or substitute with faux meat.

Instructions

1. Cook the ground pork until the meat is cooked through.
2. Mix the pork, carrots, lettuce (or cabbage), onion, salt and pepper, sesame oil, and soy sauce in a bowl.
3. Add the mixture to the wrapper, sealing the edges with the beaten egg
4. Heat olive oil in a pan; once hot, fry the egg rolls in the oil until they are brown on each side.
5. Enjoy!

Note: Exact amounts of each ingredient will vary depending on how many you are making and what type of flavoring you prefer. If you ask any Filipino, measuring begins and ends with how much you can "pinch" with your thumb and finger.

Ooligan Press

Ooligan Press is a student-run publishing house rooted in the rich literary culture of the Pacific Northwest. Founded in 2001 as part of Portland State University's Department of English, Ooligan is dedicated to the art and craft of publishing. Students pursuing master's degrees in book publishing staff the press in an apprenticeship program under the guidance of a core faculty of publishing professionals.

Project Managers
Luis Ramos
Cole Bowman

Publisher's Assistants
Alexandra Magel
Mary Williams

Social Media
Riley Robert
Alix Martinez

Acquisitions
Jennifer Ladwig
Michael Shymanski
Amanda Fink
Kelly Zatlin
Scott Fortman
Rebecca Gordon
Rosina Miranda
Claire Plaster

Editorial
Rachel Lantz
Emma Wolf
Rachel Howe
Erica Wright

Design
Katherine Flitsch
Morgan Ramsey

Digital
Amanda Hines
Chris Leal

Marketing
Sarah Moffatt
Hannah Boettcher

Publicity
Emma St. John
Alex Gonzales

Book Production
Alex Burns
Dustin Prisley
Ava Phillips
Kate Chilelli
Frances Frangela
Rachael Renz
Sarah Bradley
Elaine Schumacher
Tara McCarron
Dani Tellvik
Zachary Grow
Briana Ybanez
Glorimar Del Rio
Paige Zimmerman

Colophon

The interior of *Love, Dance & Egg Rolls* is set in LTC Goudy Oldstyle Pro, Helvetica Neue, and My Font, a font designed by an Ooligan Press master's student. LTC Goudy Oldstyle Pro is a light and classic serif font designed by Frederic W. Goudy from Lanston Type Co. for Adobe. Designed by Max Miedinger, Helvetica Neue is a widely popular sans serif typeface that's often used to spell out major brand identities on public signage. The title and chapter headings of *Love, Dance & Egg Rolls* are set in My Font, designed by Phoebe Whittington, an Ooligan Press student, in 2021 specifically for this title. Zapf Dingbats and Wingdings are both used for special cases such as heart and smiley face emojis. Benito Handwritten is also used for the handwritten style ampersands of the title and folios.